F OURTH
BLACK BOOK
OF
HORROR

Selected by Charles Black

Mortbury Press

Published by Mortbury Press

First Edition

2009

This anthology copyright © Mortbury Press

All stories copyright © of their respective authors

Cover art copyright © Paul Mudie

ISBN 978-0-9556061-3-7

Mortbury Press
Shiloh
Nantglas
Llandrindod Wells
Powys
LD1 6PD

mortburypress@yahoo.com
http://www.freewebs.com/mortburypress/

Contents

Dedicated to Michel Parry

*****

Acknowledgements

Soup © by Craig Herbertson 2009
Words © by Paul Finch 2009
A Cry For Help © by Joel Lane 2009
With Deepest Sympathy © by Johnny Mains 2009
Many Happy Returns © by Carl T. Ford 2009
All Hallow's Even © by Franklin Marsh 2009
Dead Water © by David A. Sutton 2009
'And Still Those Screams Resound' © by Daniel McGachey
2009
Love is in the Air © by Gary McMahon 2009
The Head © by Reggie Oliver 2009
The Devil Looks After His Own? © by Ian C. Strachan 2009
Bad Hair Day © by Gary Fry 2009
Flies © by Hazel Quinn 2009
Nails © by Rog Pile 2009
The Lord of the Law © by David Conyers 2009

Cover artwork © by Paul Mudie 2009

*****

Also in this series:
The Black Book of Horror
The Second Black Book of Horror
The Third Black Book of Horror
Forthcoming:
The Fifth Black Book of Horror

SOUP

Craig Herbertson

Peters stared upwards and observed, with detached serenity, the slow drip from the central rose of the sagging ceiling. The white plaster bulged in a sweeping concave that resembled nothing less than the belly of a long dead whale. The mottled patches of moss-green dissolution festered like archipelagos across the pale surface, affording the quiet mathematician uneasy images of rotting flesh. When the lights dimmed at indeterminate times, Peters would picture the bulge as the swollen breast of a cold, dead giantess, its protuberant nipple dripping foul milk directly into the slop bucket.

They had got used to *that* smell.

But sometimes, as the mind is wont to dwell on trivia under extreme duress, Peters wondered why their host had neglected to fix the broken pipe that produced the effulgence. It seemed... untidy, especially given their otherwise sumptuous and bizarre treatment.

There were low points in the whole affair of course; extremely low points, but Peters still liked the highs. As a bachelor past middle age, he lived a solitary and uneventful existence. He possessed, of course, a few like-minded friends and could point to certain bearable colleagues, but his true companions were mostly mathematical conundrums and Occidental poetry. While he recognised the perversity of his response, he had to admit that he appreciated the attention even if Jennifer Dunning did not.

She didn't look well. The simple wrought iron bench and the white chess table obscured her elegant legs and the ugly manacle around her ankle. The beautiful face that had adorned high fashion magazines was marred somewhat by puffy eyes and the tracks of last night's tears. Her husband, Captain Dunning, was gone. He had looked queasy when they had taken him.

Soup

It was probably the screams.

The screams, prolonged, ululating and piteous had impressed themselves in the small room much like the cacophony of a hidden tape recorder: Faraway, extending through the night: background noise, but not noise that sent one off to the land of nod. In fact, from their brief conversation this morning, Peters understood that he was the only one who had caught a few winks of sleep.

Farantino's sense of humour, no doubt. The reason they were all here. He had been a wit at Bellport High among his other talents. Bit of a joker. He always had style of course, something that Peters saw and admired without owning himself, but Farantino's jokes had a predisposition towards sadism. Like his introduction of the chess table in the centre of the room, apparently placed there for them to while away the long hours. But only apparently: As with the pack of cards, the crime and horror anthologies, the kaleidoscope and the set of Ludo, each distraction had an amusing catch.

The Queens in the chess set were glued irremovably to their squares rendering the game useless. The crime novels all had the dénouement removed. Nobody, of course, had so much as opened a page of the horror anthologies for obvious reasons. The kaleidoscope, when shaken, revealed various pictures of Farantino's smiling face and the little men in the Ludo set were smeared with a hot paste that irritated the skin for days after their handling. All in all, Farantino had excelled himself in creating a nervous atmosphere full of minor irritants.

Couple this with a sumptuous meal each night, clearly prepared by Farantino, a small carafe of Domaine de la Romanée-Conti, arguably one of the finest wines ever made; add the string quartet, virtuosos every one, who arrived promptly every third evening, set out their musical stands in the hallway, and performed Beethoven's String Quartet No. 10, Op. 74, in C minor for the benefit of the imprisoned. (After three nights Peters had noticed they had dropped a tone to B minor; something he found more irritating than the fixed

6

queens on the chess board.) Then there was the Thai masseur who worked tirelessly on the aches and pains engendered by their confinement but who, at irregular intervals, simply came in and watched them in utter silence.

It was difficult for victims of pained and cramped muscles to imagine anything more hellish than the reluctant masseur: Except perhaps the pursed-lipped whistler who rendered a series of bird songs and wouldn't depart until they guessed one correctly or, perhaps, the naked lap dancer who left the men in ball aching agony to stare at poor Jennifer Dunning; the Captain with a look of melancholy betrayal and Peters with shamefaced lust.

The expert mime, who had been regaling them with silent versions of Broadway films, seemed almost a treat.

This recipe of minor irritants had been balanced then, by Farantino, the maestro, with a mix of exquisite or bizarre entertainment. The resultant emotions of the entertained: a cocktail of confusion, wonder and fear. It was a conundrum of course, and Peters had spent most of the weary months trying to solve it.

Perhaps that constant dripping tap was not some negligence on the part of Farantino, because, all in all, the treatment was driving them slowly insane. Peter's suspected that that was the intention. He also suspected that they would be not quite insane before the finale. Close, but not quite close enough.

And it *was* slowly building to some kind of crescendo.

There had been six captives, initially: Captain Dunning, his wife, Peters and additionally a software programmer fresh from college, some Bulgarian athlete and a young female soprano. For a time they had been separated, the others placed in a cell some distance up the corridor. Captain Dunning had tapped out messages to the Bulgarian on the stone walls for the period of their mutual incarceration. Basically, it had achieved nothing but the solace that they were not utterly alone. Then, five days ago, the three had disappeared.

Not long after that the screams had begun.

7

Soup

How long was it since they had stopped? Perhaps three days? In that time the men's diet had been changed to a kind of sweet smelling clove, a peculiar mushroom and a sage-like paste, all unfamiliar even to the Captain, and both men had suffered an undignified regime of forcible enemas and regular emetics. Even though Mrs Dunning had been spared this indignity, Peters suspected that the end was in sight. He had no doubts the end was something awful but, after the long confinement and the refinements of Farantino's mental torture, he had managed to accept this prospect with something like a stoic calm. Not so the others. Perhaps they had more to lose: Youth, Beauty, Strength... each other.

They had been newly weds for only a matter of weeks; the disparity in their ages clearly not an impediment to their love. Jennifer was twenty years old – a perfect object, as far as Peters was concerned, of unobtainable desire. The Captain was some fifteen years her senior. He was utterly besotted with her as, in fact, anyone would be. Yes, Captain Dunning and his lovely wife were certainly suffering.

And yet the whole farce had all begun with such promise. To put it bluntly, when the invitation had presented itself, Peters had nearly come in his pants. No doubt, with all its immense social implications, the newly weds had felt much the same

Peters reached forward and picked up the black king on the chessboard. Jennifer Dunning started like a deer at his sudden movement, stared at him with wild eyes and then dropped her head. He guessed she felt less than comfortable with her husband gone. The screams too: Unnerving, and they had gone on and on. It could have been two or three days. They only stopped about three hours after Captain Dunning had been escorted from the cell. About lunchtime. Unhappy coincidence? thought Peters.

Jennifer had begun to weep again in her quiet way. His experience of consoling her had proven ineffectual on previous occasions so Peters returned to an examination of the chess man. He hadn't noticed it before, but the King's head was a small gnome-like Farantino. In its hand there was a letter and yes, the tiny symbol of that soup tureen.

Farantino? He was famous beyond mere celebrity: A legend, a myth, a living testament to the possibilities inherent in the human race. To come from a relatively humble background, son of a vicar and an Italian parishioner, and end up as the wealthiest, most sought after man, nay genius, in the twentieth century was incredible. That he should have remembered Peters, the humble mathematics pupil who had sat behind him in Year 7 at Bellport High, was unthinkable. To get an invitation from Farantino was the catholic equivalent of the pope begging to be best man at your wedding.

Even the invitations had that special magic. Farantino was principally known as the world's greatest chef. His various explorations of the lonely planet, his ballooning exploits, the numerous follies, his privately financed trip into space, the ownership of six islands, his legendary poker skills, the voice that had graced the Royal Opera and the seventeen languages with which he was familiar were all achievements dwarfed by his ability to cook. It was notorious that kings and queens, Prime Ministers and Heads' of State, celebrities, everyone who was anyone, had been snubbed by Farantino, that it was impossible to buy his culinary skills.

Farantino invited you to a banquet and whoever you were you dropped whatever you had planned and went along for the meal of your life.

The pattern of the invitation was not widely known except in a kind of inner circle. Of course, many of those who had attended Bellport High knew of it because Farantino was their most famous son. And word did get around, even to non-entities. But it was only spoken about by the in-crowd or amongst those, like Peters, who were simply in the right place at the right time. *His* knowledge was a bit like that of a villager, who never discusses the indiscretions of a local politician outside of his own village.

Still, for all his unworldliness, Peters had known exactly

what was happening the instant he had opened the door three months before.

It was two in the morning, streets silent and eerie, a little light rain. Peters had been up late, toying with puzzles in *Cheiro's Book of Numbers*, when he heard a light rap on the door.

There, in the dim-lit entrance of his suburban home, were two masked, dwarf harlequins framing, like bookends, a small golden-haired boy who bore a silver tray. On the street behind the silent tableaux, an antique silver Mercedes stood poised like a predator, white-gloved chauffeur beckoning. Peters had hardly seen the letter on the tray. He had barely observed the single silver line-drawn picture of a faience *saucière* in Rococo taste: Farantino's famous soup tureen.

The picture was the key; Farantino was known to have a 'thing' about soup. The tableaux, the timing, were irrelevant: The invitation could have come with a parachute drop in the morning, a Christmas card sent in spring, a newspaper advert, a cryptic, signed Ace of Spades delivered by a croupier at a late night casino. The variety of the invitation and the quixotic nature of its delivery were the stuff of legend. The drawing of the soup tureen was the thing. Anyone not recognising that symbol would simply not have been invited.

Peter's hadn't even taken his hat and coat. Whisked away into the night, he had almost welcomed the blindfold because it had some effect in calming his nervous excitement. He had to bite his tongue to stop repeating Farantino's name out loud. He was still rehearsing the story he would tell his friends and colleagues, trying to impress every detail on his mind, when the car had stopped. Escorted blindfold by the dwarves, they forged a path through long grass.

With the succubus brush of grass on his trouser legs and the chill on his naked arms, Peters strode blind through the still, graveyard world. He projected these mild discomforts into a distant land. Soon, in a matter of hours, at most a day, he would be sitting at a table of the great and the good. There would be displays of ostentation, creative acts, farragoes, heavenly meat and drink, wild extravagances: the lot. And Peters, the humble mathematics graduate employed for thirty years at Wellber and Sons CA, would be there amongst it all.

Even now he could only recall two or three people from Bellport High who had been to a Farantino feast. There was the deputy head master, Mr MacAteer, an amateur expert in Egyptology who had taken Farantino under his wing when he was only sixteen. MacAteer had helped with some extracurricular work on embalming techniques. It was said that MacAteer had once taken Farantino on a dig in the summer holidays but he always denied it. The two had been quite close and it was a fair few years later that MacAteer had been rewarded for his kindness. Peters could dimly recall MacAteer afterwards in a brief discussion with a gaggle of masters. He had simply repeated 'Doves in pies, Doves in pies' to the others' insistent requests

Then there was the Head boy of the year above, John Palmer, who had gone on to win Olympic bronze in the triathlon before he disappeared some years later in an avalanche on a British expedition to the Virunga mountain range.

Shortly after Palmer's legendary invitation, and many years before his loss, Peters had been in the common room tidying up. Palmer was lounging on the battered sofa; feet up in a state of euphoric bliss. The older boys had been chivvying him endlessly about Farantino. Eventually, Palmer had replied in a dazed voice. "It's not something you can talk about. It was simply spectacular. But I can tell you that I will still see mental images of that naked, dancing girl on my death bed." Palmer had slouched back further into the couch, a vacuous smile on his handsome face as he left the others scrunched up like insects. "Naked," he repeated. "Naked…"

That was how it was always described. One ingredient in the whole soup, one epiphanal moment, one slice of the cake that summarised the taste of the whole. And Peters was already savouring the *hors d'œuvre*.

A rocking motion, a tang of dampness and the feel of hollow, wooden boards beneath his feet suggested some kind of boat. Minutes later, with the blindfold removed, Peters' assumption was proven correct. A narrowboat: All the curtains drawn and only a dim glimpse through mirrors of the prow. Here Peters could discern the back of some phlegmatic giant who wielded a long oar and propelled the narrowboat silently through an unseen canal.

It was a scene he quickly dismissed in favour of the Chinese girls, dressed *hanfu* style, lit by perfumed candles, who were preparing a green tea and some light wafers. Soon, one of the girls had taken up the *pipa*, and a volume of *Chu Ci* poetry was intoned in quaint English as the strings of the Chinese lute wove their magic spell. Qu Yuan was Peters' favourite poet and lays from the *Songs of Chu* melted through his mind – like the vaguely recognised incense – in tones as smooth as the wooden belly of the pear shaped *pipa*.

Peters was aware then, that Farantino knew his intimate soul. For a second he doubted if he was even alive. Somewhere in the recesses of his mind this particular fantasy was etched on a blind wall. What else would happen, what *could* happen to improve on perfection? The music drifted on, the girl's lilting voice, the incense and the light from the perfumed candles touching, with the delicacy of moth wing, the wooden slats of the interior.

The image of the wooden bellied *pipa* brought Peters back to the cell, the lute-like shape echoing the bulge of the ceiling. It was always thus. The reveries and then the stark horror of the reality. He had drifted off again; lulled by Jennifer Dunning's weeping and the survival instinct, no doubt, of his own mind; the mind that Farantino was trying to unravel with the skill of a seamstress, and which now protected itself by focusing on better things.

The present was pretty awful and the future didn't look much better but at least Jennifer Dunning was silent: Probably exhausted. Peters put down the chessman with its little Farantino face, shut his eyes and tried to drift back in time again. He noticed with little interest that his manacle had been removed. For all he knew it could be another hallucination. There were plenty of those around.

The memory of the screams intruded for a while until he dozed into a fitful sleep.

Again he felt the rush of wind on his face as the carriage left the narrowboat behind and swept up the driveway between the sentinel oaks. Time had been suspended. Peters knew that he had slept at some point on the boat, but not until he had experienced things he had only distantly read of in exotic books, and now his skin prickled with the *hanfu* style dress. His mind still lingered on the Chinese girls and their flickering hands as they had first undressed and then clad him in their traditional costume. But for the moment there was only the wind and the beat of horses' hooves.

From all directions they came, white stallions forming a *cavalcade* before him. To the North and West along the other approaches individual setouts, teams of horses, carriages, glittering attendants scattered across the lawns as far as his eye could see. He was aware of faces that peered from the recesses of the coaches, some as bewildered as his own. Others regal; all masked like himself.

Then he saw the mansion house rearing up against the blackened sky: A huge palatial affair. Peters had heard rumours that Farantino had erected a secret country house in the North of England, somewhat on the scale of the Caprarolain Palazzo Farnese in Italy.

Here was the evidence. Lit by flambeaus and hosts of imported glow-worms, apparently imprisoned by gossamer nets, the red-gold walls of the buttress supported a gracious *piano nobile*. The huge, lit windows, open to the night sky, were darkened only by the flitting shadows of dancers. Venting forth from their capacious depths, some Wagnerian piece by a full orchestra sweetened the air with dark, melancholic chords.

Above this middle terrace, decorated with gargoyles and projecting bastions, two more floors of the central villa seemed to climb to the moon. The Villa rooms above the *piano nobile* were eerily silent. They appeared to be not so much asleep as brooding. At the time, Peters had dismissed this intrusive thought as morbid speculation. He was simply speechless with admiration. Later he was to remember.

He tried not to run up the wide marble steps. He even managed not to gasp when thousands of Red Admiral butterflies and Death's Head moths burst from the opening of the huge doorways like thrown rose petals – to the delight of those who stood by the balustrade. He contained his eagerness, attempting like a few other guests, a stately walk. It wasn't working. He was simply overwhelmed. As the huge entrance hall widened before his eyes with its massed velvet curtains, Steiner grand piano, dwarfed by huge monolithic kas, obelisks and enigmatic koras, culled from unknown Greek and Egyptian hoards, Peters felt himself on the edge of swooning. In a minute he would start to gibber like a five year old.

Chinese acrobats swung from the vaulted ceilings, silent flunkies glided with silver trays, elegant men and women, all masked, all clad in theatrical costume, drank fine wine, danced or idled by the Steiner. Some sat, bare feet dangling in the vast goldfish ponds. A festive atmosphere prevailed. No one seemed silent unless imbued with awe; no one who spoke could conceal their delight. As he wandered enthralled through the crowd, Peters became aware that all were apparently strangers to each other. This would be a one time invitation, an unforgettable experience. There could be no social dimension to this moment; the individual must simply live, for the first and only time, in a dream wrought by genius.

There was one name on everyone's lips. The Maestro, the impresario, *the* genius: Farantino!

Everything ever said about the man seemed now to be an inadequate description. Someone remarked that they thought his covert space trip had been faked at the time. Now they knew that there was more possibility that the Americans had faked the Eagle landing and that Farantino was probably conducting diplomatic discussions with Martians. Farantino had no need to fake a damn thing.

Another guest with a heavy accent had listened to one of Farantino's recordings of the nigh impossible Percaro language. "Word perfect," he said in adulation and he shook his head in disbelief. Peters paused half listening to the exotic tones. "My tribe neighboured theirs, if the vast lands of the American basin can be talked of in such terms. The Percaro occupied a hidden valley in the foothills of the Acarai Mountains. Somehow, no one knows how, Farantino managed to infiltrate their village; notorious cannibals. To have survived such a thing. To have become fluent..."

Another was comparing Farantino's majestic tenor to old recordings of Caruso. Farantino wasn't losing there either. Everywhere the talk rose and fell from cultured, erudite lips and everywhere it returned to the same focus: Farantino!

It was here, immersed in euphoria at the foot of the stairs, that Peters had first encountered Captain Dunning. Peters hadn't known at the time, of course, because Dunning was masked and clad in a Jaeger rifleman's uniform from the Napoleonic wars – green fabric the colour of pea soup, and neat little epaulettes – very dignified with the grey hose. But he recognised the military type by the stance, the erect head and the eyes searching the hall. It had to be the military or the police. Peters favoured the military. The man had a certain quality about him. His was the carriage of an officer; a man who commanded the utter obedience of elite soldiers.

Captain Dunning's wife wasn't beside him, of course. One of Farantino's jokes to have them come separately and incognito. When you were incarcerated for months with a person, you got to know their body, their movements, their carriage, even their smell and Peters remembered all these things a long time afterwards and related them to this meeting. But for the moment, Captain Dunning was some stranger in an entrance hallway.

At the time, Peters was impelled by greater needs. He looked at the vast series of steps leading to the *piano noble*, to the dancers, to mysteries beyond his ken. He actually trembled as he walked up the main stairway. The golden balustrade was about the only thing that kept him on his feet. Part of him wanted to simply remain in the entrance hall because, when he analysed his feelings, he had never been happier than now. But another part drove him to explore. Was there any limit to this?

A man of medium height stood alone at the well. He was masked and clad in a jet black Imperial Chef's coat with silver buttons. He sported checked pants and dark chef's shoes. It was almost as though the man's very presence, somewhat death-like, had cleared an avenue of space: The space that emerges when a way is open. One can walk there, but it is empty. To fill the space is sometimes to invite other energies. It is not always wise to walk paths others avoid.

The man stood at the centre of the stairs where they split like red Spanish fans, ascending to left and right. Peters walked up. He intended to slip past but the man smiled and said quietly:

"Peters. How nice to see you after all these years. How's the old counting coming along?"

Farantino! Even now Peters had no idea what he said in reply. Another of Farantino's jokes – to simply turn up in his work clothes, spectacular though they might be.

Beyond speech, Peters was aware of his elbow being taken. He was escorted up the stairs as Farantino pointed out this and that painting, all immeasurably valuable or more or less priceless. The Persian rugs, golden filigree on the wallpaper – the holders for the lamps would have cost Peters his house – But it was all so tasteful... Then as an afterthought Farantino had turned and caught Captain Dunning's eye. He waved him up and the Captain began to follow.

The next moments were a blur. Peters had a vague, single vision of an immense ballroom, colours blazoning out into the starless night, buddhistic sculpture that towered monumentally to vaulting heights, the great sweep of the string section as the orchestra proclaimed the opening movement of *Thus Spoke Zarathustra*. Beauteous dancers, whose elegant movements merged like wave and strand as they struck up a pavanne to echo the symphony.

But it was only a tableau, a single, glorious moment before they were escorted to a small anteroom. The world stilled and Peters and twenty-four masked guests stood in audience to Farantino.

The simple dignity of his costume, his unremarkable height and quaintly staged movements were the antithesis of his voice. Farantino spoke quietly, without emphasis but every word struck the core of their being. It seemed they were to be his special guests for the evening. They would taste delights that others had only heard of. Even throughout these hallowed halls, few had gained the inner sanctum. Peters felt it in his soul; a kind of rush of warmth, like the first sip of Laphroaig. And then, something of the alien in Farantino seemed to reach out like a silk glove. He began to speak in tones that caressed Peters' heart like a dead monkey's paw. This time there was no blurring of his mind. Peters was good at counting, to some extent his memory was almost photographic. He could remember Farantino's speech word for word...

But for the moment the vision fled. The chill words retreated to the recesses of Peters' brain. He coughed, his bleared eyes opening on the familiar claustrophobia of the cell. Jennifer Dunning's head lolled across her breast; asleep at last. She snored quietly. Peters shook his head, tasted his dry lips. He could see the faint pulse of the great arteries in Jennifer's elegant neck, the faint traced, blue veins.

Despite the dark circles around her eyes she was still very beautiful, beautiful like Praxiteles' Aphrodite. Even Farantino had been stirred by her great beauty, visible even while masked. Almost like a predator, the chef had circled her as he made his one, great speech. At the time Peters had got a faint echo that Captain Dunning had changed his stance. Now, on reflection, he realised that, at that moment, Dunning had doubtless recognised his wife through the mask and she him; an irony that had not escaped Farantino as he began to intone to a stupefied audience in words that had etched themselves on Peters' memory...

"Welcome," he had said. "Welcome to my life such as it is. All lives are short. We have an obligation to make of them something wondrous. You have enjoyed yourselves? Was it not beautiful?"

A murmur of assent spilled from those gathered.

"There is more to come," said Farantino, "but before the sugar, you must try a little salt. How can I express it?"

Here Farantino had paused. He seemed to struggle for words. In that instant, Peters got an inkling of the essence of the man. Like Buster Keaton, like all great comedians, Farantino existed only in the present. He had no past, no future, only an interminable 'now'. His uncontainable emotions, torn living from his soul, were manifestly visible in his tortured eyes. With a violent movement Farantino had beckoned to the opposing doors.

Slowly, at his gesture, the doors began to open on a vast dark chamber. In stark contrast to the perfumes of before, a dank smell wafted from the exposed room like old bandages and dark, dead things. Somewhere, far away, something moaned.

Farantino ushered them through the doors. There was a faint gasp from a woman, probably Jennifer Dunning, in retrospect – she was fairly fragile – But others were not immune to the chill.

At first, Peters saw only the pedestal at the centre of the room and the quaint statue of a goblin creature perched there, lit by hidden lights. He had a sensation of vast depths, unseen passages beyond. Then, he saw the iron chair and Peters knew that they had entered a room quite different in character from the others. The chair was large, laced with spikes to penetrate flesh, sporting ancient metal bands to crush the feet and hands.

He felt a shudder race through his frame.

"A German Inquisitorial chair," said Farantino, "last used in 1800."

Beyond the chair, awakening in the dim lights, a wall of shrunken heads gazed sightlessly upon three maidens of Nuremburg, the sarcophagi open to display cruel spikes stained rust-brown; bleak interiors that seemed to scream in shocking silence. Beside the sarcophagi, a garrotte. In dim, shadowed alcoves great wheels, Judas cradles, racks and strappados lurking like huge skeletal insects. A variety of smaller instruments, no less threatening for their size, were suspended from the ceiling: the branks, with its distinctive ass's ears; head crushers, cats paws, pears and spiders to rip and split the intestines.

Farantino paused then he deliberately picked up a fiendish metal cross, spiked at two ends and bearing a metal collar.

"The heretic's fork," Captain Dunning said quietly. "Place the collar around the victim's neck, one point in the breast and the other under the chin. Their head cannot move without inducing intolerable pain—"

"Yes, Captain. You know about these things. The British army trains well."

The captain nodded, "I'm not sure the ladies *should* though." His eyes, suspicious now, behind the mask.

"But why have this ugly room?" said a voice, "amidst so much beauty."

Farantino placed the fork under his chin and then smiled. "You may well ask," he said. "But then why have soup when one can eat meat? They all say it do they not? Farantino and his soup. I will tell you why." Farantino peeled off his mask. His bright, ferret eyes steeped in intelligence, his narrow chin thrust forward. "Because nothing in life is alone. All things have a doppelganger, an accompaniment, an animus. There is nothing fine and wonderful that does not have its visceral root. You have heard of the term *duende*?"

"*Duende*" said Peters, surprised to hear his own voice. "A

Spanish concept. The demon within the angel, perhaps: Emotion, expression, authenticity. They use it about dance."

"Yes," said Farantino, "but it is more than a description of dance. The artist's Muse gifts inspiration, *duende* gifts blood. The Muse gives life, *Duende* death and the struggle of knowing that death is imminent; the knowledge that death waits and the despair of that knowledge. The dancer, *tenere duende,* expresses the entire gamut of the human condition."

Farantino paused. "My life's work is only authentic because it surges up, inside, from the soles of my feet. My living flesh needs to interpret the voice of *Duende*. I like fine meat but meat is nothing without the basic simplicity of soup." Farantino gave an oddly sexual gesture towards a cracked and rusted wheel.

"Look carefully on that instrument. Imagine the broken shambles of a human being strapped upon that wheel, writhing in the splintered chamber of its own bones; a huge rag doll, screaming, slimed with blood and gore. And there, the cauldrons with which the Percaro cook their victims – a process lasting three days, three days of excruciating agony. And there just beyond. A favourite of mine…"

Reluctantly the little group advanced further into the room, impelled by the hypnotic voice. Dunning hesitated. He was looking with concern at his wife.

A huge copper basin stood just beyond the pedestal. It was concave, about the size of a paddling pool. A tracery of metal bars formed an inescapable cage above the basin. The whole appearance of the contraption was suggestive of a vast, oval bird cage.

"The slave griddle", said Farantino: "You lock the doors such. Then light the coals so. The screaming victim springs around like a March hare—"

"This is enough, Farantino," said Captain Dunning. "The ladies…"

"My apologies," Farantino smiled. "I will desist." He took one look at the revolting apparatus and then said quietly. "A musician once told me that good cannot be trusted unless it has breathed the same air as evil. Perhaps later you will understand."

Farantino smiled again and made a mock bow. The doors at the far end of the room opened. Glowing lights showed beyond. The torture chamber dimmed. Peters last saw the grinning face of the gnome like some twisted Cheshire cat above the pedestal.

As the lights died, he realised that the face was uncannily like that of his host.

Again Peters found himself fully awake. He stared at the chess man. Farantino and his jokes. His smiling visage on every artefact. But he had been right. After the glimpse of the torture chamber, the banquet was beyond words. Faced with images of horrific death and pain, the palate reacted with gusto to the superlative food. The conversation sparkled with innuendo, wit, laughter. Each guest had appeared more animated and alive. Each moment had seemed eternal. Farantino, noticeable by his absence, had forged god-like ambrosia from the smithy of his kitchen; every course a new wonder. It was only now, many months after, that Peters realised with a sudden jar, that despite all the talk of Farantino's obsession, there had been no soup.

"No soup," he said out loud and he began to laugh.

Awakened, Jennifer Dunning stared at him. Peters lapsed back into silence and continued his contemplation of the ceiling. The concave, white expanse glistened with moisture that spread from the central rose. He realised that the ceiling looked uncannily like the rust spotted underbelly of a faience *saucière*, Farantino's famed soup tureen. The laughter simmered at the edge of his consciousness. Peters was unsure whether it had a voice outside his own head.

The end approached. His fine mathematical mind was unhinging.

After an indeterminable time, the door opened slowly. Captain Dunning stood in the opening. He was naked and he didn't look good. The heretic's fork jutted from his sternum and poked under his chin, held by the metal collar. A rivulet of blood ran freely between his chiselled pectoral muscles and spread like the scummed waters of a gory marsh among the hairs on his belly. His head was forced back by the fork so that he could only speak through gritted teeth. In his hand he held a second fork. With great difficulty he spoke.

"Don't struggle Peters. I wouldn't like to hurt you. You'd better strip."

Peters was beyond struggling. He removed his clothes, looking with some regret on the soiled Chinese *hanfu*. Passively, he waited as Captain Dunning fixed the collar around his neck. The biting pain of the fork brought a fresh awareness.

"You too, Jenny. Clothes off. You're not to be hurt. Trust me."

She stripped, unseen by Peters, who now observed the world in agony, his head thrust upwards to stare at the ceiling. With care he could look through slanted eyes at the top of Captain Dunning's head. Any sudden movement dug the prongs of the fork into his chin and sternum.

"We're all to be spared, Jenny. Everything will be fine. Farantino wants to play a silly game. The man's a sadist but he won't murder us. He won't hurt you at all – gave me his word. He's gong to humiliate me and Peters but he's taken a shine to you." Peters could vaguely see Captain Dunning attempt to caress his wife. "You just have to dance for him love; play his silly game. Whatever he asks just go along with it and we'll be allowed home. It won't change anything between us, I swear…"

Peters was almost glad of the fork, he could only hear the dreadful sobbing, the whispered endearments.

After a time he felt Captain Dunning take his hand.

"Right, Peters, we walk on now. Jenny will follow."

Each step was painful; each tiny jar on the stone floor sent an involuntary shudder through his frame. The fork dug in.

Soup

Itching, scratching. It had only been minutes but the strictures on his neck were already agony.

They had gone some distance down the corridor when Captain Dunning gripped his arm and leaned in close to whisper. "There's no way out, Peters. I know my job and Farantino has every angle covered. The bastard's making soup out of us. I know you're a man and won't let the side down so I'll give it direct. Farantino explained how he does it – part of his warped pleasure, I believe – and it's far from pleasant – a long, slow process learned from that bloody Percaro tribe. I saw the remains of the others. Not nice. We'll be off our trolley before the end, hopefully, and none the wiser. Damn that sadistic bastard!"

Peters grinned like a puppet. There was nothing to say.

"For Jenny's sake we have to carry on." Captain Dunning gripped Peters' arm tighter to emphasise his lack of alternatives. "Farantino's really taken with her," he continued. "He'll let her live, I'm just praying he won't let her witness what happens to us. I made a deal. We cause no trouble, make it easy for him and... well, you understand."

Peters said nothing. They had come to the door. Beyond, he could vaguely discern a large room. A murmur of conversation, hushed by their arrival. His arms were taken. Led step by step to a large metal basin sunk into the floor, he felt leather chords tighten behind his back. Captain Dunning mirrored his every action with stoic calm, holding out his wrists passively as two robed men imprisoned his arms. Then they were up to their shoulders in warm water. Peters felt bubbles rising between his toes, a barely perceptible increase in the temperature of the water.

His head locked at its unnatural angle, Peters was only able to look with any ease at the tiers above where he could see seated guests, their faces unmasked, their mouths red and their eyes glinting with anticipation in the flickering lights. He was only vaguely aware that he, and Captain Dunning, were at the centre of an amphitheatre A huge velvet curtain suspended by a rope, shrouded some vast object placed beside their basin. Then Peters saw Farantino, clad in his black Imperial Chef's coat. He made a great flourish with his meaty hands. The crowd murmured. Farantino began to pull the rope

Captain Dunning opposite stared at the crowded tiers. No anger or resentment registered on his impassive face, not even the disgust that he must have felt. Already the soldier had taken over. He was lapsing into a state of catatonia, dropping into defences as he prepared for a long and terrible death.

"And now the dancing," It was Farantino, his voice imbued with peculiar relish.

The curtains flew upwards exposing the huge, copper-plated griddle and the open doors of its cage. Peters noticed with a gritty smile that the lower half of the contraption was remarkably like a giant soup tureen.

With the last vestiges of his rational mind, he concluded that Captain Dunning would certainly have died like a soldier if he had not seen the heated coals flare up beneath the griddle and heard the first of his poor wife's pitiful screams.

WORDS

Paul Finch

Cameron parked his BMW at the end of the wooded lane, just in front of the three concrete bollards. He'd been expecting the lane to run out. It had gradually dwindled down to a single-track and now gave out completely in rutted soil and trampled leaf-mulch. The trees on either side had closed in to a point where they were only a few yards apart. Overhead, their reddening foliage had entwined to form a dense canopy.

He grabbed his bag, climbed out and stood breathing the fresh country air. It was fumed with autumn: mildew, fungus, a rich dankness in the undergrowth. There was hardly a sound, which he supposed was only to be expected in the depths of the Forest of Dean. On the other side of the bollards, a footpath wound down towards a rippling mere. The signposts to Whitebrook had all pointed in this direction, and now it seemed there was no further access. Yet, for some reason, Cameron wasn't surprised or even disheartened. He locked the BMW, zipped his jacket up, hoisted his bag and set off walking. Above him, through breaks in the thinning branches, patches of powder-blue sky were visible. The mist, several veils of which he'd driven through to get here, seemed to be confined to ground level. But it wasn't cold. It was only early October and this was south-west England, once known in folklore as 'the Summer Land'.

When he reached the edge of the mere, he saw that it was actually a larger-than-average duck-pond, one hundred yards across and perhaps several hundred yards wide. Hourglass shaped, it was crossed at its central point by a timber footbridge. On the other side, he saw the village. Cameron hadn't smiled in months, but he smiled now, faintly – as he focused on the tall, narrow buildings with their thatched roofs and Jacobean, black and white panelling. Thus far, Whitebrook was everything he'd expected.

He followed the path along the shore, weaving between clumps of bulrushes, then started across the bridge. This too had been painted black and white. To his left and right, swans drifted lazily. Skeins of mist had extruded from the woods, and lay over the edges of the water like a translucent vapour.

Before Cameron reached the other side, a man appeared at the bridge's far end. He made no effort to come over, which Cameron realised was probably because the bridge was so narrow that only one person could pass at a time. He hurried forwards. The man was in early middle-age, and dapper in a rustic sort of way. He wore smart tweeds, a mustard-yellow waistcoat and a deer-stalker. His face was broad and florid, with a thick, blonde-grey moustache.

"Morning," Cameron said, stepping off the bridge and moving to one side.

"Good morning," the man replied, staring over the water towards the distant trees, but making no effort to cross. "You haven't by any chance seen a dog?"

His accent was pure Gloucestershire, that peculiar mix of Welsh and West Country, but slightly gentrified.

Cameron shrugged. "No, I'm sorry."

"Can't find the blighter anywhere. Oh well, not to worry."

"I wonder," Cameron said. "Is there a hotel in the village?"

"There's an inn. The Whitebrook Arms."

"Do they take guests?"

"I believe so."

"Thanks." Cameron set off up a stony track. "I'll keep an eye out for your dog."

"Yes. If you would. Rather scruffy beggar, he is. A mongrel. Looks more like a stray than a pet."

Cameron would have expected a chap like this to own something more imposing; a mastiff or Great Dane. But then what did Cameron know? He'd written about the countryside many times, but he'd never lived here. He glanced back once as he strode up the track. The man waited beside the entrance to the bridge, scanning the opposite shore. He still made no move to cross over.

On entering the village proper, Cameron at first wondered if it might be one of those preserved historical villages, the sort you normally had to pay to gain access to. Its thoroughfares were all neatly cobbled, its buildings exclusively of the antique variety – comprised almost entirely of white plaster and black beams. Many had projecting upper floors and were stunted with age, leaning giddily towards each other, blotting out the sunlight in the narrow alleys between them. The shops, of which there was only a handful, had mullioned front windows and colourful shields hanging over their doors. It was all exquisitely clean and well-kept. There were no vehicles in sight except for a cart and two shire horses waiting alongside the inn, while a drayman handed casks of beer down through a trapdoor.

The village square, which fronted onto the inn, was a small, circular green surrounded by flower beds and a fence of low iron hoops. Paved paths led into it from north, south, west and east, converging on a central dais of white stone. Ordinarily, he'd have expected to find a cenotaph or statue located here, but instead saw an object that stopped him in its tracks. It was an upright wooden post, about five feet tall; at the top of it there was a heavy cross-piece, which opened on a hinge like a pair of jaws. Grooves were cut in both the upper and lower sections so that once the device was closed, three holes were neatly aligned in the middle of it, the central one slightly larger than the other two.

It was a pillory.

He had no doubts whatsoever.

The three holes were clamps for the neck and wrists.

Cameron walked up to it, fascinated. Many country towns in England maintained their stocks as curiosities for visitors. Here and there, on lonely crossroads, there was even a gallows or gibbet, a left-over fragment from the arcane past. But seldom, if ever, had he heard of a pillory being preserved. Felons would have been forced to stand here for hours at a time, sometimes days if their offence was deemed serious enough, and local people would shower them with rotten food and animal dung. Of course, it was debatable whether or not this was an original.

If so, it might it be the very same structure on which Alice Fairwood was beaten to death in 1634, though in truth it looked too new for that. Its wood was smooth and solid, and in keeping with the rest of the village style, had been painted black. Its ironwork – its hinges, the steel facings within the clamps – bore no mark of corrosion.

A replica then. But an impressive one all the same.

The pillory was a central character in the Alice Fairwood story, which is why Cameron had come here in the first place. Back in 1634, it hadn't been intended that she die. In fact, contrary to popular belief, even at the height of the witch-hunting craze, it was never permissible in English law for accused witches to be executed unless it had first been proved that they'd used their powers to commit murder. And torture was forbidden under all circumstances. But Alice Fairwood's actions had caused such ill-feeling that, once a local magistrate had ordered her to be fixed in the pillory, a mob descended on her with such ferocity that she was dead within an hour.

It was a grim tale, but a strangely enticing one.

Cameron took in the rest of the village, with its ancient houses and narrow ways, and it suddenly seemed very likely that the atmosphere of this place would prove the perfect antidote to the writer's block that he'd suffered for the last eight months.

It might seem strange that he was pursuing the story of one dead woman to soothe pain caused to him by the death of another. But Alice Fairwood and Cameron's late-wife, Sarah, had been two different people. The latter had been the world to him, had meant more than he could ever possibly describe in words. The former had died so long ago that she might as well be a fictional character, and that was how he intended to use her: to rekindle a career, which, though it had seemed unimportant after Sarah's death, would leave him on Skid Row if he continued to neglect it.

He walked towards The Whitebrook Arms. Its front door stood open on red firelight.

*

Inside the inn there was indeed a real fire, crackling away in a massive stone hearth. But this was only part of the ongoing Jacobean theme. It was a warren of small rooms and narrow passages, all with low, beamed ceilings and doorways standing aslant.

Thankfully, there were also modern conveniences: the window panes, while divided into multiple diamonds by criss-crossing strips of ornate leading, were clearly double-glazed; there were radiators in every room and the bar was modern and well-stocked. Behind it was a woman of about forty, wearing a T-shirt and jeans. She had a cuddly if shapely figure, and a pretty young-old face, which needed only touches of makeup. Her bright red hair was cut in a fetching pageboy bob.

"Jeanine!" she shouted, as Cameron approached. "Jeanine, where the heck are you? Oh, I'm sorry, sir. What can I get you?"

"A room, if that's possible," Cameron said.

"Oh... right." Her reaction suggested that she hadn't had a request like that in some time. "I'll not be a sec. Jeanine!" She glanced at Cameron as she came around the bar. "Daughters, eh! What use are they?"

He smiled politely.

She led him back to the lobby, a wide hallway adorned with old leather furniture, its walls decorated with implements of the past: farming tools, hunting horns and even Cromwellian-style weapons and armour, all kept in fine condition. Cameron had already decided that the inn, and most of the other houses here, were reconstructions probably designed to replicate historic buildings that had decayed to the point where they'd needed to be demolished. But it had been lovingly done.

The woman slid behind a counter of polished walnut. She took a register from a drawer, blew a coat of dust off it and handed it to him, along with a gold fountain pen. He signed the register on a page otherwise empty of names, and pushed it back to her. She glanced down. If the signature 'Cameron Wade' meant anything, she didn't show it – which surprised him a little. Okay, he was no Ian McEwan or Martin Amis, but after writing eight best-selling novels in the last ten years, he'd have thought she'd recognise him. Not that it troubled him unduly.

"How long are you planning to stay, Mr Wade?" she asked.

"That's the thing. I'm not sure. I've come here to work rather than for a holiday."

"Fine. Just as long as you let me know a day or so in advance before leaving." She turned to a row of five pigeon holes, and took out a heavy brass key with the number '2' notched into its wooden tab. "This is the best room we have. It's got a nice view over the village square. Will that suit you?"

"Assuming the price is right."

"Of course. It's thirty pounds a night, and that includes breakfast, which we can make for you between eight and ten. How's that?"

"Excellent," he said. Though actually it was more than excellent. It was astonishingly good value. Of course, he hadn't seen the room yet, nor sampled the food. Though as it turned out, neither would disappoint him.

The room, which was located directly above the inn's front entrance, was not en suite, but was very elegant. Its walls and floor were of bare wood panels, though a large rug occupied the floor and an even larger tapestry hung on the wall facing the bed, which was big and four-posted; beneath its pristine white sheets, the mattress, quilt and pillows were of sumptuous duck-down. In front of the window, there was a chair and writing desk, both of carved oak, which might very well have been antiques in their own right.

"Okay?" the woman asked.

"Great. Thank you very much."

She offered him a well-manicured hand. "I'm Martine Culpepper, the licensee. Anything you need – anything, just give me a call."

He said that he would, and tried to ignore the suggestive glint in her eye as she smiled and closed the door. At forty-two, Cameron was still a handsome, rugged man, and Martine was undoubtedly a handsome woman, but there was no room in his life for romance just yet. He dumped his bag and paced across the room to the window. Its view over the village was indeed splendid: the thatched roofs and shaggy eaves, the weathercocks. To the east there was a larger building – its aged stone turrets suggested that it might once have been fortified; the village meeting-house perhaps? Beyond that was a small car park; a single vehicle was visible there – a Rolls Royce if Cameron's eyes didn't deceive him. Directly below, villagers were out and about, greeting each other pleasantly, nobody in a hurry. The pace of life here was very sedate.

It certainly didn't look like a community plagued by a hideous curse.

In fact, it seemed laughable associating this place with something so unpleasant. Not that Cameron knew the exact details of the so-called 'Whitebrook Curse'. He wasn't even sure when he'd first heard about it, though it was reasonably famous among English folklorists.

Apparently, Alice Fairwood had uttered it with her last breath, and it had afflicted not just the villagers at the time, but the many generations of villagers who'd followed. Few present-day scholars were exactly sure what form it was supposed to have taken, but it had pricked his authorial interest immediately – mainly because with this next novel, he'd wanted to veer right away from his normal subject-matter, which tended to be contemporary thrillers with a psychological angle, and into the realms of the supernatural. The idea of a remote English village where, thanks to an ancient hex, mysticism ran rife, bizarre deeds were practised, and horrible, inherited deformities were on view, was ideal. Okay, it was hardly cutting-edge, but with his name pasted on it, it would sell. In addition, the writing would be painless; it'd be a world away from the real England inhabited by his other books, which would only serve to remind him of his former, happier life.

He watched the people below: an elderly couple walking arm-in-arm, a teenager carrying a skateboard. No one was limping suspiciously, or had eerie facial features. There were no webbed fingers or sealed up eye-sockets. Cameron chided himself for already thinking in clichés.

Then he saw the woman.

She was on the far side of the green, in the process of turning a corner.

A chill touched his neck.

She was slim and of medium height, though she looked a little taller because she was wearing heels. He only saw her from behind, but her long, honey-blonde hair was astonishingly familiar. As was her beige mac, and the way she was wearing it: cinched at the waist with a belt, her hands tucked into its front pockets.

Cameron blinked and she'd moved out of sight.

He had to lean on the sill for several seconds. Whoever the woman was, she'd looked so like... but this was bound to happen. He'd been told that by everyone. He'd hear her voice, see her face, mistake other people for her. And it would owe to nothing more than a completely natural and desperate longing for her to somehow be returned to him.

He sat heavily on the bed, and then the tears came. He wiped them away with his fingers, but they came again. He continued wiping. Eight months and still he couldn't get over it. They'd warned him this would happen too: you'll never recover from a loss of this magnitude. You'll learn to live with it, but you'll never truly recover from it.

"I will," he growled at no one. He had to get his life and

career back on track.

Defiantly, he returned to the window and peered down.

The square was now empty. There was no sign of the woman, which was what he wanted. Instead, he focused on the pillory. Sarah was gone, and there was nothing he could do about it. But Alice Fairwood was a different matter.

He would make Alice Fairwood live again.

*

"Did you find your dog?"

The man with the blonde moustache and tweed jacket looked up from the corner of the snug, where he was sitting with a pint of bitter and a magazine. "Er... no. Thanks for keeping an eye out, though. He'll turn up. He usually does."

Cameron nodded and went to the bar. It was now mid-afternoon. No other customers were present, but Martine was behind the counter, mopping it with a cloth.

She smiled as he approached. "Drink, is it, Mr Wade?"

"Not yet. I've had to leave my car outside the village. I couldn't work out which way to bring it in."

"The other side of the footbridge, would that be?"

"Yes. I saw from my bedroom window that there's a car park. How do I reach it?"

"It's easy. Just back up from where you've left your vehicle for about two-hundred yards. You'll come to a crossroads. The right-hand turn will take you around the north perimeter of Whitebrook. There's a road in from that side."

"Thanks." Cameron moved away.

"Motoring chap, are you?" the moustached man asked him.

Cameron stopped. "Well, yes."

"Don't get much call for motors round here."

"There's a very nice one on the car park. A Roller."

"Hmmm, yes." The moustached man pondered this. "Not sure who owns it, to be honest."

"Really?" Cameron had considered the possibility that this

fellow himself might be the owner. He had a sort of 'village squire' aura.

"It's always there," the man added quietly, as if talking to himself. "No doubt someone will eventually claim it."

Realising he'd been dismissed, Cameron moved outside. There was a Rolls Royce here and no one knew who owned it? That was a turn-up. He'd have thought that, in a village like this, everyone would know everyone else's business. Still, it was nothing to do with him. He threaded back between the cottages and crossed over the footbridge, meeting no one en route. The air was fresh with October damp. Aside from the clipping of his shoes on the woodwork, there was barely a sound. On the other side, he followed the path by the water's edge, veering back into the woods and between the concrete bollards. His BMW waited there. Opening up, he slid behind the wheel and stuck his key in the ignition.

There was no response.

He tried again – the same.

He wondered if he might have left a door open, or even the boot. But he hadn't. He tried the engine a second time – still nothing.

He climbed out. It wasn't a major problem. He hadn't intended to drive anywhere. But there'd been no sign of a garage in the village, and he'd need to get help of some sort. He put his mobile phone to his ear, but found that this too was silent. He flicked the 'on' button – again, again. No response. He walked a little way along the road to see if he needed to pick up a signal. Eventually he'd covered forty or fifty yards. The phone gave a faint buzz, but promptly died again. Cameron swore under his breath as he remembered that he didn't have the charger with him. Okay, if he needed to make calls, he could use a land line from the village. But no one knew he was here – not even his agent – which meant that no one would know where to reach him if something came up. Then he glimpsed movement. He glanced left.

Some distance down a woodland path, a woman was

walking away from him. It was the same woman he'd seen circling the village square. As before, she wore a beige mac belted at the waist, its lower skirts flaring out around her shapely calves and high heels. Also as before, she walked with a slow sensual motion that was reminiscent of...

"Sarah," he said under his breath.

It was ridiculous. How could it be Sarah? But the way she'd tucked her hands daintily into her coat's front pockets, the way her fair hair shimmered in the forest twilight.

"Sarah?" he said more loudly.

She was too far away. The path was bending around a mass of rhododendrons. Even as he watched, she strolled out of view.

"Sarah!" he called. His heart hammered in the base of his throat; his brow was suddenly moist with sweat.

It wasn't Sarah; it could NOT be.

But he had to check. The resemblance, even from behind, was too great. He started in pursuit, all thoughts of his car and phone forgotten.

It might have occurred to him that following a woman he didn't know down a lonely wooded walk was not perhaps a sensible thing to do, but briefly Cameron was in a world of his own. He hurried onwards. When he rounded the rhododendrons, there was no sign of her, but the path was still visible. It led deeper into the woods, looping out of sight again about fifty yards ahead. Cameron began to run. Coincidences happened, of course. Incredible coincidences; coincidences that no one would believe. Yet somehow, for some reason, he didn't think this was one of those. Even if it was, he had to know who this woman was.

Not that it would be easy, because there was now no trace of her at all.

The path continued to weave between the trees, but these were oaks, their trunks cathedral-like pillars, their high canopy largely intact despite the waning season. As such, ground-cover was almost absent, yet still he couldn't see her. He gazed in every direction. Mist seeped along the peripheries of his vision, almost like a movie special effect. But surely she hadn't been so far ahead?

"Sarah," he said again. He'd meant to shout, but it came out more of a whimper.

Breathing hard from his brief exertion, he continued forwards at a walk. The path swung left. By his reckoning, it would soon bring him back to the road. But it didn't. It brought him to the edge of the village pond.

He stared blankly across at the bushes on the far shore and beyond those, the black and white structures with their steep, thatched roofs.

Puzzled, he turned and glanced behind. As the afternoon advanced, the mist was closing in. It folded over the path to his rear like a dingy curtain. He was certain he'd been moving in the direction of the road, but apparently not. Presumably, in the heat of his confusion, he'd lost his way. Annoyed with himself, and not a little relieved that no one else had been around to witness his burst of irrationality, he walked back along the shore until he reached the bridge, then started across it.

Slowly, the self-pity crept it – as it always did after he'd let his thoughts linger on Sarah. He paused and watched the swans on the water, roughly knuckling a tear from his eye. Overhead, the blue sky of late afternoon was deepening to the violet hue of evening. He knew he had to progress with his life; he needed to move on. But eight months, and it still seemed like yesterday.

When he finally reentered the village, lights had appeared in some of the cottage windows. The air was noticeably cooler, the people moving about quickly as if eager to get in doors.

"Jeanine!" Martine was calling, as he came back into the bar. "Oh, evening Mr Wade. Drink for you now?"

"Yes please, and I'd like to look at your menu."

"Certainly." She passed him a card.

Cameron read it carefully. It was crucial to make sure that

everything appeared to be normal. The first rule of stopping feeling like a widower was stopping behaving like one.

As he perused the menu, he ordered himself a pint of bitter and a double-measure of malt whiskey. He glanced around. The fire, which had been built up to a blaze, crackled deliciously, glowing rose-red on the white walls and leather upholstery. The chap who'd lost his dog was still in the corner, in conversation with an older man, also in a tweed jacket, this one with leather patches at the elbows. Despite the smoking ban, the older man was puffing contentedly on a pipe. And frankly, Cameron didn't care.

"Nice little village you've got here," he told Martine.

"We don't complain," she said, drawing his beer from a brass-handled pump.

"I've never known as peaceful a place. Though I suppose it can feel a bit isolated."

"You get used to it." Another pair of customers now came in. "Jeanine! I need you!" She took Cameron's money and handed him his drinks. "Mind you, we're none of us averse to a little company now and then."

She smiled at him and moved away along the bar.

He wondered what she'd meant by that. Had he misread her comments early on, and was he maybe misreading them now? He didn't think so. A woman living and working here with only her daughter for company, her husband or boyfriend either having left her or died; it wasn't impossible that she wanted another man in her life. He eyed her as she served the new customers. Now that she'd dressed for the evening, she looked even better than before. She had broad hips under her tight-fitted black skirt, but she was slim-waisted, and an ample bosom pushed at her pearl blouse. She sensed him watching, and gave him another pleasant smile. Her red hair shone in the firelight; she was exceedingly pretty – green eyed, scarlet-lipped. Her face was scarcely wrinkled, given her age.

Cameron went and sat in a corner, where he drank thoughtfully and wondered if a bit of harmless, no-strings sex would mess him up as much as he suspected. It wasn't as if he'd be falling in love with someone else – as if such a thing was even possible. But it also occurred to him that maybe, in his current self-centred state, he was overstating his own attractiveness. It could just be that the landlady was being friendly and chatty, as indeed – and he watched her again – she was being friendly and chatty to her other customers. In the end, he decided that it made more sense, at least for the moment, to spend his nights sleeping rather than engaging in some other activity that wouldn't just tire him out physically at a time when he was hoping to reenergise his working day, but would likely have an emotional impact as well.

The beer and whiskey went down like nectar. After he'd eaten, he ordered himself another round, and then another. As the clock ticked towards midnight, he warmed to his decision. Yes, a good night's sleep was the best possible thing under the circumstances. In truth, he couldn't remember the last time he'd had one.

And unfortunately, that coming night would be no different.

*

His eyes snapped open. Footsteps sounded somewhere overhead.

The room was pitch-dark, and he had to fumble around until he found the bedside lamp. He switched it on and glanced up at the ceiling. Someone was pacing back and forth up there. What was more, they were wearing high heels. Each impact was double-barrelled: first a light *clip* as the heel descended, then the heavier *thud*.

Cameron threw the quilt aside and sat up properly. Surely the only room above this was the attic? It could be Martine putting stuff away, but a glance at his watch revealed that it was after four in the morning. He swung his legs to the floor. Overhead, the feet continued to pace.

It wasn't Martine; it was someone else. And he knew who.

He pulled his shorts and T-shirt on, and moved out onto the landing. The passage was dark. A couple of other bedrooms opened off it, but their doors remained closed. Somewhere at the far end, near the stairs leading down to the bar, there was a narrower stair leading up. He crept towards it, feeling along the wall for a light-switch, and only locating one right near the end. When the light came on it was dim, its bulb flickering.

The upwards stair had the look of a utility stair – its treads were bare wood, its walls ordinary plaster. There was no sound from up there, but, whoever it was, they couldn't have come down yet. He padded up. At the top a door stood ajar. The room on the other side was in blackness. He reached forwards. The door opened silently. More of the room became visible, faint beams of moonlight penetrating through what were probably chinks in boards placed over an old upper storey window. There was still no sound.

He had to work his lips together to moisten them sufficiently to speak. "Hello?"

There was no response.

He reached in and around to the side, where a light-switch ought to be. To his surprise he encountered one. He flicked it.

Another dim bulb came on, showing a large, untenanted room. It was indeed the attic: the ceiling was a heavy wooden framework, supported by timber joists, which stood like columns at regular intervals; in its turn, this supported other joists above, which held up the sloped masses of roofing thatch. The room was spacious, running the entire length of the upper floor. It was also empty, except for a few bits of furniture in the centre. One of these was a rocking chair with its back turned. A figure was sitting in it.

The little hairs on Cameron's arms began to prickle.

He could only see the back of the figure's head, which seemed to be covered by a black hood or cowl. It was completely motionless.

"Are you supposed to be up here?" he asked. "Because you're making a lot of noise."

The figure neither moved nor spoke.

"Even if you've got permission, you're keeping me awake."

Still there was no reply.

He ventured nearer. Now that he was close, he could see the spread of the figure's cloaked shoulders; they were immense.

Cameron swallowed nervously. But there was no backing down now, not when there was an entire hotel to call to his assistance.

"Alright, you've been warned." And before he could change his mind, he lunged forwards, grabbing the backrest of the rocking chair and swinging it around to face him.

He stared at the figure face-on, repelled but at the same time bewildered.

It was a toy: a great stuffed ape with glass buttons for eyes and crooked stitches for a mouth. Its face was pallid pink, like the colour of undercooked pork, its fur an odious grey-green, like old men's hair when they've let it grow long and greasy. It was horrible but it was almost life-size, so he could easily imagine some kid clamouring for it in a shop. Of course, it couldn't have made the sounds he'd heard. The only other item nearby, somewhat incongruously, was a coat-stand from which hung a white sports jacket with a pink carnation in the buttonhole.

He turned, scanning farther afield. A piano stood against one wall – an ordinary everyday model, rather battered, with an ashtray stuffed with dog-ends on top of it. On the opposite wall, there was a closed wardrobe.

Cameron approached this latter object more cautiously. It wasn't huge, but it was tall enough for a human to hide inside. When he came within touching distance, he halted. Sweat was damp on his palms again. He took a breath, then grabbed the handle and yanked the door open. With a roar, a vast deluge of materials fell on top of him: footballs, cricket bats, fishing rods, but also plant pots, a child's bike, a scooter, an articulated metal stork that looked as though it belonged in someone's garden, a cardboard box scattering jewellery. The impact on the wooden floor was thunderous, and no sooner had Cameron scrambled back to his feet than he heard someone on the attic stair.

Martine, slightly tousled, in a blue silk dressing-gown and matching blue slippers, burst in. "Mr Wade! What on earth is happening?"

He was more frustrated than embarrassed. "There's a woman I've seen in the village. I think she's staying here."

"I'm sorry?"

"Is a young woman staying here at the inn?"

Martine looked perplexed. "You're the only guest at present."

"She lives nearby then." He tried to describe the woman, mentioning her beige mackintosh, her lovely honey-blonde hair.

Martine was clearly listening, but a little distracted by the wreckage all over her attic floor. "There's no such person in this village."

"Maybe your daughter knows her?"

"I assure you she doesn't."

"You're bloody lying!"

Martine looked stunned, even horrified. "I beg your pardon?"

Cameron had started and now he couldn't stop, and why should he? It wasn't a matter of imagining things. He knew what he'd heard – and what he'd seen, and it was all getting a bit much. "What're you people up to, eh? Earlier on, you knew I was going to my car, so you sent this woman over there ahead of me. Is that what you did? Now you've allowed her to come into the inn, so she can walk around over the top of my damn bedroom!"

"Mr Wade, what are you…"

"You can cut the innocent crap. You act as if you don't know who I am. But you must know. Everyone knows. I've written eight best-selling novels."

"And I'm supposed to have read them?"

"You must have heard of them at least. The last one was…" Fleetingly, he couldn't remember his latest title. But it didn't matter. "The point is I'm famous. And maybe that's your motive? Are you doing this to get one over on me?"

"I have no idea what you're talking about."

"Maybe you don't want me to write about your village? I planned to change the name, but now I don't think I will."

"Why would anyone want to write about our village?"

"Why the hell do you think? Because of the curse!"

"Mr Wade… what curse?"

She looked genuinely nonplussed. But Cameron wasn't buying it. He wasn't buying any of it. Still in his shorts and T-shirt, he raced past her downstairs and, after banging around with the bolts on the front door, crashed out into the village square.

"The curse that you commemorate with this thing!" he shouted. "This hideous thing!"

He pointed at the pillory, a spectral, cruciform shape in the half-darkness. Martine followed him outside, now looking concerned rather than confused. Lights had appeared in windows. Cottage doors opened; other villagers emerged.

"It's just a relic of the past," she said.

"Hardly that," he retorted. "It's brand new."

"Well I've never known there to be a different one here."

By the expression on her face, she was completely sincere. They all were. He halted briefly – could she be telling the truth? He shook his head. Of course she couldn't. Not only had the mysterious woman looked like Sarah, she'd vanished into thin air. Then she'd vanished from the attic!

"Are you ashamed? Is that it? You know all about the atrocity that happened here and you don't like the way it tars you?" He approached the pillory. "It's this thing, isn't it? You're happy to take the money of the tourists who come to gawk at it, but you don't want anyone digging up the grisly details…"

His words stuttered out. He'd just placed a hand on the

wooden upright, and now felt what seemed like a bolt of fire searing down his arm. He body went rigid, his tongue caught between his teeth. Then a stench assailed him: of blood, sweat and human faeces.

Firelight suddenly glared on all sides. There was smoke in the air, a chorus of shrieking voices. Alongside him, a figure was pinioned in the pillory. Even as he watched, its filthy, ragged clothes were stripped away by raking hands. A curved spine was exposed, white skin already blemished with bruises. The figure gargled for breath as its struggles tightened the clamp around its neck. And now the blows began to rain down – belts, whips, birch rods – in a relentless assault, which split and cross-split the naked flesh and soon was tearing it away in great bloody chunks. The gargles became choked squeals. But the blows fell mercilessly; the feral roars increased in volume.

Cameron twisted away, sickened. Men's faces thrust at him; bearded, pock-marked, their eyes ablaze; there were women too, giggling or screaming, their unkempt hair hanging in strands from under their grubby linen caps.

He wanted to stop them. But how could he? To make a stand now might turn their fury on him. So he stood back and watched as the fire-lit form writhed and gibbered; as slowly but surely, in a welter of blood and hanging tissue, its exposed musculature was shredded from the gleaming bones beneath…

Unable to stand any more, he clapped a hand to his face – which drew mumbles of polite confusion. Warily, he parted his fingers.

The night was quiet again. Various worried faces peered down at him.

"He's alright," someone said. "Must've fainted."

Weakly, Cameron allowed them to get him to his feet and steer him into the inn, where they placed him on a sofa.

"A brandy should do it."

Cameron shook his head. Things were already blurred enough; he didn't want alcohol, he wanted answers. "You're trying to keep it hushed up, yes? I understand that. Just tell me… this business with the woman, it's a trick, a hoax? You've been trying to scare me away?"

"Poor chap's still not himself."

"Tell me about the curse then!" A glass was pushed into his hand, but he slammed it down on the nearest table. "Everyone knows there's a Whitebrook curse, but no one knows what form it takes. Why do you keep it secret?"

"He's lost his marbles."

"Don't piss down my back and tell me it's raining!" Cameron shouted.

"Mr Wade!" a female voice said firmly. It was Martine. She was now sitting alongside him. She put an admonishing hand on his arm. "There is no Whitebrook curse. Now where have you heard such nonsense?"

She seemed sincere, as did all those around him. He glanced from face to face, and for the first time wondered if maybe he was wrong. Where had he actually heard about Whitebrook? Surely he must have had good information otherwise why would he have gone to the trouble of coming here?

"Maybe you've just had a nightmare?" someone suggested.

It was the elderly man in the patched tweed jacket. He was still wearing that jacket, now over the top of his pyjamas. It was the same for the others; they'd all put coats or dressing-gowns over their nightwear. They seemed like honest people. Their expressions were of concern rather than annoyance – though maybe that in itself was too good to be true. For all that he was being cordially treated, Cameron still felt that he was among enemies.

He stood up abruptly. "I have to leave."

"In the middle of the night?" Martine said.

"As soon as possible." Some primal instinct now warned Cameron that he mustn't stay here a moment longer. But for the sake of civility, he tried to make light of everything that had happened. He half-smiled. "Good thing I didn't have that brandy, I've a long drive ahead…" His smile faded. "My car, damn! Look… I need a phone."

44

There was a dull silence.

"You do have a telephone?" he asked Martine.

"Yes."

"I need a garage, my car's broken down. Don't worry, I'll pay for the call."

"It doesn't matter about that." For the first time, she sounded cross, maybe insulted. "It's on the bar."

He followed her over and sat on a stool, as she slipped back behind the counter and handed him a telephone. It was an ornamental piece, Edwardian-looking. He hadn't memorised any relevant numbers, the AA for example. But again Martine came to his rescue, giving him a piece of paper with a number scribbled on it.

"These people are pretty reliable. They provide emergency night-cover."

"Thanks… thanks very much." Quite possibly, once he got home he was going to have to make a long and very apologetic phone-call to The Whitebrook Arms. But for the meantime *this* phone-call was all that mattered.

He tapped out the number. It rang for a minute before a man answered. "Hello?"

"My name's Wade. Do you do roadside repairs?"

"Whereabouts are you?"

"The Whitebrook Arms, Whitebrook. My car's stuck on the south side, the road that stops at the bollards. Can you help me?"

"I dare say so." Oddly, the voice sounded familiar.

Cameron glanced around. The excitement over, the villagers were drifting away. "How long will you be?"

"Difficult to say."

"I need to know. So I can be waiting there for you."

"Want it doing tonight, do you?"

"That's the point of this conversation, isn't it?" The voice was definitely familiar. Suddenly Cameron had the suspicion he was being humoured. He glanced around again; aside from him, the bar was now empty. Even Martine had disappeared.

"Can you do it, or can't you?"

"That depends."

"Who are you?"

"Beg your pardon, sir."

"I'm supposed to be talking to a breakdown service. What company are you?"

"Does that matter?"

"Can't you give a straight answer to a simple question?"

"I was wondering the same about you, Mr Wade?"

"Eh?"

"Have you seen a missing dog? I asked you that quite clearly. He's a small mongrel, a rather scruffy looking beggar. You didn't help me at all…"

Cameron slammed the phone down, jumped from his stool and backed away. The bar area was still empty. The door behind the counter stood open and there was a light on in the room it connected to. But there was no sound. Where'd they all gone?

He had the distinct feeling it wasn't very far.

In fact, he was certain they were listening to him right now.

He edged towards the hall, then turned and ran. He passed the bottom of the darkened stairway, but he wasn't risking going up there even to get his clothes.

Outside, he was tempted to head across the footbridge towards his BMW, but that would be an obvious direction. Instead, he circled the meeting house and emerged on the car park where the Rolls Royce stood unguarded.

Could he hot-wire it? He wasn't sure, but one thing was certain – he'd followed miles of silent, wooded lanes to get here. It would be no easy thing escaping on foot.

He grabbed up a large stone. It was heavy, and he had to heft it with both hands as he approached the Roller. Glinting in the moonlight, it was a silver-blue Phantom, beautiful, ultra luxurious. It would be a crime to damage such a vehicle, but what choice did he have? All he'd need to do was put the passenger window through, rip out the panel under the dashboard…

But wait. It *was* a crime.

What the devil was he thinking?

There was no proof these people had been playing games with him. To all intents and purposes, they'd been kind. It would be bad enough that he'd run from a hotel without paying his bill. But to then steal a quality car? He could see the headlines now:

Bereaved author goes crazy in quaint village
They welcomed him with open arms; he repaid them with violence

He dropped the stone and crossed the car park on foot, entering the foliage on its far side. Immediately, he was in trackless woodland. He advanced determinedly, but was ill-clad for such a venture. Tendrils of freezing mist lay across his path; as the first rush of adrenaline faded, the sweat plastering the shirt to his back started to turn icy. He winced as his unshod feet landed on sharp stones or prickly twigs. He had no idea which direction he was headed in. The north perhaps? But even if he was, where would that take him to – a road, another town?

Whichever, wild horses wouldn't drag him back to that village of lunatics. All he needed to do was keep reminding himself that this was not some vast wilderness; it was modern England, and he'd find help soon. But the mist continued to thicken, the temperature to drop. Soon his feet were bruised and cut, his toes numb.

Then he heard voices approaching.

He halted, panting.

There were a number of them – men and women together.

Cameron's flesh began to creep.

They were shouting to one another. He imagined them spread out, like a skirmish line in a battle. But that wasn't the main problem; the main problem was that they were approaching from the front.

Had he come round a circle?

Mist hung on all sides; the trees were ethereal shapes, black stanchions glistening with dew. There was nothing distinctive, no point of reference. He could be going in any direction and wouldn't realise it. The voices drew nearer: they sounded coarse, guttural. Then he saw the torchlight. Initially it appeared as a row of glowing blobs in the gloom, but soon he saw the flames, and then he saw the people themselves. They were only silhouettes, but they were clearly armed – with clubs, farm tools, ropes.

Cameron fled.

Not back the way he'd come. Nothing would induce him to go that way. Instead, he went left, plunging though thickets and thorn breaks, clawing himself, plucking his underclothes, which were already bloodied and damp. Again he envisioned that tortured form, bowed and quivering in the pillory, its flesh hanging in gory ribbons.

All the time he could hear the voices behind. Whenever he glanced back, he saw shadowy forms in the glowing mist. As such, he almost collided with the building that suddenly loomed out of the night in front of him. This too was fogbound, only vaguely distinctive, but he saw black beams, white plaster. He also saw a door – a heavy one, made from oaken planks studded with nail-heads. He didn't imagine for one second that it would be unlocked. Yet when he twisted the steel ring that served as its handle, it opened. He slid through and closed it behind him. Fumbling in the dark, he found a bolt and rammed it home. Then he stood listening, soaked with sweat, barely able to suppress the dragging sound of his own breathing.

Almost immediately, he heard voices on the other side. Through the gaps between the planks came the glint of firelight. There was a growl of argument, which seemed to last an age. Cameron expected imminent blows on the wood.

But that didn't happen.

At length, the voices faded. Soon he could no longer hear them. Was it a ruse? Was someone still there, listening for him? Sweat pumped from his brow as he strained his ears. But there was no sound. Minutes ticked by and at last he relaxed a little.

He looked around. He was in some kind of village outbuilding. Spears of moonlight revealed stacks of what looked like mouldering paperwork. There was a passage leading through the centre of it towards another door. He had to turn sideways to move along it, but then began stubbing his toes on angular objects littering the floor. He picked one up. Moving into patch of moonlight, he saw that it was a book, very old, its cloth binding frayed around the edges. Printed in gold leaf, its title read: *West Country Lore*. He glanced at the encircling stacks. They smelled musty, mildewed, and now that his eyes were attuning properly, he saw that these were also mainly books.

He took a couple down. The first was: *The Gossip of Dean (amusing histories of the great wood)*. The second was: *Yarns of the Summer Land*. He flicked into it. It was an A-Z of West Country legends. With a vague sense that he was doing something he was going to regret, he worked his way through the Ws and found: *Whitebrook: A Curse*.

He had to hold it close to read it:

In the early 17th century, a series of misfortunes befell the small rural community of Whitebrook, Gloucestershire. It was a toilsome life at the best of times, but when milk was delivered sour, animals began to stray and crops developed blight, local people became suspicious that witchcraft was the cause.

A woman called Alice Fairwood lived outside the village because she was said to have loose morals. Though described as 'comely', she had been born with one eye green and one eye blue, which in a superstitious age indicated that she'd been marked by the devil. She became implicated in the disasters when a poacher was arrested and, to save himself from punishment, made a statement that he'd followed a rabbit after it had escaped from his snare, only to see it enter a mass of undergrowth and emerge on the other side as a naked woman. The poacher insisted the woman was Alice Fairwood, and that, as a result of being snared, she'd limped as she'd walked away. Another witness then came forwards, a village scold whose husband was believed to have had adulterous meetings with Alice, and claimed to have seen her riding over the tree-tops on a hurdle.

The resulting trial led to uproar. The villagers were convinced the evil in their midst had been uncovered. But the magistrate, a level-headed man, dismissed the charges as ludicrous, and described the poacher and the village scold as the most unreliable witnesses he'd ever heard. However, to calm the angry mob, he acknowledged complaints about Alice's 'licentious behaviour' and ordered that she be placed in the pillory for two days and two nights.

The villagers were not satisfied and took the law into their own hands. That first night, Alice was beaten so brutally that she died, but not before uttering the famous Whitebrook curse. What form this took has been debated for centuries, but the general belief is that one generation of Whitebrook villagers after another would be struck with a conviction that they had lost something dear to them – even though the item in question had never been theirs in the first place – and would thus pine away in misery.

When he finally stopped reading, Cameron's mouth had gone dry. He dropped the book and went quickly to the index of the next. There was an entry for Whitebrook in this one too. The story, though worded differently, was identical in content. Its final paragraph read:

The curse was a dread scourge. The villagers ran about, searching in vain for things they believed they had lost, whereas in fact they had never owned such articles. The anguish of this drove some mad and sent others to their graves.

Cameron grabbed another. It was aged, its pages cracked and desiccated. This too dealt with West Country lore. It had a section on Whitebrook:

They fully believed they had each lost the dearest thing they owned, when in truth they had lost nothing. No amount of reasoning would sway this irrational belief.

He glanced again at the mouldering book-stacks. Little wonder the scholars had been scratching around in the dark. It was all here – hidden in this building, every book or scrap of documentation that detailed the Whitebrook curse. Not that filling out the blanks in history was Cameron's prime concern now. He fought his way down the aisle and yanked the next door open. Suddenly he was desperate for fresh air. The stench and must of that dingy repository had become overpowering. Outside, dawn had broken – a chill, ice-blue dawn where thin curls of mist provided the only movement. But it had broken over the village car park.

Cameron had emerged from the meeting-house.

He tried not to let this faze him, which wasn't difficult as his mind was still reeling from he'd just read. He stumbled into the main square. There was no sign of life. All doors were closed; all lights extinguished. He glanced up at the window to his bedroom, hoping to see Martine gazing down at him, wrapped only in a quilt. At that moment, he'd have done anything for the warmth of a female body, to feel sweet breath in his ear, soft lips on his cheek. But with Martine it could never be – never, ever, and for that reason it was no disaster that the window was dark and empty. He turned and looked at the pillory, seemingly the one immovable fixture in this place of spatial confusion.

It was smeared all over with fresh blood.

Even this didn't surprise him. Nor did the bloody footprints that led away from it, meandering across the square and vanishing around a corner. They'd been made by bare feet, and he wondered briefly if they might be his own. But then he rounded the last building and saw down to the edge of the village pond, and his throat tightened.

The woman with the honey-blonde hair was standing there, her back turned, gazing over the water. The bloody tracks led straight up to her, but she was as immaculately dressed as before: her beige mac, her glinting high-heeled shoes.

This time as Cameron approached, she didn't walk away. He stood alongside her.

It was several moments before he could bring himself to say: "You should realise, the villagers refuse to accept this."

"It's not that they refuse, it's that they're unable." Her voice was soft, her accent faintly rural – like Sarah's he was sure, if only he could recall Sarah's voice. "They lack your power of imagination, your instinct for terrible truths."

"I refuse to accept it too."

"Are you certain?"

"I was definitely married. I'm certain about that."

She turned to look at him. She was beautiful, as he'd expected, despite one eye being blue and the other green. "How long were you married for?"

Cameron struggled to put his mind back. No answer came to him.

"Very well, how did your wife die? Surely you remember that?"

"I remember everything…"

"You remember nothing, Cameron. Because it's all a delusion."

She wasn't being cruel, saying this. There was no gloat in her enigmatic little smile.

"I can learn to live without her," he said, choked. "You're not all powerful."

"I never claimed to be."

"I can get on with my life. I'll just walk away from this."

"Through the mist?"

He glanced across the water. The mist was now so thick that it completely hid the opposite shore. That would be a challenge; it had been difficult enough to penetrate the woods even in light mist – especially when every path had seemed to wind its way back to the village. But at least the footbridge was still visible, ten yards to their left.

Cameron moved towards it, reassured. When he stepped onto it, it was solid. Even though its far end was concealed, he started across.

"I'm only trying to save you from yourself," she said. He glanced back. She'd followed him onto the bridge; in fact she was right behind him. "This time, the other side of the water will be less pleasant for you."

He laughed and continued forwards. "Words, Miss Fairwood. Nothing but words."

"Words are the only power I ever had. And now that you've found the truth, even their effect is nullified."

He stepped ashore, half-expecting to find himself in the village again. But now it was difficult to tell where he was. The vapour enveloped everything.

"Hardly nullified," he replied, distracted by the whiteness swirling around him. "The pain of losing Sarah's as real as ever, I assure you."

"That's because Sarah is real."

Cameron was feeling strangely light-headed. It took several seconds for that statement to strike him. He spun around. The woman was still on the bridge, but now receding across the water as if the bridge was somehow retracting.

"As real as the poor mutt that lives on the backstreets of Whitebrook," she added. "Bedraggled by rain and frost, desperate for the return of the kindly master it had never actually had. As real as the delinquent teenage girl, a hopeless case, in and out of care, always hankering for the pretty mother and cosy home she'd never known."

Cameron heard each word, but now was too dizzy to

respond.

"You think that Rolls Royce is in grief for something it believes it's lost, Cameron? How about the ape in the attic?"

Incredulous, he held his hands to his face: they were dissolving, trailing off in streamers of milky ectoplasm, which, even as he watched, were mingling with the mist.

"Sarah is not your non-existent dream," the woman said.

The terror inside him ought to have blown his chest apart, but his chest no longer existed. His T-shirt fell away in gossamer threads. His ribs followed in light, frothy suds.

"Cameron... *you* are Sarah's dream."

The whiteness filling his eyes was now beyond white.

"Or rather, you *were*."

A CRY FOR HELP

Joel Lane

The train journey to Harrogate took nearly four hours, including an hour in the metal and concrete maze that was Leeds Station. It was an overcast day; the sun flashed occasionally through the leaden clouds like a police car on a city street. Between the railway line and the bare fields were various small industrial units that resembled factories without walls: engines, pipes, steel walkways suspended in mid-air. Plastic huts where people stayed.

Carl should have been looking through the conference programme, briefing himself on who to talk to and where to be. Networking didn't happen by itself. But as usual on trains, he kept shifting into and out of sleep. There'd been too many late nights recently. He needed to sharpen up his attitude. The conference would help. Janice had never understood why work was so important to him. It did more than pay the rent: it kept him sane.

The moments when he fell asleep, or almost fell asleep, while travelling were when he really missed her. His phone and laptop enabled him to contact everyone who counted – but who did he want to talk to? There was no e-hand you could reach out and touch, no e-mouth you could kiss. At least not yet. *He travels fastest who travels alone.* He didn't need company. What he did need, he wasn't sure.

By the time he reached Harrogate, night had fallen; the town centre had the trustworthy glow of electric light. Carl walked down through the main street, past the elaborate facades of theme bars and restaurants. The pink silhouette of a crouching woman with cat ears and a tail advertised a gentlemen's club. A camera flashed on the steps of a hotel, where a young couple were leaning into a stage-managed kiss. The air was thin and cold.

Beyond the conference centre, the streetlamps were further

apart and the buildings mostly dark. Trees, stripped by autumn, trembled in the headlights of passing cars. Rain brushed Carl's face gently. His hotel was set back from the road, a small renovated building with flawless off-white pillars. As he walked up the path, carrying his briefcase and overnight bag, an early firework exploded behind the hotel and wept silver tears over its roof.

His room, on the third floor, turned out to be a twin room charged at single rate. The wall behind the beds was plasterboard; he hoped his neighbours were quiet. The TV offered terrestrial and satellite channels, plus classic films and pay-per-view porn. He wanted to lie down and catch a few minutes' sleep, but the room depressed him: it was too obviously prefabricated, like a stage set.

Hotels always made him think of Janice. How she'd make herself at home in a double bed, turning her head from side to side as if they were already making love. How utterly still she was when sleeping. One of the signs that things were coming apart was that she stopped sleeping well. Had he done the right thing to let her go? Or would it have been even worse?

Janice lived on her own, and had recently lost her job. It was a fortnight before they found her. The unanswered phone calls led her sister to contact the police. Her neighbours had put the smell down to a blocked drain. She'd opened the veins in her wrists. There'd been a note, but Carl had no idea what it said. Her family hadn't invited him to Janice's funeral – just sent him a cutting about her from the *Express & Star*.

It still chilled him to think about, nearly a year later. He tried not to. Shit happened, people broke up. People broke down. Janice had been quite irrational at times – and not only *those* times, though mostly then. He wasn't responsible for that. The real world was there to be lived in.

The rain was heavier when he left the hotel. To save getting wet, he ate at the nearest restaurant: an up-market Italian place that served pizzas with balsamic vinegar and olive oil. His beer came in a frosted glass that stuck to his hand. Despite its cost (his company expense account took the pain away), the food didn't seem to taste of anything. Through a glass pane, he could see two chefs at work in the kitchen. One of them must have spilt some oil, because a flare like a magnesium ribbon lit up the corner of his eye. He could still see it when he rubbed the eyelid, and soon he smelt the burning. His mouth felt dry.

Leaving the restaurant, Carl decided a short walk would clear his head. The rain had stopped. He ran through the essentials of his presentation as he strolled up Cheltenham Parade towards the train station. *We see private health insurance as a contract between provider and customer, a doorway to security and wellness for all. We're taking the ambitions of the discredited NHS model and rebranding them for a society freed from the shackles of state control.* The rest was PowerPoint and some free DVDs of the corporate video for potential contractees.

The dryness had spread to his throat. A bad cough was the last thing he needed for tomorrow. Carl dropped into a crowded basement bar and downed a quick vodka and tonic, then another. A few young women in business suits were gathered at the bar; their eyes and teeth gleamed as they talked, but the music soaked up their voices. He was getting too old to fancy his chances, these days. How much did the porn channel at the hotel cost? But however they disguised it on his bill (and he wouldn't claim it), Carl's manager would know what he'd done. He didn't want to pay for an escort – and it worried him that he was even considering that. At what point did you become capable of something?

Suddenly angry with himself, Carl walked out of the bar and turned back towards the hotel. Except apparently not, because – as often with alcohol – he'd swapped left and right on his inner map. A few minutes later, he was completely lost. An old man was standing under a railway bridge just ahead, smoking a thin roll-up. Maybe he'd know the way back to the station. The smoker looked up at the roof of the tunnel, then turned away. Carl ran to catch him up.

Under the bridge, rainwater was dripping through brickwork. Mercury tubes in wire cages gave off a weak unreal light. The old man had stopped to put out his cigarette underfoot. He was wearing an old check jacket of the kind Terry-Thomas would have worn. Carl stepped past him and said, "Excuse me. Do you know the way to the train station?"

The old man glanced at him. "Can you help me?" he said. There was some kind of growth over his left eye. He fumbled in his jacket pocket, took out a coil of plastic-covered wire. One end was tied crudely in a noose. "I need to fix this to something." He gestured towards one of the wire cages. "Do you think that will take my weight?"

Carl couldn't stop himself looking up. He doubted it. "I'm sorry," he said. "I can't help you." As he walked on, embarrassment stiffening his face, he wondered how long the guy had been waiting there. How many people he'd asked.

There was no-one in the street beyond the bridge. None of the houses were lit. This was clearly a less wealthy part of town: the cars were grimy, the houses narrow and run-down, the front gardens overgrown. But he couldn't face going back past the old man. There had to be other routes. Carl walked up the road, turned right. A skinny teenager in a combat jacket was waiting to cross the road as a long goods vehicle passed. Carl felt his hands tense involuntarily. He could do some damage if he had to defend himself. "Hey," he called.

The youth turned slowly. His face was stained with yellow light. "Please help us," he said. Carl stared at him, unable to answer. The boy pointed to the roadway. His left leg was distorted, the foot caught in a futile dance step. "Push us under a lorry. I can't jump." Another long vehicle approached and he leaned forward, his face taut with longing. Carl backed away, then turned and ran.

He was afraid of not finding the bridge, but panic restored his sense of direction. The old man was still waiting there; Carl ran straight past him. A few minutes later, he reached the cluster of bus shelters outside the train station. A black cab was approaching; he waved it down. The driver didn't ask him for help.

A couple of large brandies in the hotel bar took the edge off his fear and let his exhaustion soak through. The amber light of Remy Martin glowed in his unsteady hand. Near midnight, he stumbled to the lift and went up to his room. He chose the left-hand bed, because he'd always slept on the left when sharing his bed with Janice. She liked to be nearer the wall.

The couple in the next room argued all night, the wall too thin to keep their business private. Fireworks went off somewhere behind the building. Carl's mattress was flimsy and too short for him; it felt like a bunk bed. He got up a few times to drink water or piss, a cycle he often fell into when tired. At last he drifted into a dull, inert blankness that passed for sleep.

The sound of ragged breathing woke him. He opened his eyes and saw two figures on the other bed. Just enough light filtered through the curtains to show him one figure was a man. The other was a blurred grey thing, terribly incomplete. They were locked in some intense congress, both a death-struggle and an act of love. He watched them for a couple of minutes, afraid to prove the vision real by moving. Then his alarm clock began to shrill. He turned it off, and when he looked back the other bed was empty. Then he switched on the light. The unused bedspread was smooth, but flakes of ash were scattered over it.

The conference was a long, hard day of networking – or, as they called it in these parts, chiselling. Shaking hands, exchanging business cards and corporate brand messages. Carl's presentation was well received and earned him a pocketful of contacts, at least half a dozen of which he expected would lead to business. By the end of the day, he'd filled three pages of his notebook with other people's thoughts to be digested, assimilated and passed off as his own. From a health insurance consultant: *The American model is a visionary healthcare system that lights up the way for Europe.*

And from a university lecturer in marketing: *Health and safety legislation is an attempt to mimic the effect of market forces in a state-run economy.*

As he left the conference centre, the streets were getting dark. His throat was burning from the dry air and the amount of talking he'd done. But if he stopped for a drink, he wouldn't get back to Solihull before midnight. He could get a beer and a sandwich when he changed trains at Leeds. A hard day, but worth it – and not just from his company's point of view. It helped him not to think about Janice. Coming through like a bruise.

He was near the station when a violent flare drowned the street in red-gold light. No sound followed it. Was that a firework or something going up in flames? Or the night itself splitting open to reveal its fiery heart? He kept walking, but the light didn't come back. By the time its afterimage had faded, he was at the bridge. A young woman was standing in the tunnel.

This time he didn't run away. There were people who needed his help. Their voices, like the rose of fire, had been trying to reach him for a long time. Whether they knew it or not. The girl under the bridge had ash-blonde hair; she was dressed in a long fabric coat. As he came closer, he could see that her hands were severely burned. The fingers were shrunken claws. She turned to face him, holding a razor blade in the scarred palm of her left hand. "Help me," she said. "Please." She mimed putting the blade to her right wrist. The sliver of metal fell to the pavement.

Carl looked at the darkness of her eyes. He crouched to pick up the razor. The light from a passing car flared in it, blue and white. He stood up and touched the girl's thin arm. "That'll be fifty pounds," he said. "I can take a card."

WITH DEEPEST SYMPATHY

Johnny Mains

"Beautiful."

Mrs Primrose Hildebrand smiled and reached across for the red biro and circled a small notice that had been posted that day in the obituaries section of the local paper.

> Mr Terry Buddock
> Died peacefully at home
> Aged 69 years.
> Funeral will be held at...

Primrose scanned through the rest of the recently deceased, but Terry was the only one for that day. It made sense now why his wife Jean hadn't been helping out at the church for the last day or so like she normally did.

Primrose got up from the solid oak dining table and walked across to the ornately carved mahogany writing desk that used to belong to her husband. She had never been able to bring herself to part with it. Reaching up behind her neck, she undid the clasp of her necklace – a small black key dangled lazily on the fine silver chain. Pulling the key from the chain carefully so as not to break the links, she bent down and inserted it into the lock of the main drawer and as it clicked, she pulled the drawer open, revealing a small stack of finely decorated sympathy cards and envelopes. Also lying by their side was a large leather bound ledger and a fountain pen. Taking them out, she relocked the drawer and went back to the table.

Sitting down, she flicked through the book, peering at the minuscule handwriting that filled nearly every page. After going through a good ten of them, she finally came to what she was after. She reached for her pen, opened up the condolence card and started to write.

With Deepest Sympathy

Dearest Jean,

I'm ever so sorry to hear about Terry's passing. I hope that he didn't suffer, but if he did, it's probably his punishment from God for creeping about with that floozy that he used to work with all those years ago in the needle making factory. You know the one? Gretchen Banks her name was. If I remember rightly, she suddenly left – transferred is one word – though I like to call it pregnant.

Tell anyone about this card, and I'll make sure that the Vicar finds out about the time your hand dipped into the Starving Children from Africa fund.

What, you think I didn't know?

I'll see you at the funeral.

With deepest sympathy,

Primrose.

Chuckling to herself, Primrose put the card into its envelope, sealed it and stuck a stamp on. It would have been easier to post it herself – Jean only lived around the corner, but it was all part of the game.

At the funeral, Primrose was there, elegant in her finest funeral wear. As was to be expected Jean couldn't or wouldn't meet her eye. And when everyone went back to Jean's house for a few drinks and nibbles it was up to her brother Ronald to hold court as his sister retired to her room as she was feeling 'delicate'.

Primrose loved it.

*

Primrose lived in a 4 bedroom detached house in the village of Effingham-on-the-Stour and had lived there since she was married, but had lived in the village all of her life. As far as she was concerned, she *was* the community.

At 67 she had been widowed for the last forty years – there was never any thinking that she would find another man, her husband Ralph was and would be the only one in her life. They had been married only two years when he died in a fire that swept through the factory where he was a manager. He had his sights set on actually owning the factory when his father passed on. She had carried herself well, all the way through her defined mourning period – up until the moment the postman delivered a parcel to her door six months after Ralph was in the ground. Opening it up on their kitchen table, the same one where she wrote her sympathy cards, the parcel revealed her late husband's passion for producing Victorian-style pornography books. Going through the house, Primrose ended up in the loft, covered from head to toe in filth looking at three boxes of porno books that her husband had produced and had been producing before they had ever met. There were also photos. Photographs of Ralph in different positions with lots of women. Positions he hadn't even tried with her.

The betrayal destroyed Primrose, and after she had burned everything she retreated into her own little world, and never ventured outdoors. She prayed a lot.

Ralph, in life had been wise and while he wasn't producing books for the mass masturbators – had invested carefully and considerately. Primrose soon found herself receiving an income which entitled her to a living way beyond the means she was accustomed to. She was rich, but soon she was obscenely rich and with the help of her bank manager who received a handsome cut she further invested and then sold when the time was right.

This was still when she was housebound. She had made arrangements with her nearest neighbours, the Probes, who made sure that she had shopping in and that all other affairs were catered to. Her life had settled into a routine which was such that she felt that she could stay indoors until the day she died. She could feed off her bitterness quite happily.

One day, she was in the bedroom polishing her dressing table when she heard her neighbour, Ewan Probe, the newly qualified doctor talking to Sheila Winthrope one of the Circle ladies, down on the street below.

"I'm pregnant, Ewan."

"I'll arrange for you to come in next week for an appointment," Ewan said in an arguably quieter voice than was his normal demeanour.

"It's yours, Ewan."

Stunned, both Ewan and Primrose reeled back, she into the room, covering her mouth so she wouldn't let anything escape lest she was overheard overhearing.

"You're having the abortion, Sheila. Or I swear by God, I'll destroy you," Ewan nearly shouted.

Scandal! Well how delicious! Primrose wondered who she should tell first then stopped herself. Ralph, her husband had his secrets that he had kept for her and what trouble they had caused. Would she still be married to him if he had told her that he published dirty books? After thinking on it for a while, Primrose decided that she wasn't in the business of breaking marriages. But an idea of sorts started to form in her mind.

Five months later, and after knowing what she would dedicate her life to, Primrose decided that the time for her to finally go and brave the outside world had come. She had secrets to collect.

*

The phone rang and Primrose got up from watching a documentary on the glue sniffers of Hull to answer it.

"Hello, Stour 61230 speaking, how can I help you?" she asked in a fresh but clipped accent.

"You bitch!" a voice screamed down the line to her. "How could you do this to me?" The voice burst into tears as Primrose smiled gleefully.

"Well *hello*, Jean," Primrose absently brushed away a fly that came too close to her face.

"Everyone knew; everyone but *me*!" Jean whispered. "Do you know what it's like to live a lie? To know that the man that you love is… why would you do such a thing? Why would you do this to me? I thought that we were friends."

"Not friends – just two people that get along every time they happen to meet. I'm counting on you to do the decorations for the Thanksgiving Day feast of course. Next Wednesday, 3:00 p.m."

Primrose scrunched her nose with distaste as the fly buzzed past it.

"Are you insane?" Jean said, her voice sounding truly amazed at the brass neck of this harridan. "I wouldn't go there for all the money in the world!"

Primrose giggled. "But you will go there to safeguard the money that you stole from the church fund. I hear that those unwashed jail lesbians would just love your *hausfrau* frame. Wednesday. 3:00 p.m. sharp."

Primrose slammed the phone down and her hand darted into the air and caught the fly. She squashed it, then walked through to the kitchen and washed her hands, knowing fully well that Jean wouldn't say anything to anyone.

*

When Primrose ventured out into the outdoor world after her self-imposed sentence she seemed to gather up every little bit of gossip; no matter how trivial it seemed at the time. She bought a leather bound ledger and started to write everything down. Sometimes she would stumble over big secrets, other times she would have to add up all the little bits together before she had something tangible. She began to read behaviour, and see things that others were blind to. Primrose became for the want of a better word, a sponge. Years passed, decades passed and the amount of information that she had amassed was truly staggering. And if someone died and Primrose had information on the deceased and the deceased's next of kin, she would strike – sending a beautifully decorated *With Sympathy* card detailing all of the gruesome information that she had been able to get. And so that her gleefully distasteful pastime didn't come to an abrupt end – she would scare the bereaved into saying nothing by threatening to expose them for whatever mistake or arrogance they had been responsible for.

Primrose Hildebrand had a little bit of something on everybody. Half of the town lived in fear of her, and the other half were blissfully unaware of the damage that she could do.

*

"She's dead? Oh well – that is fantastic news!" Primrose sat back in her chair staring at the Obituaries and clapped her hands with unbridled joy. Maria Makepeace had died aged 53. Now, this was a biggie – she didn't need her book for this one. Maria's husband was going to get it with both barrels.

Illtyd Makepeace was a self-made millionaire who was said to have had dealings with the Devil himself. He lost his fortune twice, and had bounced back both times as if nothing had ever happened. He used and abused and hurt and destroyed everyone who had the misfortune to be in his way.

Reaching for her pen, she opened up a rather spectacular looking sympathy card, one bought especially for such an occasion.

Dear Illtyd,

I am heartbroken for you at such a time in your life. It must be worse still for you to discover that for the past five years Maria was having an affair with your younger brother Crane. You seriously didn't think that it was you who gave her that smile on her face? The brother that you trusted completely was screwing you and your wife over.

Now, just in case you go shouting out – I would like to remind you about your fascination with animals, and more so – the private little film you made out in Bulgaria last year. And yes, I have a copy – don't ask me how much I paid for it –

you can rest assured that it was worth every penny.
I'll see you at the funeral, of course.
Primrose Hildebrand.

While the first part of the letter was absolute dynamite –
Primrose was taking a calculated risk with the second part.
There were only whispers of a certain film in which Illtyd got
it on with a female German Shepherd when he went on a
business trip a few years back.

Throwing caution to the wind, she sent it off anyway and at
the funeral, while Illtyd looked at her like she was shit on his
shoe – he didn't approach her, she also noticed that his brother
Crane was nowhere to be seen. So the film *was* genuine!
Primrose smiled beneath her black veil and wondered about
having a poke around his house during the drinks and nibbles
and seeing if she could find it. She wasn't surprised and not in
the least bit put out though when she was told by some cousin
of Illtyd's that she wasn't welcome.

*

Three weeks later and Primrose was ill in bed with the flu. It
was something she hardly ever got, and she was annoyed at
herself for catching it. She was drifting in and out of a feverish
sleep when she heard the postman open her gate, and whistling
that high pitched drivel he was always so keen on doing. He
rattled the letterbox loudly as he pushed the mail through.
Primrose slowly got out of bed and trudged down the stairs
and went to the door. There were a couple of letters, one of
them most definitely a bill of some sorts. She walked through
to the kitchen and put on the kettle and opened the first one
that hadn't been postmarked.

It was a card that had *With Deepest Sympathy* emblazoned
ornately on the frontispiece, with a sunset scene underneath the
gold leaf lettering. Grinning and wondering who would have
the temerity to send her such a thing, she opened it up and was

taken aback for a moment at the blood red copperplate handwriting.

Primrose,
  Deepest Sympathy on the loss of your foot.
  Regards,

A shudder of cold paranoia swept over her, but then she shrugged it off and put the card in the bin. She would have to go over her journal and list of cards sent to see if any of the deceased had death due to amputation. And if so, she would have the sender and reveal all of those dirty little secrets on them.

Once the kettle had boiled, she made herself a cup of coffee and opened up the other letter and it was a water bill from the council.

*

Primrose coughed into her handkerchief and decided that it was time to go to bed. She looked at the television briefly and was loath to switch off the program on the homeless dog eaters of Peterborough. Getting up slowly, she turned off the box and paused at the cabinet, wondering if she should look through the ledger to see who sent her the card. Thinking it would be easier done when she had a clearer head, she made her way upstairs and got into her nightgown and slipped under the covers. Within moments, she was fast asleep.

*

Someone's gate rattled, not hers, waking Primrose up. She looked across at the alarm clock and was mortified to discover that it had gone nine o' clock. She sniffed experimentally and was thrilled to discover that her cold had all but gone. She threw back the quilt and moved her legs off the bed, and wondered why her foot had remained where it was.

She looked down at her legs. Her left foot was there, lavender painted toes wriggling. Her right foot… was still on the bed.

Primrose screamed for a very long time indeed.

*

A week later and Primrose lay in a bed that was too hard in the local infirmary. Dr Ewan Probe, the hospital's silver fox, and her neighbour, was talking to her gently.

"We've done some tests on your foot, and it was totally drained of blood. The police don't seem to have any leads on who did this to you. Do you have any ideas, Primrose?"

Primrose looked at the doctor blankly. "Someone managed to take my foot off, drain the blood from it and somehow cauterise the stump without taking a blowtorch to it, all when I was asleep and all without any residual pain of any kind. How the FUCK would I know who took my FUCKING foot?" Primrose screamed and reached for an orange that was in the bowl next to her and threw it at Ewan.

"The sympathy card, did the police find the sympathy card?" she breathed heavily as he knelt to pick up the orange.

He looked at her and shook his head. "No, they say they haven't found it in the bin where you said you put it. I don't know, Primrose…" He shrugged apologetically.

After he left, Primrose fingered the little black key that hung from her silver chain. The answer was in there, she thought. Whoever it was; was in there. God knows that she had made enough enemies in her life, but for someone to do this… it was beyond sick. Primrose closed her eyes and Illtyd's furious face at the funeral flashed through her mind. Was it him? Had he taken his revenge against a defenceless old lady?

Primrose drifted off again, and woke up to see a petite nurse bending over her.

"There's a letter here for you," the nurse said, placing the heavy grain envelope into Primrose's hands.

Primrose knew what it was, and didn't want to open it. But then she realised that she was in hospital, and no one could get to her with all the nurses and doctors and even staff security around. She tore the envelope open and it was another expensive card, not unlike the ones that she sent off on those special occasions.

Written with that expensive red ink:

Dearest Primrose,
Thoughts are with you on the loss of your hands.
Warmest Regards,

The bastard was being familiar with her! Primrose pressed the call button next to the bed frantically and the nurse came back into the room.

"What's wrong?" she asked, her brow crinkling up as Primrose thrust the card at her.

"It's him! It's the bastard who took my foot; he says that he's after my hands next!"

"I don't understand," the nurse said, giving the card back to her, "the card's blank. Nothing's been written on here, Mrs Hildebrand."

"Don't be stupid, girl, look here," Primrose stabbed at the ornate handwriting. "And it's not the work of a simpleton! Look at how elegantly he writes! Get me the police now!"

Primrose descended into hysterical babbling and the nurse hurried out and got the elderly Dr Probe. Ewan came in with a shot and stuck Primrose with it, calming her down.

"Tonight my hands will go, mark my words," she whispered, her eyes glazing over.

"Don't be silly," Ewan said, looking at the card that was at the end of the bed. Picking it up, he looked inside. No inscription, nothing. Strange though, who would send Primrose an empty sympathy card? Ewan left Primrose to sleep her hysteria off.

When he came back the next morning to do his early rounds, he found out that Primrose was indeed right. Her hands *did* go.

*

Three days after she lost her hands, Primrose was sitting by the window in her private room, looking blankly out at the back car park when Detective Crow came in with her black leather ledger. She had let the police take the key from her the night before and they had spent the time presumably going through all of the people she had ever sent cards to. She hadn't wanted to say anything, her shame was too great, but the police were manipulative buggers and before long she was singing like the upper class canary that she was.

Edmund Crow looked at the lady hard, and wondered what would possess someone to go to such obsessed lengths as she had.

"We're getting in touch with everyone involved, but Illtyd has a strong alibi; he was hosting a dinner party for 30 people the night that you, uh... lost your hands." Edmund spoke softly, mindful that Primrose's marbles were rattling around a little bit too freely after her latest amputations.

"It's okay, I know who it is." Primrose said in a sing-song voice. "I know who it was that took my hands."

"Really?" Edmund took his notebook and pen out of his pocket. "Who was it, Mrs Hildebrand?"

Primrose looked Detective Crow squarely in the eyes and said with all sincerity, "It was my husband, Mr Ralph Hildebrand."

Edmund sighed and closed his notebook. "Your husband is dead, Primrose; he can't come back."

Primrose smiled the most insanely sweet smile. "Yes, he did. He took my foot as a warning, but I sent another card off. How stupid was that? I couldn't help it, I was looking through the obituaries and I saw that Edna Biscuit died. I sent her husband a sympathy card with some choice views on what Edna call her charity work. Her 'charity work' amounted to giving random gentlemen services down dank alleyways. How did I know this? Too much money and time on my hands. I hired a private detective to follow her after a rumour came my way. And there it was, her life exposed for me to catalogue.

"So I sent off the card, and my hands are gone. My husband came to me in a dream and told me he did it. He's said that he'll take off my head if I spill any more secrets!" Primrose lifted her arms and showed off her bandaged stumps. "He did a pretty good job of these; I'm sure my head will be an even better one!"

Edmund sighed and wished that she had only lost one hand. The case for self-amputation would have been so much easier to prove and Primrose would be lording it up in the mental hospital.

*

Dr Ewan Probe was doing his rounds with the nurse when he bumped into his wife Amanda who was crying her eyes out.

He went to hold her, but she pushed him away. Ewan told the nurse to go and get her a cup of water.

"What's wrong with you, Amanda?"

"*All these years.* All these years you kept that secret from me," Amanda hissed, her eyes blazing with raw anger.

"What secret? I don't know what you're on about!" Ewan said, his mind going into overdrive.

"Sheila Winthrope, and the child of yours that you terminated!" Amanda slapped Ewan across the face.

"What? Who told you that?" Ewan blurted, already knowing the answer. The stories of Primrose's dirty little secrets were the talk of the town. All over, people were being exposed and talked about and ridiculed left, right and centre. The press had even been leaked the story of Illtyd's animal sex film from a source inside the police force.

"Why, Ewan? I was only coming here to pay her a visit and keep her spirits up like you asked me to. Thirty years we've been married. And those thirty years extinguished in a moment through talking to that bitter old bitch in the room through there. Don't bother coming home."

Amanda stormed off, leaving Ewan who promptly started to cry. The nurse came back with the water in her hand. He told her to fuck off and then went into Primrose's room to have it out with her. All he got were some blank stares and the occasional giggle.

*

Primrose woke and looked at the alarm clock whose digits were glowing a ghostly green in the darkened room. 3:24 a.m. She groaned, and tried to get back to sleep.

"Primrose, you should have kept your mouth shut," Ralph Hildebrand, her dead husband croaked.

Primrose pushed herself up on her stumps.

Ralph stumbled towards her, his funeral suit ragged and torn, his destroyed and rotted features only hinted at by the light of the clock. Primrose tried to scream but nothing would come out.

"All the hassle I've been getting from the folks whose relatives you've been torturing. Years it's been going on. Well, you won't take no for an answer, so we've decided to pay you a visit."

Primrose looked on in terror as the door to her room was flung open and four shambling corpses came in. One was wearing a brooch which the now completely insane woman recognised as once belonging to Louisa Kibble. Primrose had some real dirt on her once, what had it been?

"I can't help it, you hurt me so much, Ralph," she managed to wheeze.

Ralph and the others descended upon her and one of them

73

had a knife and started to cut the pale white wrinkly skin of her neck.

*

Dr Ewan Probe was doing his early morning rounds when he heard a scream coming from the direction of Primrose's room. He ran towards it, and one of the early shift nurses burst out, and threw up.

He went in and looked on in complete shock.

Primrose Hildebrand was there; well her head was. The rest of the body was nowhere to be seen. Her eyes were wide open, and there was something crumpled up and shoved into her mouth. Reaching forward, Ewan plucked it out and smoothed it out against his thigh.

It was a card. A condolence card.

He opened it up and was confused at the message it bore.

Deepest Sympathy about being the scapegoat.
  Regards,

Dr Ewan Probe showed the card to Detective Edmund Crow when he arrived, and of course there was nothing written on the inside of the card. Edmund looked at the doctor very strangely indeed and it wasn't long before he found out about what Primrose had done to him in regard to spilling the beans to his wife about the affair and the abortion. So what, if the police couldn't hang the previous amputations on him – they had motive for the murder. And that was more than enough. There was a slight problem with finding the rest of the body, but they had the head – and that was more than enough too.

Ewan was protesting his innocence when he was arrested and was still protesting it, three years into his prison sentence when he died of a heart attack. No-one sent his ex-wife any condolence cards as she was in Brazil, shacked up with a lovely ebony skinned pool boy called Rico, who was 25 years her junior.

MANY HAPPY RETURNS

Carl T. Ford

Crouched at the corner of Maitland Avenue, Dan surveyed the front porch of the house. The evening shadows lurched forward to engulf him whilst he watched and waited. From his vantage point, the dwelling appeared little changed from that in his dreams though much of the surrounding area had succumbed to urban decay. East Deacon had seen better times. Now, instead of neatly cut emerald lawns adorned with ornamental ponds and birdbaths, there stood a desert of cracked rubble and broken furniture that formed drab tombs lamenting past splendour. The grey debris and ravenous overgrowth obscured what had once been a desired stepping-stone for more affluent couples seeking some form of respectability away from the council estates at the south end of town. Today the three-floor townhouses appeared mostly vacant. Few residents had remained and fewer still wished to move here.

Things had been different back then. Could it really have been sixteen years? Dan had no need to count time via past vague memory posts for he recalled his twenty-first birthday, and could vividly see the profusion of hurried cards from the well-wishers that lay on the doormat. Their abundance had come as a surprise. Perhaps this generosity acted as some form of cathartic release for them, although people were often given to kindness following dreadful events. But there had been one too many; the hastily scrawled messages a guarded nod to the events that had befallen a mere week or two before; each blurred signature a defiant statement of unity from a community that had attempted to suppress the inevitable social breakdown that tragedies of *this* kind foreshadowed. This simple act of kindness, they hoped, might feign a communal return to normality in order that folk could get on with their lives as if *nothing* had happened. Or was this just a feeble pretence to demonstrate to society that the town would continue its banal day-to-day existence without collapsing? It was all people could do to fend from shame and ruin, and the abandonment of what had once been, for many, an idyllic suburban lifestyle.

Despite the cards, there had been no celebrations. Dan recalled the shocked faces that bore whispered tears and angry voices, and the sensational words writ large in red marker on the newspaper bulletin boards caged to the brick outside Turkey Neck's grocery store on Massey Street that told the ugly truth. Turkey Neck had typified the community, with his old-fashioned views and an intellect fashioned from empty mornings buried in the tabloids and evenings at the local Gala hall exchanging half-baked politics between bingo calls. The shop's decrepit owner had acquired the unflattering moniker by way of the thick white hairs and leathery sinews of saggy pink skin that covered his scalene muscles and disappeared under the white starch of his open necked shirt. Turkey Neck's was the first store to close in the area. There was no talk of why? Or utterances of regret from the stifled residents, eager to feign blissful ignorance as their world fell apart around them. Now the derelict premises had become a haven for heroin addicts, whose thin, broken syringes lay strewn about carelessly like shattered glass teeth, and served as another warning that this town ought to be forsaken.

Others had entirely failed to come to terms with events. As soon as the television crews had left, and the radio interviews had ceased with the psychologists, authors and oddballs that tainted the airwaves with obscure ranting, the community, mindful of the scourge that had invaded their lives, had begun its exodus. East Deacon had become a ghost town in less than a year, with the surrounding area following suit soon after, its economy unsustainable with the collapse of its wealthy neighbour. Rats jumped ship leaving behind hardened sailors who'd weather the storm.

All this had transpired in less time than it had taken the

authorities to catch the young girl's killer.

But had they?

Dan was sure he hadn't been the first to realise something was still wrong with the community after all these years, but even he had failed to come to terms with the outrageous truth that had warned him and, he suspected, others. So, he had kept quiet and minded his own. When the local church had been vandalised, Dan preferred to believe it was the junkies; the police were uninterested for there had been nothing of value to steal and only Reverend Thomas was distraught when the statue of a crucified Christ in the yard was found beheaded. The incident was relegated to filler for the Deacon Gazette that now relied heavily on cut-price colour spreads from estate agents to stay afloat. Everyone else stayed away from the church. When Reverend Thomas moved to greener pastures four weeks later the church doors were locked for the final time.

Dan had caught sight of a police cordon around one of the semis on Bateman Street the next morning. He slowed his walk to take in a few more details and had watched patiently as paramedics ferried two bodies from the house into a couple of waiting ambulances, one appeared dead for a white sheet covered its head. The second appeared to be a female, though a respiratory mask obscured most of the facial features making a positive identification difficult from the opposite side of the street. Dan could, however, make out the purple blotches that covered the bare arms and several nasty lesions that cracked across her face like snapshots taken of a thunderstorm. A third paramedic carried an oxygen tank that fed the shaking woman vital supplies. Her eyes fluttered in and out of consciousness and Dan feared the worse. Later that day he learned that the victims, a middle-aged married couple, had both died from porphyria. But the event failed to ignite the passion of the press, and the matter was hushed up by the locals, perhaps in light of recent events those left in the town preferred to keep afloat the chances of a business revival, no matter how daunting prospects might appear.

Barely three weeks had passed when the body of a woman was discovered on the tracks half a mile from Deacon South Station. Despite much consternation from members of the community, the local coroner declared the death a suicide. Sarah Harding had been distantly related to the murdered child though several close neighbours had professed that she hadn't displayed any outward signs that would account for the taking of her own life. A news bulletin taken at the scene of the carnage appeared on local TV, with one interviewee recalling how he had discovered her mutilated body whilst walking his dog alongside the tracks. The reporter had announced that if a train had hit her, the driver had failed to stop – perhaps he hadn't seen the woman stumble into the locomotive's path. Much of the route in this region lay unkempt, with the stretched resources of the national rail services preferring to concentrate on the maintenance and clearance of routes and sidings of towns that offered more commerce and not on abandoned tracks such as this that lay away from the mainline. The trackside was now a designated 'Nature Reserve', for better or worse. It would have been difficult for a driver to spot a lone figure half-swallowed by gorse that stretched for miles alongside the open tracks and now trespassed upon the adjacent footpath. Maybe the driver had been half asleep? It was a journey of several hundred miles, the track here was dark, and the lampposts along the pathway lay in disrepair. Or perhaps she had been struck by one of the diesel shunters that passed through Deacon during the night, ferrying gnarled cars to scrap merchants in Merseyside. What was certain was that the victim had suffered extreme blood loss, something inevitable given the prospect of being hit at sixty-five miles an hour by thirty-plus tonnes of locomotive. But why did the eyewitness say there was surprisingly little blood at the death scene? What if a train hadn't hit her, the body parts having been carried to the railway line in order to conceal the true cause of her demise? A mangled corpse in an area that was a haven for foxes and carrion would be no laughing matter for a team of forensics.

Watching the detached building for signs of movement was now Dan's priority. Like one or two others in the street, the land on which the house stood was enclosed by a tall hedge that shielded its lower windows from the gaze of passers-by and the light of the sun. Whilst above, the interior lay hidden behind thick purple curtains that closed over their arch fashioned portals like bruised eyes. Were they truly closed, or was *he* being watched from within?

It was the same in his dreams.

He'd find himself in the building. He knew not how he had come to be there or why?

Only that it was night.

It was dark

He was not alone.

Something was stalking him.

Dan sniffed at the dank tang of blood that pervaded the air. To his right, spiders of light penetrated the black at sparse intervals weaving tightropes that revealed more of the shapes around him. Two long walls lay two feet away on either side. Manoeuvring along the corridor silently, proved haphazard. Here and there, he would bump an item of furniture or a picture frame on the wall, but as the seconds desperately fought to keep apace with his heartbeat his eyes slowly adjusted to the gloom. The wooden boards creaked under the weight of Dan's footsteps and a momentary thought crossed his mind that perhaps he would be better served by standing still, or hiding so that whatever it was that pursued him might lose track. But some strange force, perhaps wild curiosity, compelled him forward, and he reached the top landing with four large strides. At once, he became all too aware that his pursuers were closing. Was that the cellar door he heard opening far below? Dan fumbled his way along the passageway both palms flat against each wall like an advancing crucifix. It was colder up here, and the hairs on his arms felt like fine wires as he nervously made his way past two closed doors towards another that stood slightly ajar at the far end. Inimitable shrieking danced inside his head. The sound was familiar, like some insane duel between wildcat and bird. The scream was meant to paralyse, but he knew he must press onwards. He reached the door and stepped inside the room to face the wraith that lay on the bed in front of him. It must still be daylight outside, for the monster was resting – its youthful complexion, pallid and serene, with raven hair framing its soft features. In their sleeping state, the creatures appeared beautiful. Dan stooped forward in order to gaze at the pursed lips for a physical sign of evil when its eyes suddenly opened. Without warning, the monster on the bed had leapt upon him. Frenzied claws whipped the darkness and slashed at Dan's cheek. Its black mane smothered his face as the demon's breath painted fetid clouds that danced in the air. Dan felt his body give way to the onslaught and came crashing down in the darkness.

Dan woke with a silent scream lodged in his throat and a curtain of sweat draped around his body. His nightmare had been the first of several. In each, he'd find himself in the house, pursued by something or some things as he made his escape before stumbling upon the ghoul lying in bed. But with each successive dream, his attacker's sly, wet lips inched nearer, its breath ever colder along with the knowledge that the unseen things that stalked his every move were closing in.

He was sure that the nightmares were a form of warning, a message from his subconscious telling him that the evil that lurked in East Deacon knew that he was aware of their atrocious secret; that their numbers had grown. Dan posed a threat to their reign of terror; a dwindling taper that must be extinguished so that darkness was consummate.

The past three weeks had been spent at the library in Critchet, where Dan had perused the old newspaper files for anything untoward in the town that he might have missed and utilised the free Internet service where he read of similar slayings, sinister cults, and creatures that thrived on blood. This in turn led to Dan recollecting tales from childhood that his father would read to him at bedtime, legends from around the world of boogeymen, chupacabras, aswang, and the undead. The stories had scared him so much as a child, that on many occasion he had slept with the bedside light on, in case they should return once his father had quietly closed the door, leaving him alone to stare unblinkingly at their hunched shadows and long spindly arms that scratched at the windowpane as they waited outside for his father to leave him.

Dan noted the comings and goings of strangers to the town and watched for anything unusual. As most of the town was deserted, keeping track of any newcomers was relatively straightforward. He watched the people go about their business, recorded the names and addresses of anyone that stayed clear of the streets in the daytime hours, and the faces of those he didn't recognise. Any outsiders who moved into the area would warrant special attention for sensible souls would avoid East Deacon at all cost. Surveillance had eventually led him to 26 Maitland Avenue. It was here, sixteen years previously that the initial horror had begun to weave its evil – it was here that a child had been brutally slaughtered. Sylvia Marriott had been only nine, when the monster had struck, a sweet, blonde girl whose parents worked shifts at the South Deacon Infirmary. The child had been grabbed from the front garden in the early evening and dragged into the kitchen. Her father was working the late-afternoon shift, whilst the mother slept upstairs in preparation for a stint later that night. No one had seen the assailant but clues and forensic evidence collated during the following month had led to the arrest of the child's cousin. Despite fierce protestations of innocence, his subsequent conviction was, according to press reports, a mere formality. The jury upheld the prosecution's case unanimously; contrary to the fact that the judge had pointed out that much of the evidence had been circumstantial. The defence had even presented a relatively sound reasoning regarding the possibility of there having been more than one attacker, but these claims were dismissed and the killer was given the mandatory life sentence. The outcome had not been one that most of the town had expected. The Marriott family moved away from East Deacon within months of their daughter's murder, and the house had remained vacant until very recently.

The fact had come to Dan's attention quite by chance whilst returning from one of his sojourns at the Critchet Library. Maitland Street wasn't usually on his route home, for the hourly bus to and from Critchet took in the more scenic route, winding a path through the main town of Critchet and North Deacon via a series of leafy lanes and parkways, running alongside the Deacon Canal before coming to a halt, usually passenger-less, outside the old Roxy Cinema at East Deacon Square. But on this occasion, there had been a detour due to road works at the foot of North Deacon Bridge, and the driver found himself steering the bus through the deserted streets of town and along Maitland Avenue. It wasn't a region Dan particularly liked to traverse due to its desolate appearance, but he knew the area well enough from snapshots of houses and wasteland from the ads in free weeklies. An old, weather-beaten 'For Sale' sign had once staggered in the garden, peering lopsided over the hedges like a drunken scarecrow. But now it stood, loud and proud, emblazoned with the letters 'S O L D' in crimson sans serif, a gesture of defiance to the dilapidated houses around it.

Recent weeks had been spent watching the house's inhabitants for any signs of strange behaviour that might lend weight to his theories. Peculiar figures within appeared to shift along the walls in the half-light and Dan swore that the shapes that came and went throughout the day did all they could to avoid detection. They wore dark clothes, hats, scarves and shades and held their heads low, preferring to pass by on the shadowed side of the street. Watching the house for patterns of movement by day proved futile – for the newcomers seemed to only emerge at night. A cliché, but Dan had already begun to sense that he would only truly catch them under the cloak of night whilst the town slept, when wandering citizens or lone members of the community would be at their most vulnerable. He was sure that his dreams were portents of the horror that waited within the house, he knew the very idea of blood drinking monsters pacing around in the darkness was absurd, but he couldn't risk waiting any longer. They were on to him now. He must act swiftly, and now was as good a time as any.

Dan removed from his person, all the items which were surplus to requirements and bundled them into the blue 'Bag For Life' carrier. He smiled briefly at the irony before burying the package under a pile of crumpled brown and yellow leaves that marked Autumn's arrival. Glancing in both directions, and satisfied that no one had seen him Dan crept catlike across the road, manoeuvring between the bumpers of two abandoned vehicles, and moved swiftly along the kerb. Pausing for a further look and safe with the knowledge that the street was deserted, he nervously made his way to the front gate of number 26, and reached over the top to unlatch the bolt. Fortunately, the entire gate had been recently replaced, and Dan released a sigh of relief that the sound of the shifting iron would be inaudible from more than a few feet away. He reached the relative safety of the porch, and peered through the letterbox, mindful not to drop the three-inch reel of silver gaffer tape and tungsten carbide knife that lay in his right hand. Dan had planned things carefully, and released four six inch ribbons of pre-cut tape from the spool, arranging them diamond fashion on the lower left glass panel of the door, directly above the latch. Using the knife, he scored the glass surface running parallel to the inside of the duct and then softly elbowed the glass, with just enough force to stop the cutaway glass falling to the floor. By manoeuvring the newly formed cracks with his thumbs, the diamond gave way in one piece, with a minimum of fuss. Having removed the glass from the pane, Dan eased his left arm through the broken panel, inching his fingers towards the latch that lay above the lock. With a flick of the thumb and a gentle prod, the door opened quietly. Dan laid the remaining gaffer on the porch, making a mental note to retrieve it on the way out and stepped inside the house. The layout of the place was familiar from his dreams, and he felt his eyes adjust to the gloom more readily than in the nightmare world.

If his visions were correct, the monsters lurked in the cellar and upper bedroom – he would deal with those upstairs first, that way if anything should go wrong he would be able to make his escape more readily. The stairway was void of carpet. Thick dust and chippings gathered at the corners of the treads, despite the house's newly inhabited status. As silently as possible, Dan climbed the stairs, taking the steps two at a time. He found the landing unoccupied. A siren caused Dan to start, and his first thought was that he must have triggered an alarm, but it was just the sound of a services vehicle in a distant street. He looked along the landing, and saw three doors separated by radiators, upon which lay wet clothing. Dan moved along the passageway and sniffed the stale air. There it was again, unmistakable, the dry stench of blood. He paused outside the third door. The siren still wailed in the night; growing louder. He hoped the junkies had their hands full. He ran through his plan a final time, and heard what must have been the cellar door open with a shuttering crash way below. The monsters were here! Spurred in to action, Dan slammed open the door and it banged against a cabinet. The entity that lay on the bed woke with a startled cry.

Dan faced his enemy. There would be an end to the evil tonight.

The young boy shrieked as his eyes caught sight of the erect rod of flesh that rose from the naked man stooped over his bed. He screamed one final cry before his cowering body was torn asunder in a delirious onslaught of carbide and muscle. The killer was spent within seconds, and sat, in a puddle of blood, sinew and semen with a grin punctuated only by swiftly drawn mouthfuls of breath that marked his handiwork. The siren in the street outside was now almost deafening.

And then the monsters came bursting in.

ALL HALLOW'S EVEN

Franklin Marsh

Some people hate Christmas. Some hate their birthday, or bonfire night.

Giles De Ray hated Hallowe'en. So much so that, this year, he'd decided to kill everyone in the village.

The village was Muffin-in-the-Marsh, population thirty. Occasionally swelling to sixty when all the second-home tossers could be arsed to show up.

Giles had settled on the thirty permanent residents. They loved Hallowe'en. Mums and kids trick or treating. Ghosts and pumpkins everywhere. The acceptable face of horror. People who liked horror were fuckwits. He'd lived with horror all his life. Real horror. Well, tonight he'd spread it around.

He ascended the stairs of the small house he shared with his parents, and walked into their room. They sat, as usual, in their armchairs, one on either side of the chamber.

Giles raised his glass of sherry.

"Tonight, I am become Death," he intoned, "and the denizens of Muffin-in-the-Marsh will dance to my tune."

He drained the tiny glass, coughed, gagged and walked out.

His parents didn't say anything. They couldn't. They were dead. They'd been dead for quite a while now.

Giles's mother had passed away in her sleep. Giles's father, overcome with grief, and an enthusiastic amateur taxidermist, couldn't bear to be parted from her.

Giles considered his inability to relate to women stemmed from his only sight of a naked one – his mother, being slit open, eviscerated, filled with sawdust and stitched up by his dad.

His father explained every step, letting his son know that, although he had preserved his only true love, her lack of animation would cause him to pine and die quickly, and he wanted his only child to do to him what he had done to the child's mother.

Unfortunately for both of them, Giles's father didn't pine and die, but developed lightning dementia and lasted another eleven years.

Giles would wake in the morning, shower, dress, breakfast, clean his teeth, clean the pool of waste and drool from around his father, go to work, return, clean the pool of waste and drool from around his father, eat dinner, undress, bathe, clean his teeth and go to bed.

It was only when congratulating himself on having three days of not having to clean the old boy up, that Giles realised his father had died.

He tried, he really did try. The lapse of time between his parents deaths meant that he couldn't remember his father's instructions. He should have paid more attention, or taken notes or something.

His mother actually looked better than she had when alive. His father made the Elephant Man look like Brad Pitt. Lumpy wasn't the word.

He could have put his mother in a wheelchair, taken her anywhere, and people would have commented on her beauty. Since getting his dad upstairs, Giles couldn't bear to move him again. He'd leaked sawdust from every orifice.

*

Downstairs, Giles donned his Death outfit. The normal flowing robes were sculpted to his body to prevent those who weren't keen on dying from getting hold of him. The skull mask fitted tightly, accentuating his piercing blue eyes. He then hefted his weapon of choice.

A gun or flame-thrower would have made things easier, but wasn't really playing the game. A scythe would have been more traditional, but he'd found it too unwieldy. This Death carried a machete. He'd practised for weeks on melons, grapefruit and bastard pumpkins. A succession of mice, hamsters and gerbils had prepared him for the taking of life. He was ready.

Giles peeked through the drawing-room curtains. Dark already, and it was only 6:00 p.m. He stepped through the front door, and took a deep breath. He saw the flash of a torch. Yes! Heading for the house of the Misses Stalybridge were Amanda Bruen and her three children. He had to get there first.

Death straddled the garden fence, tiptoed across the flower beds and knocked on the front door. The two elderly spinsters were the village seamstresses, and loved the children in their costumes trick or treating.

The door flew open. It was Edna.

"Oooh! You're a big one. What a smashing costume. Lily! Chocs!"

She looked him up and down again, frowning.

"Bit old for this, aren't you, son? Go on, then. What do you say?"

"I am Death."

The machete rose and fell. For a first effort, it was a belter. The blade split Edna's head from crown to neck. Disappointingly, the two sides didn't flop down. Edna fell backwards, slipping from the blood-christened blade.

"Here we go, my dear, lots of... Aaagh!"

Death got a faceful of inappropriately named fun size choc bars, as Lily stepped from the kitchen, took in the scene, and retreated in fear. Death followed her into the kitchen and screamed himself, as a kettle full of boiling water struck him. Lily backed up towards the far wall. An enraged Death struck. More beginner's luck. Lily's head came right off, surging toward the ceiling on a tide of crimson arterial blood. As it descended, Death chested it down, knocked it back up with a knee and unleashed a thunderbolt right foot. Lily's head soared back up, crashed off the underside of a kitchen cabinet, and flew into the sink, completing a few circuits before coming to rest upright, and facing her destroyer.

"Back of the net," intoned Death, swivelling and walking

into the hall.

He filled the front door just as Mrs Bruen and her trio of childish exuberance showed up.

"Good Lord, Edna – or is it Lily? That's a bit much. My children are…"

Death's machete sliced off the top of her head. A hat-trick! From inside Death, Giles stared in amazement at the half Ping-Pong balls filled with vitreous humour. Gawd, that blade was sharp!

As Amanda's body toppled earthwards, Death towered over the three cowering infants. His hand stayed. The innocence, the tiny stature, the pleading eyes… They started to cry.

That bloody noise. In the supermarket, on trains, buses, even in the pub when you were trying to enjoy a quiet pint. And their costumes were really shit. You couldn't even tell what they were supposed to be.

Death laid into them with a vengeance.

"Hoi! What the bloody hell do you think you're doing!?"

Death looked up from his enjoyable infanticide. This would be the ultimate test. His most fearsome adversary had arrived.

Cyril Jackson. Big, strong, red-faced, loud, the man who thought he owned the village. If Death could take him, it was all over.

Jackson vaulted the Stalybridge gate and hurtled towards the Ultimate End, arms outstretched.

Death feinted, then thrust his blade forward. Jackson ran onto the machete. It slid into his stomach, up to the hilt. Yeah! thought Death, receiving a thick ear from Jackson's left fist. They fell to the garden path.

Jackson was gasping, eyes protruding. He gained his knees, staring down at the hilt protruding from his stomach. His Viyella shirt and cavalry twills turning scarlet.

Death selected a large white-washed stone from the line flanking the path, and brought it down on Jackson's skull. There was a satisfying crunch, and a lot of greyish brain matter leaked out. Far more than Death would have expected from a bruiser like Jackson. He picked up another stone, and brought the two together, crushing Jackson's cheeks. Giving the would-be village headman a literal fish face.

"Give us a kiss," lisped Death. He retrieved the machete from Jackson's innards and stood over the dying man. With a blood-curdling shriek, he brought the weapon down on the kneeling figure with all his might. A berserker rage gripped The End and he rained blow after blow on the helpless shape beneath him. Jackson became chutney, then mincemeat.

Soaked in gore, gasping for breath, Death looked from his most satisfying conquest yet, into the petrified eyes of the one person in Muffin-in-the-Marsh more despised than Giles De Ray.

A disgraced ex-Headmaster known locally as Pete the Peedo.

Death roared. Pete fled. Pausing only to check his watch, Death followed. Still only ten past seven. This'll be a doddle.

*

Giles peeked out of his grave. Well, strictly speaking it wasn't his grave. It belonged to Arcadia Gravel, upon whom Giles was standing. He looked at the front of St. Jacob's church. A number of people who had fallen before Death relatively unmarked had been propped up as corpse-like scarecrows outside the church.

Giles smiled. The final victim of Death's sweep had been the Reverend Montague Groyne. The cowled avenger had stalked up the aisle silently, eyes fixed on the holy man, sat in a front pew, head bowed. Death paused, slightly disgusted, as he realised that Monty's trousers were round his ankles, and the vicar was playing his organ whilst perusing religious periodical *Norty Nuns on the Job*.

Death strode in front of the priest. Monty looked up in mid-stroke, had a massive one, ejaculated, turned purple and fell from the pew.

Death became Giles once more. He cleaned up Monty with a Book of Common Prayer, dressed him as Death, and laid him upon his own altar.

After setting up the scarecrows, Giles leapt into Miss Gravel's grave, soon to become his own. One useful thing Cyril Jackson had done was to create the self-filling grave. His robust build made him an ideal grave-digger. He would hurl the displaced soil into a large wooden trough angled upward beside the grave. The trough had a wooden door to release the soil once the deceased had been placed in the hole in the ground, by the simple expedient of pulling a piece of string.

The string was in Giles's grasp. He took a last look around. Goodbye Muffin-in-the-Marsh. I have destroyed thee. And now will die with thee, undiscovered when Fat Stan the Porky Postman does his rounds tomorrow and finds Hell On Earth. Giles sat down and pulled the string. It came off in his hand. That twat, Jackson! Couldn't the wanker get anything right?

Giles stood up and examined the wooden door. Faint whispering caught his attention. He looked toward the scarecrows, realising with a start that they were staring at him. He shook his head. Idiot. Get on with it, De Ray. You haven't come this far…

The door sprang open suddenly catching him a glancing blow on the forehead, and sending him reeling across the grave as the soil poured in. Dazed, he propped himself up against the far side of the Gravel grave. He suddenly felt compressed, unable to move.

Looking down, he realised that the earth had poured into the hole at incredible speed, burying him up to his neck, like some cretinous father enjoying a day at the beach. Shit! This wasn't supposed to happen.

That whispering again. He struggled to move his head in the clinging soil. The scarecrows were facing the church door. Death walked out.

That shithead Groyne, cursed Giles. He'd been faking, he'd…

Death's black robes were long and flowing. He carried a scythe. Behind him tottered the late Monty Groyne, purple of face and tongue protruding.

Giles whimpered as they approached his head, the scarecrows detaching themselves from their supports and lurching in his direction.

He heard the church gate latch click. His peripheral vision showed him Edna and Lily Stalybridge, one head stitched on with garden twine, the other head stitched together with same, both carrying two shopping bags each apparently filled with offal. As they neared Giles's early grave, Edna shouted into a bag, "We're nearly there, Mr Jackson!" A squelching sound came from the bag.

Behind the spinsters came most of Amanda Bruen, and her mutilated children. And behind them, the ultimate horror. Giles saw his achingly beautiful Mother, holding on to the arm of what he assumed was his father. The sawdust had settled badly. His dad looked like a fat-arsed Popeye. The sunken eyeballs latched onto the son.

"Bshlsdhglsgclhbcl," the lurching penny for the guy gabbled, spraying sawdust.

As the dead villagers gathered around the grave, Death unfolded a small deck chair and sat down.

"Mother," wept Giles. "You can't let this happen to your only son."

His mother looked down her nose at him.

"You were adopted," she sneered.

Giles agony knew no bounds. His fevered gaze flitted from corpse to cadaver.

"Go on, you bastards!" he screamed. "Do your worst!"

"Oh, they will," rumbled Death, as the church clock struck midnight. "There's no hurry. We've got all night."

DEAD WATER

David A. Sutton

Brian stared at the gloriously vivid sunset across the salt marsh. Nature, he imagined, was in harmony with his emotions. In his fifty-two years he couldn't remember a holiday that had been more tranquil than this was turning out to be. Dreamy contemplations of environmental equilibrium basked him in a warm glow and filled him with contentment. And the holiday was not over yet – only half way through in fact. For a while he wasn't tormented about pollution, biological diversity out of joint, or his carbon footprint. The haze-rippled sun was low in the sky and red light flickered through the gently swaying reeds, stands of black spears silhouetted against the waning day. Through a gap in the reed bed the still water of the lagoon perfectly reflected the sky; crimson shading to pale azure blue above pink-tinted smears of cloud. The surface of the lagoon was so motionless Brian saw that sky and water might be interchangeable and if he stared at the mirror images for long enough he might never be able to tell the difference and the world would be topsy-turvy and changed to omnipresent exquisiteness forever.

The holiday in France was a first. For years foreign holidays had been packaged and parcelled for two weeks in the summer, separating the working year. Managing personnel statistics for consumption higher up the chain of management was an endless round of achieving month-end deadlines and he was ready for a change, both personally and at the coal-face. The latter was harder to achieve now that the years made him less eligible for promotion. Yet he was happy, nonetheless. And the holiday was a refreshing change from the all-inclusive, structured trips he was used to.

He and Harry had gone off for odd days or a weekend of bird watching, but this was the only time he and Jane had taken a two-week holiday abroad with Harry and his wife

Brenda. When the idea had been mooted, Brian had been keen but wary, knowing from the experiences of other acquaintances how a friendship might be wrecked by the close proximity of those who had, a mere few days earlier, been the best of friends. Harry had retired early, and his holidays seemed to take place with alarming frequency now he had more time on his hands, and *he* could afford, therefore, to have the odd unpleasant jaunt. And – which added to Brian's initial hesitation – though he and Jane were very happy in their marriage, Harry and Brenda were having problems with theirs. Jane talked him around, however, and dispelled his qualms. Bless her. The two couples shared a car to the south of France and were staying in a chalet on a campsite in L'Espiguette, which, despite its relative luxury, still meant they were getting under one-another's feet for a couple of weeks. But neither disagreements nor arguments had arisen.

And the sunset was blessing that triumph, Brian thought. Jane was a gem, he freely admitted.

Harry was starting to pack up, folding his piece of canvas, capping the lenses and putting his binoculars in their case. Brian would have liked to stay, basking in meditation in those final minutes before darkness decisively descended. He'd had a lovely day, but if they were to avoid ending up wading home through the marsh in the pitch black, they *should* really get a move on.

At least he might savour the day's salient moments while he packed up his kit...

The afternoon had begun sensibly enough and it wasn't until they had ridden out past one of the reserve's bird hides and left it far behind, that Brian's head began to feel the wrong shape. The sensation, he supposed, had either something to do with the landscape and the powdery smell of salt permeating the atmosphere, or there had been something wrong with the *moules marinière* he'd eaten last night at the restaurant. There had also been the curiously beckoning hand at the bird hide, which disconcerted him initially. Out of the dim interior,

95

through the viewing flap, a solitary hand had gestured. Harry had dismissively declined the hand's invitation as they freewheeled on along the causeway, but then it presented its palm and splayed fingers, and shook wildly, as if waving goodbye. Or urgently summoning them back. The hand may even have been gesticulating at the warning signpost they cycled past.

Later, as he peered through his field scope he began to feel decidedly odd; that sort of muzzy sensation that precedes a bout of vomiting and diarrhoea. He mustn't permit himself to become ill, he told himself, there was too much at stake.

He couldn't allow Harry to win the day, if indeed it was to be won at all. Harry always took a malevolent delight in getting the upper hand at bird watching, and most other things in life.

Brian attempted to shrug off his growing queasiness and concentrate on the distant circle of landscape within the orbit of the scope's eyepiece. Although in sharp focus, the field of view appeared to be blurred. The scenery had an indistinct texture to it, as if it wavered slightly out of focus from other, more expressive patches of countryside. Something to do with the scarcity of trees, the lack of hills and the serene lagoons. The shimmering sheet of water bombarded the sun's rays back off its surface like an enhanced mirror, turning an almost unbearably bright silver. Tall brownish-yellow reeds stood like a cluttered, thin army in disorderly ranks, motionless before the battle day to come.

"I wonder if the ladies are enjoying their ride?" Harry spoke quietly, edgily, without taking his eye away from his scope. His scope's tripod was firmly positioned and he was sitting comfortably in his fold-up canvas chair. Somehow he'd managed to collar the best pitch on the small scrap of rough terrain. Brian's tripod stood on less firm ground and his own seat squelched into the soggy surface whenever he shifted to make himself more comfortable. Yet they'd both agreed that the territory beyond the bird hide might yield better results, despite the deteriorating state of the paths and the warning notice they'd chosen to ignore. It was the instinct of the seasoned naturalist to find the optimum locations, rather than previous experience of this particular countryside.

Brian answered his companion's question with a grunt of acknowledgement, but he didn't say anything. Both their wives had opted for a horse ride, one of their must-dos on a holiday in the Camargue. He could see them in his mind's eye now, on their white horses, riding through grassy tussocks and along the beach, through gently foaming surf. Not his cup of tea, or Harry's. But that suited both couples. The wives could do their tourist things and he and Harry could get on with their preoccupation as twitchers.

And the *competition*.

Harry was one bird ahead. Brian needed to catch up with a sighting and it must be a positive identification. It mustn't be any old bird. The Camargue was awash with, say, flamingos. They were a beautiful sight – white and pink, elegant walkers among the gleaming waters of the *étangs*. No, no, no. Brian needed a spectacled warbler. Or a collared pratincole. They would be worth twenty other species, even if there might be a bit of an argument between them as to whether a particular bird was in fact rare enough to qualify for the contest.

The friendly rivalry had been going on for years.

"Jane hasn't been on a horse for donkey's, has she?" Harry piped up again, seeming not to have noticed his inadvertent witticism. Brian wondered if his friend was trying to sabotage his concentration. He *had* been concerned about the rather casual way the riding stables had allocated the horses. And the two women found they needed specifically to ask for hard hats; they weren't handed out as standard practice. This was France, though, and their way of doing things were different to those in Blighty. The other riders, German and French mainly, had seemed rather surprised by the request, and to a man none of them called for protective headgear. Some of the younger riders wore their own cycle helmets admittedly, so Brian supposed their parents had foreseen some potential danger in riding unfamiliar horses.

"She'll be all right," Brian whispered grudgingly. He'd have preferred complete silence, both for the bird watching and his woozy head. Mind you, he allowed that the distraction might take his mind off the nausea. "They both will," he continued, and then paused, squinting through his eyepiece. "Your Brenda's not been riding for years either. None of us are teenagers any more." Harry was Brian's senior by four years, yet was more haggard than his age would have suggested. Although nothing had been said or discussed, except between him and Jane, Brian believed that Harry and Brenda were no longer happily married, which might account for his occasional gloomy moods. Or perhaps it was simply that their marriage had reached that affectionless plateau that comes with years of living together. If Harry was anxious, Brian deemed it was more to do with maintaining the marriage and stability for their two adult sons – who still lived at home – and hoping Brenda didn't have a riding accident, because that would upset their domestic arrangements.

Brian made sure not to lift his head from the eyepiece of the scope while they spoke. Perhaps Harry really was a little apprehensive about Brenda riding her first horse in twenty years, but was reluctant to admit it. Anxiety wouldn't be his style. Either way, both men were here now and should be concentrating on the job in hand.

After dropping their wives at the riding stables, seeing them off with a wave and a few photographs as mementos, they had parked the car for the day and hired two pushbikes in Aigues-Mortes. With panniers loaded up with their equipment they cycled out into the wetlands of the Camargue. It was mid-September and the weather was still incredibly hot, which usually suited Brian. Except that now the heat was exacerbating his light-headedness.

He stared intently through his scope at the distant reed bed across a stretch of open water. Something, a bird hopefully, had been trembling the upright stalks and the thick clumps of grasses and might reveal itself in a moment. Unconsciously he scratched at a mosquito bite on his ankle, one of several that he had acquired last night at the campsite. He had forgotten to use the 'Jungle Formula' insect repellent and was suffering the inevitable consequences. He was sweltering even in T-shirt and shorts and the cloying heat seemed to intensify the itching, inflamed skin around the bites.

After a while his right eye tired of gazing through the spotter scope's eyepiece and he sat back in his chair and used his binoculars instead, to obtain a wider field of view, in the hope of catching sight of anything that might be flitting across the water. Surprisingly, there were hardly any interesting birds about. Three egrets stood dotted on a mudbank, as if waiting for a hand out of food. To the far left, in a wide expanse of water, a small conglomeration of flamingos with their heads below the surface, were sweeping the shallows for crustaceans. Whatever they did they seemed to do in unison. Whilst agreeing that they were a beautiful sight, especially in the great numbers you often saw in the Camargue, Brian always thought their thin legs and sinuous, down-turned necks made them resemble a bizarre art installation.

Harry had opened a lunch box and was spreading some goat's cheese on a chunk of baguette. Brian decided to wait a little bit longer before he ate, just in case his light-headedness *was* a precursor to the collywobbles.

The reeds managed to tremble in the afternoon heat, whispering and clicking. Old ghosts, Brian thought, their voices as reedy as the rushes themselves. Lean, skeletal wraiths, leaning together and murmuring about the two new visitors in their midst. In the far distance, wading through the salt marsh, he watched a group of horse riders pass by, rippled by the heat haze. Training his spotter scope on them he confirmed that this was not the party in the company of Jane and Brenda. Nine white horses and their riders trotted across his field of view, water spraying the flanks of the horses.

Abruptly he realised that his attention had been diverted, and leaving the scope to idle on its tripod, he returned his binoculars to his eyes once more and scanned in slow, wide sweeps for fauna of the avian type.

They were in the west of the Camargue, not far from the *salin* d'Aigues-Mortes, situated in an area that combined salt lagoons, coastal salt meadows and small lakes. The topography was level and rather extraordinary. Colours were muted and defined by the yellow reeds, green grass, the pale blue sky and water, and the whitening effect of the salt. Most of all, Brian reflected, the relative seclusion made a person quiver, almost, with exhilaration, at the wilderness. Tall reed beds served to hinder his inspection of far distances in almost every direction, bringing on a sense of claustrophobia. The water was still and silent, except for the occasional muted sounds made by waders or muskrats swimming to and fro. There were three hundred and sixty square miles to this peculiar country, formed by the delta of the Rhône, the river itself creating a huge wetland island as it split into its petite and larger partner. The two spurs of the river meandered down to the Mediterranean, isolating the marsh from the disturbance of roads, traffic and casual tourists.

Above distant rushes, Brian trapped a bird in his sights. It was gliding effortlessly and flew over the edge of the reeds and across the clear water in front of him. Then it dived with a sudden acceleration that was attained with breathtaking effortlessness, and he panned with the bird as it swooped low and nipped a dragonfly out of the air and then swept off back over the reeds and out of sight.

"*Hobby!*" Brian almost shouted. "Did you see it take that dragonfly? That's some kind of flying."

Harry failed to respond straight away, so Brian knew that he had seen the bird too, though not as quickly as him, and could confirm its identification.

"We're square methinks!" Brian said with a delicious satisfaction, taking a leaf out of Harry's book.

"Mmm. Not that uncommon though, Brian."

"Nor was your marsh harrier yesterday." Harry had been lucky too, as they hadn't actively been bird watching then. They had been touring the *salin*, seeing the process of manufacturing the sea salt when the raptor came sweeping across the pans of drying salt, the crystals tinted by the action of microscopic algae. The harrier's silver-grey wings and black wingtips starkly drawn against the surface colours of what had the appearance of diluted blood saturating the saline layers.

"Both birds are pretty much in the same league in this neck of the woods, wouldn't you say?" Brian's riposte was quick, before Harry could downgrade his sighting even more. "And the hobby is smaller and was harder to spot here, compared with where we were yesterday, I think you'll agree."

Brian slowly removed his notebook from his pocket and began to jot down the details, a description of the location, heading the entry with the bird's name and, taking out his GPS, noting the grid reference. He wrote slowly, waiting for Harry to reply, guessing the negotiations might take a while yet.

"All right. I'll let you have that one," his friend said surprisingly. Brian looked up to see Harry performing his theatrical knowing wink, creasing one cheek and curling his lip in the process. As if he was allowing a young novice the benefit of his doubt, in the full knowledge that both of them knew that Harry's magnanimity came out of sheer good will and not agreement on the point in question. "It's *too* hot to argue one way or the other," he said heavily, scratching the long bushy sideburns that gave him the appearance of a country yokel, rather than a townie. "Shall we try another spot? I don't think we're going to see much more here." Harry paused. Brian sensed he was restless, but perhaps not on account of the rather paltry sightings. "We should be bagging a lot more birds!" he complained.

Brian smiled to himself, despite Harry's discomfort. Level-pegging! "Right-o," he replied cheerfully; raising his cap, he used it to wave across the water. "The path off to the left, if you can call it that, looks like it skirts round and closer to the other side of that clump of reeds. We might be able to add to our tally around there."

All of a sudden he felt better. His light-headedness was gone. And he even didn't want to think about Harry and Brenda's relationship any more. Harry regarded him as a bit of an old woman, with his fussiness and caution, but he wasn't going to mither any more about the misfortunes of others. Jane was right: he shouldn't fret about how others were feeling, deferring his own emotional needs to the greater cause of group harmony. No wonder his still abundant hair was turning grey. He couldn't hope to be able to penetrate Harry's thick skin, even if he might have been in a position to offer domestic guidance. His own relationship with Jane was a happy one, full stop. That's what life was all about.

So as not to make too much noise they loaded their pushbikes as quietly as they could and pushed them along the boggy path that circled the *étang*, eventually finding themselves in an area of much softer ground, with islands of reed breaking up brackish pools of water. The location appeared to be a very good one, if they could situate themselves in the wedge of reeds without either disturbing the fauna or sinking into a quagmire.

Both men left their bikes on the raised bank and sloshed quietly though shallow water that smelled of decay and brine. They took just their binoculars with them this time and a piece of tarp to sit on, taking up position in the little stand of short reeds surrounding a tamarisk tree, whose drooping, grey-green wispy leaves would break up their outlines, yet allow them to scrutinise the nearby beds. They had been so careful that even a heron idling nearby had not thought to be disturbed by their approach.

The downside to the location was the number of flies, which appeared to prefer where they were sitting rather than discovering the abundant horse manure along the causeways.

At least they were not the Camargue's notorious mosquitoes at this time of the day, although Brian wasn't sure whether the mossies hereabouts kept regular hours. The flies could be put up with, though their buzzing twanged a train of thought that threatened to take his mind completely off bird watching.

Earlier in the week, when the four of them had been touring the ancient fortress town of Aigues-Mortes, he had learned about the 'Tower of the Salted Bourguignons' and a horrific episode during the Hundred Years' War. Planting the bodies of the defeated Burgundians in the shallow, foetid swamp in the thirteenth century was not an option if the rest of the population wanted to remain in good health, so the Armagnacs stuffed the corpses in the tower and preserved them with layers of salt. But Brian never found out what happened to them later on. It was never explained, but at some point those bodies would have had to be removed from the tower and be disposed of. What if they *were* secretly deposited in the salt marsh? To be feasted upon by fish and birds and muskrats and flies... Getting rid of your enemies in the marshes seemed somehow the more sensible option to Brian. He could imagine that down the centuries enemies, robbers, vagabonds, murdered waifs and the politically assassinated might become the disappeared of their time. Rotting, stinking, maggot-bloated corpses, floating to release the multitude of flies, then sinking and decomposing, eventually providing nutrients for the swamp's flora. And so with that grisly image, Brian's day wound leisurely towards its end...

Thankfully the magnificent sunset had diverted his thoughts.

By the time both men had packed up their belongings and it was very nearly dark, they discovered – and sod's law determined it be so, as Harry tut-tutted – that their hired pushbikes came without headlamps. Ordinarily, if they had been at home, Brian would have carried the torch he always kept in his rucksack along with a first aid kit and penknife.

The threads of cloud that had made the sunset so fantastic had metamorphosed into a grey duvet. The light was fading fast as the Earth turned its back on the sun.

"We'll have to walk the bikes back out." Harry said wisely, if rather tetchily, realising that it would be foolhardy to try to ride the narrow uneven causeways between the swampy ground and the salt pools.

"I think I can retrace the path we took just to this spot," Brian said uncertainly, "but I'm damned if I can remember all the other twists and turns we've made today." He then recalled the location of the bird hide, and the warning notice they'd passed near to it. A worn, hand painted wooden sign, a crude red circle with diagonal and with faded words below: *danger – passage interdit*. There had been some sort of illustration within the red circle, but it was so worn away it was impossible to say what it represented. It might have been a depiction of a mosquito. That would have made sense, Brian reflected.

"If we can get back to that hide," Harry said, also remembering its position, "the paths should be pretty straightforward." The nervous pitch of his voice didn't convince Brian. "Besides, from there we'll be able to see the lights of the salt factory," he added with more confidence.

If the salt factory was working at night and *if* the buildings had external lighting, Brian thought.

"I've got my mobile, if we need to phone..." Brian remembered, thinking aloud. Jane would be concerned if they were late arriving. They had set off without further thought and Brian was already sloshing in the brackish water as he attempted to keep his bicycle on the narrow track.

Harry was striding carelessly ahead, disappearing in the darkness, making Brian hurry. In a moment of distraction he slipped and went down on one knee, but still somehow clinging onto the handlebars of his bike. The moon made a brief appearance through the clouds, reflecting off the spokes of the bike's raised front wheel. As it rotated slowly above him, flickering across the face of moonlight Brian could almost believe he was watching an old black and white silent film. In the illuminated space between the spokes, the reeds and the moonlight, black speckles were cascading down. Almost like drifting seeds, Brian surmised, but more aerodynamic, as if seeds could launch themselves in unison and move in formation, like starlings. Despite assuming this was a perfectly natural phenomenon in these lagoons, he instinctively ducked, to avoid the flying formation.

Something landed on his neck and involuntarily he brushed it away. Whatever it was, it fell off.

"Hang on, Harry!" Brian called. He slapped the back of his neck for good measure, recollecting last night's marauding mosquitoes. And as if on cue, the itching started again with a vengeance. And yes, he could expect their attentions soon, if they weren't circling him already.

A sound came back through the night as the moon's light disappeared once more behind the sky's blanket. A squeal of noise, blaring and then juddering as if someone was blowing inexpertly on a saxophone. It had to be Harry's bike wheels squealing, or something else, not Harry. Leaning forwards to right his bike, Brian felt the front wheel tyre thud comfortingly on solid ground. As he stood up he began to push the cycle forward, with more care this time.

"Is that you, Harry, making that god-awful racket?" Brian shouted out to the silence that filled the open space like a vacuum. For a moment he wondered which species of owl or other nocturnal wildlife might have been calling out in that saxophone voice, in the dark, if it wasn't Harry.

A few more metres of solid ground were gained before water was spraying against Brian's ankles and in moments he was knee deep in swamp water. Trying to balance, he lost his grip on the bicycle and if fell over and sank. He began to fish around with both hands, like a flamingo dipping for shrimp. But his feet were stuck in the mud and he toppled over backwards trying to extract one of them. Both his legs came up as he fell, his feet kicking free, but minus their sandals. There was no panic, but Brian was not a strong swimmer and he spluttered, thrashing, until he was able to stand up again in the shallow water. He decided that if he had to pay to replace the damned hire bike, that would be preferable to drowning in a couple of feet of water and leaving the bill unpaid. As for his expensive spotter scope in the bike's pannier – well the salt water would have ruined that anyway. Flailing about, somehow he managed to struggle through the almost impenetrable, crackling reeds that barred his way, as if they were the ultra thin skeletons of the long dead Burgundians, resisting his passage. Finally he stood on the causeway, dripping wet and gasping.

"*Harry*! For Christ's sake, I've fallen in! *Wait will you!*" His voice resonated as if it shouted against an absence, as if Harry was no longer there to reply.

There was another odd sound from farther along the path. He scoured his memories for an identification, a bird-call that sounded like someone on their deathbed loudly drawing in their last two breaths. *One*, pause. *Two*. Then silence. Brian wondered if Harry had fallen in the water as well, but the noise hadn't been anything like splashing.

His T-shirt and shorts clung to him as if they were a second, loose, wet skin, chilling him. Water was dripping from his sodden underpants, but a warmer oozing from the back of his neck and down his forehead was more worrying. He reached up with one hand and touched his forehead. Warm, sticky liquid smeared his fingers.

He tasted it and the metallic flavour was confirmation.

He must have hit his head on something as he'd fallen into the water, though he didn't remember a jolt of pain. Yet, come to think of it, there *was* a tingling sensation on his scalp. Combing his fingers through his hair, he yanked his hand away as if he'd received an electric shock. What it had encountered was two or more, indeed many, globular objects firmly *stuck* to his scalp.

If they had been mosquitoes he could have slapped and slapped. But these... things on his head were... disgusting. Tentatively he felt his hair again. Like very small *eggs*. Warm, alive. A heart beat inside each one, Brian was sure.

Brian was an ornithologist, but he knew a bit about invertebrates. He'd half expected Jane, having gone horse riding, to perhaps unluckily succumb to the attentions of one of what he believed was on his head and neck...

And what now appeared to be crawling up his bare legs.

Legions of them.

Ticks.

Gorging on his blood and fattening themselves. The ones he now touched gingerly on his midriff, below his sodden, rucked-up T-shirt *were* bloated. They'd been there a while without him noticing. His groin itched painfully and several things squirmed, along with his testicles. These were *not* your everyday horse ticks, that was for sure.

Brian experimentally tried pulling one off his paunch with thumb and forefinger, but despite being quite hard, it eventually burst open, smearing his fingers with half-congealed gore. The mouth-parts of the thing were still attached to his skin and where it had sucked, it hurt like hell, as if the animal had injected him with venom at the point of its death.

Blindly, he flicked another of the creatures off him and the skin surrounding where it had suckled contracted with pain. He tried removing a few more to see whether he could stand the cumulative soreness of their embedded, harpoon-like probes, while he ran barefoot along the causeway. Within seconds came an agonising immobility. Brian could envisage nerve poison being injected into him in small, cumulative doses with each of the creatures he disposed of.

Dropping to his knees, he began to examine his exposed skin more methodically... and found there was not that much of his flesh left uncovered. Perhaps if he could remove them one at a time... acclimatise himself to the excruciating throbbing... manage to walk to civilisation and a hospital?

Just then he thought about Harry. Light he hadn't noticed before was shafting through the reeds in front of him. Perhaps Harry was right, the salt factory security lights were on! His surge of hope was dispelled when he saw a bicycle lying on its side and beside it, stretched out on the path, a humped shape, highlighted by thin beams from the distant lights. And as he watched, in the pallid illumination, as if drifting from the reeds with the determination of a group mind, more little speckles cascaded. He comprehended that this was unquestionably a dispersal of sorts, but *not* the nocturnal scattering of seeds.

The body on the causeway wasn't moving, but the black spider-like clusters that concealed it were constantly twitching. Whether Brian's strength was diminishing because he knew it was Harry beneath the parasites, or because his own blood was being methodically drained from him, he wasn't sure. Shivering, with shaking fingers he began to examine his skin with a good deal more attention now that he could also see. *Everywhere* he touched, everywhere he looked, there was no familiar pale skin. Instead, warm, pulsing ticks, all distended bodies and squirming atrophied limbs, hanging to him tenaciously by their mouths.

Not just a few parasites. A *plague*.

Frenziedly, he dug into the wet pocket of his shorts and prayed as he scrolled through his mobile's phone book. Jane's number came up and the backlight began to flicker intermittently. He pressed dial and waited. Even at the speed of light, delay occurred as signals were routed and rerouted through a multitude of phone masts. He bit his lip and shuddered anxiously. The stubble on his neck itched uncomfortably and his beard tingled as if he had a rash. Jane's voice suddenly burst in Brian's ear and he screamed her down wordlessly in his fright. Then silence. He looked at the display and screamed again. It was as black as the lagoon water. Violently thumbing buttons at random, the instrument unfailingly failed to come to life. The salt water had finally managed to seep into the innards and wreck it.

Jane would be dialling him frantically now, frustrated and scared when his phone did not respond. Not nearly so scared as him. His terror brought Brian near to tears. A yearning swept through him. Desperation to reach out and hug Jane, to tell her that everything was going to be all right. But it wasn't going to be all right. Brian closed his eyes but was unable to close his mind to how inhuman he must look. A breeze rattled the reeds around him. Bones of the dead clustering to watch the show. The gathered ghosts of the earth goddess nodding wisely while nature began its rebellion.

At last, when the torment intensified so much that Brian began to lose all sense of his surroundings, he rolled over and sat down. But even with the satisfaction of crushing many of the blood-sucking creatures beneath his buttocks, he knew, assuming he was still able to move his arms and legs, it would be pointless to try anything so dramatic and excruciating with the rest of his body. Even less so with the vigorously gripped, unbearably pulsing skin of his face and lips.

'AND STILL THOSE SCREAMS RESOUND…'

Daniel McGachey

In the past I have spoken of my friend, Dr Lawrence, and some of the accounts of the supernatural that have, in his duties as an antiquarian, been presented to him. In each case Lawrence has acted, much as you yourself do, as little more than an audience for some peculiar narrative. But his particular interest in that field of study has seen him record the details of these accounts, and this has led to many a long evening's discussion with friends as to the significance of the events to which he had been made privy.

As one of that group of friends, I regard myself as privileged to have been consulted by Lawrence, even if it was in no more exalted a position than a sounding board. For, although I can claim no real knowledge of folklore, and while I prefer to maintain a neutral stance on the existence or otherwise of ghosts and their ilk, it was certainly an experience to witness my friend as he regaled his company with whichever tale had been freshly brought to his notice. He would not only narrate each account in precisely recalled detail, blessed, or perhaps cursed, as he was with a remarkable memory, he would literally reenact it; impressing the tales upon all who heard them so that even those of us not equipped with Lawrence's agile memory found them impossible to forget.

I can picture him now, prowling the floor of his study, assuming the mannerisms and vocal intonations of whomsoever had imparted their story to him. During the course of a single evening, I saw him alternately hoist himself up to seemingly beyond his own full height and assume the bellowing tones of the retired military man who had cornered him in a clubroom to confide an unpleasant incident in the Indies, and shrink in on himself, dropping his voice to the tremulous whisper of the spinster he had shared a train compartment with, and who had, rather brazenly, told him of the suitor who was still as ardently attentive to her as he had been before his death, five decades earlier.

So convincing were the doctor's displays of mimicry, and so compelling were his accounts, that even the most avowed sceptics would find themselves startled to realise that the night had deepened perceptibly while they sat entranced, and that the chills they felt creeping at their spines had little to do with the dying down of the fire in the study's grate.

There were, though, those occasions when these reports merely left his audience hungry for more, and Lawrence would find himself pressed to provide a more personal account, one taken from his own first-hand experience. In one such instance, he was persuaded to recount his experience with a haunted phonograph, wherein he discovered that a portion of the wax utilised in the manufacture of the recording cylinders had been recovered from the remains of certain black candles involved in a particularly grotesque occult experiment. On another memorable night, I heard the grim chronicle of the travelling mausoleum, and its awful, grinning proprietors, and to this day I cannot pass a cemetery by moonlight without feeling a shudder coursing through me.

It was on a night such as this that my friend was faced with the question, "What would you consider the most evil being your investigations have brought you into contact with?"

"There is, I would say, an evil presence that I have felt my work has brought me into close proximity with. Yet it remains vague, unformed and insubstantial, hovering only on the edges of my awareness." With that, Lawrence would have been happy to let the matter rest. But his interrogator was not to be put off with hints of shadowy, amorphous presences.

"Are you saying that you have never come into contact with genuine, corporeal evil?"

A troubled look clouded the scholar's eyes, something that this interrogator seized on as an affirmative response, and one that demanded elaboration. As it became apparent that he could not escape this line of questioning without providing satisfaction, the usually animated Lawrence seemed overtaken by a sudden heaviness of spirit and of limb, and he dropped into a seat and seemed reluctant to meet the gaze of his company. When he finally raised his head, the face he presented was nearly as white as that hair of his that so belied his relative youth, and when he spoke, it was in a quiet and almost emotionless voice.

*

Yes, I have encountered what I can only describe as evil. An absolute lack of what most humans would consider goodness.

I should, I suppose, begin by admitting to you that my interest in what may be described as unearthly matters began with the influence of one man; my old History tutor at St. James's, Professor Lucius Shadwell. It was he who first opened my eyes and my mind to the possibilities of forces beyond that which may normally be perceived. Not just mine, I would add, but all of those under his tutelage, as he was given to proffering his theories at any moment; often wandering away from his intended topic of this particular battle or that particular medieval reform. In some of us boys he found a rapt audience, but from most, I recall, he received only bemusement or scorn as he eagerly detailed legends of wailing nuns sealed in abbey walls, or of ancient bloodstains that resolutely declined to dry. Even so, he appeared to accept the unkind laughter and whispered comments in good stead, his own delight in the topic and the attention of those few of us with a less sceptical response evidently outweighing the criticism.

But, for the professor, the uncanny was more than a mere interest. More than a passion, even, and before long even my open-minded fellows grew weary of his regular digressions from our studies. I, however, remained an exception, and in me he saw a fellow enthusiast. He would return my essays with additional notes in his markings to suggest I seek out a particular book with an intriguing entry or a specific history with a pleasingly terrible legend attached. It became increasingly more common for me to stay on after his classes had concluded to chat about such matters, or for him to send word that I was required urgently in his study whenever he was to happen upon some fresh piece of lore.

Of course, this had not gone unnoticed amongst my peers, and their mockery of our eccentric master was soon directed in equal measure at me. But the subject was of such overwhelming fascination to me that I shrugged off their remarks and they, seeing the lack of effect they were achieving, gradually transferred their attentions to other targets.

Despite our relative status, the professor was only ten years or so older than me, and he felt more akin to an older brother than a teacher. Therefore it seemed only natural that I was soon a regular guest in his home. There, I would dine with him and his young family, before joining him in his well-stocked library to pore over books and manuscripts. Often we would talk at such length, dissecting that which we read, that I would find myself running after dark across the playing fields that separated the married staffs' residences from the main school building, in order to make it back to the dorms before lights out.

Shadwell's wife, Meredith, was as welcoming as he, though I believe I detected a trace of weary indulgence in her smile whenever his excitement would begin to grow as he propounded on his favourite theme. But I think she was happy that her husband, to whom she was so obviously devoted, had found an ally of sorts. And, over those months, I began to feel almost part of their family, occasionally joining them for church services or for Sunday strolls, where their infant daughter would delight us all with her wide-eyed, innocent reactions to the sights and sounds of the park.

But it was within that book-lined inner sanctum of his that, after months of companionable friendship, Lucius Shadwell let slip his mask of contentment to reveal a private sorrow. "Lawrence," said he, putting a volume of translated French ghost stories to one side and lighting a contemplative cigarette, "I fear the situation is becoming all too unbearable."

What was this? Had he grown weary of my company? Did I impose myself too freely on his domestic affairs? Or had I somehow caused him some offence?

He waved these concerns away, with earnest reassurances that such was far from the case and that my kinship was a relief to him. "You and I, we are not blinkered. We accept that the supernatural is not only a possibility, it is the only sane probability in such an as yet unfathomed universe. I have always accepted it, welcomed it, sought it, but my frustration lies in the simple fact that it has not welcomed or accepted me!

"You see how I surround myself; how I have immersed myself. You might think it enough to have such a treasure trove of stories to hand at all times. But what I desire most of all is to experience these things I have studied so zealously for myself. To examine the evidence at close quarters, and to see the truth revealed before my own eyes! And it's not as if I haven't tried!"

And he told me then of what he referred to as his 'pilgrimage' around as many of the reputedly haunted sites this country has to offer that his post and his salary would permit. He told of damp nights encamped in monastery ruins, or under canvas on ancient battlefields, of being turned back at the doors of Scottish castles, and of a near-arrest upon trying to gain entry to a notorious house in a London square where several alarming deaths had occurred. And all his efforts to no avail.

Sharing this revelation had, however, a positive effect, and he crushed out yet another cigarette, declaring, "No avail thus far, perhaps? But I have no intention of giving up, young Lawrence, you just mark me! I'll continue to seek out these places until I succeed, no matter how long it takes. Indeed, I may yet end up as a restless spirit myself, haunting one of these gloomy spots. Hah, now wouldn't that be an irony, m'boy?"

From then, our friendship resumed its regular course. But time must pass, and boy and master must, of course, part company. Yet, still, I was aware of him, watching my course through life from afar with interest and, I'd liked to believe, approval. And once or twice a year I'd receive a message, with the familiar St. James's coat of arms upon the envelope, that I knew would point me to some new and exciting find. And each new missive would remind me of that long past confession, and I would wonder to myself if he had ever come closer to achieving his goal.

Which is why, when I received the telegram reading simply: '*It has happened… Shadwell*', I knew instantly to what it referred. The message's arrival at my rooms in college had come as a surprise, it having been a period of some years since our correspondence had slowed and then stopped. The lack of James's stationery had me double-checking for an address, and there it was; '*Wraithvale*'!

A suitably portentous name, I'm sure you will agree. Indeed, it was no difficult task in surmising why such a place would have drawn Lucius Shadwell. And I did not have to reach for a gazetteer to establish its location. The name was already familiar to me, as my old tutor was surely aware.

Wraithvale Priory, situated in the border country, has a reputation that has preceded it like a particularly long and crooked shadow; from the disappearance of its original architect upon the building's completion, to that more recent scandal of the church minister found hanging in the family chapel, with his family, what was found of them, propped up like a mouldering congregation. If there was any one place in the land where my old friend's goal to encounter a ghost had a better than average chance of succeeding, I thought, it was in that house known as Wraithvale.

Before the day was out, I was on a Northbound train. Although the telegram didn't say as much, it was clearly an

115

invitation, and it was not one which long-standing loyalty left me capable of declining. And, I may as well own up to the fact, I had long harboured a desire to visit the notorious priory myself, though my previous visits to that part of the country had afforded me little opportunity.

I had left so quickly on receipt of Shadwell's message that I'd had no time to send word of my imminent arrival. Therefore, as I stepped from my compartment several hours later, I was somewhat surprised to perceive the familiar figure of my tutor striding toward me down that lonely platform. I should not have been so taken aback for, after allowing himself a moment's mirth at my expression, he explained, "Unless my young friend Lawrence had grown into an entirely different man, I knew he would be unable to resist immediate action regarding my summons. And as this spot is scarcely well-served by trains, I could fairly accurately predict the hour of your arrival. You've packed for a few days, I see. Splendid, then let us have your baggage on the cart and be off. I'm sure you're very keen to see my infamous house!"

It was a grey, chill evening as we drove, he at the reins and I beside him, through the twisting streets of the drab little town, then out into the open countryside that separated the town from the house. I couldn't help but wonder if the inhabitants of that place were not happy for that distance between themselves and the priory, with its attendant reputation. As we rode, Shadwell answered my questions as to his activities in the years that had intervened since last we had communicated. He was, he admitted, no longer at St. James's, no, nor at the nearby university, nor indeed at any educational post. His interests had apparently proved of such embarrassment to James's ruling cabal, they had felt compelled to offer him a more than generous settlement to go without a fuss.

"Generous enough to net you a country estate?" I laughed, incredulous.

Shadwell joined me in my laughter. "You would be surprised how a notoriety such as the one Wraithvale has nurtured can adversely affect the price its owners may seek. I think my taking it off their hands may count as an act of charity."

We were by now approaching the edges of the woods beyond which, in a narrow valley, the priory awaited us. "And Mrs Shadwell," I enquired, "How is she taking to being the lady of the manor? I look forward to seeing her again."

"Meredith?" His voice was oddly flat as he said her name. "She has not been at all well of late. There is a weakness there, a physical one, and it has an effect on her moods. If she is strong enough, of course she will be thrilled to see our old friend once more. I fear she misses her previous existence, with the young people close by, so full of life. And Sarah, naturally."

I was suddenly aware of the passage of years. That happy infant of my memories would now be a young woman, quite beautiful and charming if she had inherited her mother's looks and manner. She might possibly even be married and with a family of her own. I felt an overwhelming sadness that it had taken so long for my friend to have fulfilled his cherished ambition, though it was driven away by a sense of admiration at his determination over a period that would have seen weaker wills surrender to defeat.

But these thoughts were sharply interrupted when Shadwell, after taking his watch out and squinting at it in the gloom, let out an oath and spurred the horse on into an unexpected burst of speed. I merely gaped at him, and he once more let out a braying laugh at my surprise, yelling above the clatter of hooves and wheels on the rutted road, "We don't want to miss it, do we?"

We were passing now through the gates in a high, forbidding wall, now along a curving carriage drive through yet more trees, and I was holding on for dear life as I yelled back, "Miss it? Miss what?"

"Why, what you came all this way to see, m'boy," he grinned. "My ghost, of course!"

When we were through the trees, I had my first view of Wraithvale itself. How did it look, you no doubt wish to know? It looked, as best I can tell you, how you would imagine a haunted house to look; turreted, stark, grey, and shadowed by the hills that surrounded it and in whose shade the trees, deprived of light, had grown twisted and stunted. Looking away from the house, across the lawn I saw what I first took to be a cemetery, though a backwards glance revealed the gravestones to be statues, bone white and crumbling with age.

Though the evening had grown cold, I felt no sense of imminent comfort as we drew nearer the priory. I tried to tell myself that it was only what I'd already heard of that place's history that made me think so irrationally. But I could not dismiss the feeling that here was a house that had never offered warmth, or comfort, or had rang with the sounds of life or laughter.

I waited with my cases on the shallow steps leading to the heavy doors, and Shadwell deposited our transport in a small stable block, before returning to escort me over the threshold and into the house beyond. Had the interior been thick with gloom, bedecked with cobwebs, and coated with a century's worth of dust, I would have been less surprised than I was to find myself in a warm, brightly lit and spacious hallway. True, the stained glass window that towered above the staircase appeared a little too grotesque, from what I could see of the battling angels and demons against the night sky beyond, but my notice was drawn to my host, and my mind returned to my previous thoughts on time and its passage.

Under the dim glow of the railway platform's lighting, my former professor had appeared quite unchanged, and our twilit journey had shown me little to dispel that belief. But here, in the light of the great chandelier, I saw more clearly that time had not quite stood still for him. His blond hair, always rather fine and wispy, was even finer and more scant around the temples. It was now evident that it had whitened, and that its yellow tint owed more to nicotine than any vestige of youth.

Then there was that hollowness to the cheeks and eyes and, as he hung his overcoat, I saw that his figure, though slender before, was now positively skeletal. Thankfully he seemed unaware of my scrutiny, looking once more at his watch and smiling before saying, "It is beginning."

I was about to enquire as to what was beginning when he waved for hush, glancing between his watch and something, I could not yet tell what, at the top of the vast staircase.

Thus it was that I heard it before I saw anything. A thin, high-pitched whine, the source of which I had to strain to perceive. It wavered, then dropped, then rose again, resuming with more strident force, before falling silent once more. Whatever it was, it was issuing from somewhere in the darkness at the top of the stairs. And when it rose again, it was unmistakably a shriek of absolute, abject terror.

I turned to Shadwell, a whisper of, "What on earth is it?" barely escaping from my lips, for he was already on the stairs, racing up two at a time, giving me no option but to follow, else be left alone with that hideous shriek ringing around me. "What is it?" I demanded once more, following in his wake.

But his only response was, "Come, there is little time!"

A long and ill-lit corridor led to yet more stairs and, as we moved further from that unexpectedly inviting entrance hall, the house reverted more to the image I'd held of it as I'd waited outside. Dusty panelling of some dark wood added to the dimness, before giving way to the bare stone walls of the staircase as it wound its way upwards. Despite his gaunt appearance, the professor was as sprightly as in his youth and clearly energised, while I struggled to keep him in sight as he rounded each turn. Our destination, I realised then, was in one of those looming turrets I had observed, and at last, just on the point where I feared my stamina would give out, the door to the upper chamber came into view.

The door was sturdy and studded with iron, and it creaked most appallingly on its hinges as Shadwell wrenched it fully open. That screech of metal, though, was as nothing in comparison with that other screech that blasted out of the chamber and down the spiral staircase. It buffeted around me like a gusting wind. As I instinctively clasped my hands to my ears, I lost my footing and feared that I was to be swept back down those perilous stairs by the sheer anguished force of the cry. But a bony hand gripped my arm, dragging me on and upwards, before slamming the door shut at our backs. Shadwell had sealed us both in that chamber with whatever it was that shrieked there.

We were in darkness. The only sensations I was aware of were the ringing that persisted in my ears after the scream had died away, and the pounding in my chest as I strove to regain my breath. Little by little I registered that there was light, even if it was just a dull shaft from a feeble moon, struggling through more stained glass mounted high in the opposite wall. I could see no lamp near to hand, in fact saw little of my surroundings. So little that, when I insisted my companion tell me what I had just experienced, his reply of, "Wait and see," left me perplexed.

"At first there was only the sound," and the excitement was evident in his voice, even if I could not see his expression. "To begin with, a merest whisper of a sound. Always at the same precise time, every evening without fail. Every evening for the past six weeks. And every evening it has grown stronger, louder, more… vibrant. But it has only been in this past week that the manifestation has altered, from purely audible phenomena to actual apparition. You see?"

And I did see. For while he had been speaking, the light in that turret chamber had changed. A circle of pale yellow illumination had formed on the floor in front of us, though the moon beyond the narrow window was still sickly and pallid. In this eerie half-light I could now see that the chamber was as narrow and cramped as it was tall. The claustrophobic lack of space, coupled with the bare, black stonework and that solid door put me at once in mind of a cell or dungeon. My attention was drawn from the starkness of my surroundings as, there in the centre of the uncarpeted wooden floor, I saw first the ring hazily ripple and form, then the flickering of unseen candles that seemed to surround it and fill it with its unnatural luminescence.

Once the image had grown more defined, the ring was shown to be more than a column of projected light. It was clearly outlined by a perfect circle that looked to be traced in white powder. Instantly I thought of the ritual protection afforded by a circle of salt. At this point, my inherent curiosity must have overtaken me, as Shadwell had to nudge my hand back even as I attempted to pluck up a sample of those white grains. "You can't disturb it," he insisted. "You must... you can only let it act itself out!"

As I drew my hand away, those awful sounds began again, though there was something more than the shrieking now that whatever we were to witness had begun in earnest. I heard the ragged breathing, the painful gasps, practically sobs, still emanating out of thin air; a voice without a mouth. But the mouth would come. That gaping, clamouring pit of a mouth would come soon enough.

The first movement was of something white at the heart of the fluttering glow within the circle. It might have been a maggot that had writhed its way out of the floorboards. Only, within seconds, it had grown larger than any maggot; longer, thicker, yet still with that same shimmering whiteness to it as it continued to twist and to wriggle and to swell. And the worst of it was that darkness at one end of it that also grew, splitting apart in time to let out that all too familiar shrill of horror.

As the mouth let loose its piteous yell, the distended body twisted in on itself, and folds of some white matter flowed out from it. Then the limbs took shape that filled out these folds like some shroud. The pallid flesh that formed itself around that dark mouth was now fringed with hair that sprouted and then cascaded down to frame the oval of a face. Even though the features were blurred, more a suggestion than anything solid, the eyes that opened and stared out of that recently

121

formed head pleaded with just as much intensity as the voice that once more sobbed.

"This is the most complete manifestation yet," whispered Lucius Shadwell.

I struggled to find my voice. "Who is she?"

When I dragged my eyes away from that newly gestated thing with the appearance of a young girl, I saw that my tutor's watch was once more in his hand. "A whole minute longer than last night," he noted, more to himself, I thought, than me.

When I looked back to the apparition, with a jolt I saw that, through tear-rimmed eyes, she was looking directly at us. Had she somehow heard our talk? Was she aware of some other presence there? But her gaze then shifted, never blinking, seeming to watch something unseen by either of us observers outside that now rapidly dimming ring of light.

She was gone in a matter of seconds, not coiling up again into that maggoty swirl of ectoplasm, but simply fading from sight, her silent cries still hanging on her lips. And, before the room was even fully dark once more, the professor brushed past me, opening the door onto the stairs beyond, declaring, "It is over. Come. We have much to talk about, I think."

But an hour or more was to pass before we had that chance to talk for, on opening the door to his ground-floor study, we were greeted by the insistent jangling of a bell-pull. Ushering me in and indicating where I could find both cigars and a stiff drink, he left, his only word of explanation being, "Meredith."

I sat alone in that study, its shelves full of well-remembered books, with a generous measure of brandy providing a deal more warmth than the fire's feeble efforts. What I had seen… What I had heard… It had shaken me. I thought, though, not of myself and how I had been affected, but of the professor's poor wife, uprooted from a life of routine normality and bedded down in this blighted plot. How must it have taken its toll on her health, to share a home with such a powerful disturbance? Particularly if, as her husband had divulged, there was already some deficiency in her health? I grew angry then, angrier than I had felt for many a year, angry at my old friend for subjecting his loving wife to such a strain simply to satisfy his single-minded, selfish obsession! Had he walked into the room at that moment, I felt sure I would have struck him. But I was alone there with my fury and, as minute by minute ticked past on the mantel clock, and the occurrence in that lofty cell crept inexorably back into my mind, my anger dimmed and curiosity flooded in again to take its place. Here I could sympathise once more with Shadwell, for I knew curiosity to be a powerful guiding force.

There was one more incident before my companion returned. As I sat musing upon the identity and plight of that apparition, with all her terrifying despair, from somewhere far off inside that old house came a cry, one which I immediately assumed was to lead to yet more unearthly clamour. However, only silence followed and, after a minute or two, the echo of a door closing somewhere overhead and, in time, footsteps on the staircase and approaching across the hall.

When Lucius Shadwell reentered, he displayed a guarded smile and offered an apology. "This is not one of her good nights, I'm afraid," he confided, the cigarette already lit and at his lips. "She'll sleep now, don't worry. But sometimes she needs someone to reassure her. She gets confused, you see. I wouldn't leave her alone here, don't ever think it. There is a nurse. Not a local woman; I don't think you need ask why. She's good at what is required of her, but she's practically deaf, and sometimes she doesn't hear…" He allowed himself a small chuckle. "Which is possibly a very good thing, considering, wouldn't you say?"

I had to laugh with him, and my bitter feelings were forgotten when he, after pouring us both a stiff measure of whisky, settled back and asked, "So, what do you make of her, then; my white lady, if I may borrow a somewhat clichéd and mundane term?"

"I've been asking myself that single question since we left the tower," I only half-lied. "So let me ask you, instead, who is she? Do you have any history of her? I thought I'd read all of the available reports on this house, but a lady in white or screaming maiden, or whatever you want to call her, I don't recall. There was something about a turreted chamber, but it involved a disfigured nobleman, as I remember..."

"Who skinned his victims and drank of their blood, believing himself to have been cursed by an Ursari gypsy to carry the taint of the 'Strigoi'," he interjected. "You forget, I've read all of the legends too. But, as I told you, this manifestation is new, though how long she has waited up there to make her presence known I couldn't say. That dress or gown she wears... she wore, it looked, would you say, seventeenth century?"

I had to admit that her mode of dress had not been foremost in my mind as she'd screamed and howled herself in and out of existence before me. "However, you also say that her materialisations are a nightly occurrence, and that her powers of apparition are growing stronger? Then more details may quickly make themselves apparent to us."

He let out a great roar of a laugh and clasped my hand warmly in his. "You'll stay, then, and help me record the sighting? I can think of no better man to have by my side, and your practical expertise will, I'm sure, prove invaluable. Come, don't look so abashed, m'boy. You think I don't know of your... pursuits? I may be merely a near-disgraced ex-tutor but I still do have some contacts in the educational establishments, and such outré achievements as yours don't go unremarked. You may also spy certain monographs with your signature to them taking up space on these shelves. You see, I've never lost interest in my young apprentice, yet now I fancy you are the master, and it is you who will be giving me the benefit of your experience. Though I thank you for not gloating about your exploits when we were in closer contact."

We talked that night through. Before long those shelves had been raided of their books, and it felt as if the preceding two decades had melted away and we were once more in my

History tutor's house across the playing fields, man and boy, master and pupil, friend and friend, talking and arguing and laughing together.

It was the jangling of that bell, long after dawn had bleached the sky, that dragged us back to the present, and reminded me that everything was not as once it was. Unlike on the previous evening, however, the bell rang only once and my old friend was gone from me only for a matter of minutes, before returning with a smile across his weary face.

"All is well?"

"All is very well," he affirmed. "She has slept and is in a good frame of mind. Just this moment, she's taking some breakfast in her room. The nurse doubles as a cook, you know, though thankfully only charges a single wage. Yes, Meredith is quite hale, and she's asking to see her friend of fond memory." My face must have betrayed how unexpected this request was, for he continued, "Unless, of course, you're too tired and would like some rest yourself. What a host I am! I've kept you up chattering all night."

I bade him dismiss his concerns, as I was entirely uncertain if sleep would have come following the visitation of the night before. Indeed, I was anxious to see my hostess. Not merely to convince myself that her continued presence in the confines of Wraithvale was having no damaging effect on her, but because I too held her in fond regard.

Although the bed was screened by a thin curtain of gauze, I could see quite well enough that the woman within it was sitting, propped up on cushions, and the tray of empty breakfast plates showed that her appetite, at least, was healthy. "My dearest Master Lawrence," Meredith Shadwell laughed. "Or shouldn't that be Dr Lawrence? How good it is to see you again. Lucius told me you were to visit, and I am delighted you could make it. Please, sit awhile. I'll ring Paskins to bring you some tea... No, I think it had better be coffee, and strong, as I know my husband won't have given you a moment's rest."

With coffee duly served by the monolithic, monosyllabic

nurse, and with Shadwell hovering ever attentive, I enquired gently as to Meredith's health.

"Yes, I must apologise for not greeting you last night. No, no, I insist, and also for dragging you up to this gloomy room." Here she indicated the heavy curtains that were only partially drawn, letting but dingy light into the bedroom. "I'm afraid I'm prone to the most infuriating headaches, and I find the darkness rather soothing."

"If you're feeling unwell," said I, rising, "I'll go and let you rest in some peace."

Her response astonished me. It may have been intended as a laugh, but it emerged as a cackle. "Rest in peace? In this house? You always were a funny little boy, Lawrence. Full marks! Top of the class!"

Shadwell shot me a terse smile as he strode across to his wife's bedside, striving for her hand through the filmy folds and clasping it gently. "Dr Lawrence is, I think, a little tired, m'love."

The laughter from within the bed fell silent, and there was a pause before Meredith's voice returned, its usual bright tone restored. "Of course, Doctor. You should have said so. Or maybe you did say? I can get a little muddled at times. Wherever is Paskins with that coffee?"

But before she could reach for the bell-pull, her husband stayed her hand, holding it tenderly in his. "You know coffee stops you from resting properly. You need to sleep, m'dearest heart."

"But I've only just woken. Haven't I?" There was irritation in the voice, annoyance at her own uncertainty. "I will try, Lucius. Has Paskins left me my pills? Ah, I see them there. I'm sorry, Dr Lawrence, but I'm a little tired. Would you please excuse me? So kind of you. Always a kind boy."

I left them then, the professor and his bewildered wife. I could see only too clearly that her confusion was causing her no little distress. And it was not only her confused state that was the cause, I deduced, as her words to her husband before I had fully closed the door were a pleading, "But what if, while I sleep, she comes back?" I had no need to wonder on who was meant by 'she'. "You will tell me, Lucius? You'll tell me if she comes back again?"

"Some houses, some places; places with something of the dark about them, you might describe them; can have a psychically damaging effect on both body and mind." I spoke these words to Lucius Shadwell over a cold luncheon some hours later.

He threw down his knife, and the face he turned on me was furious. "Don't presume to lecture me, Doctor!" He virtually spat the last word. "I know about these dark places! Or do you choose to forget he who opened the door to that knowledge you now parrot back at me? And I know my wife! What ails Meredith is both physical and psychological, but it is not psychical. She just gets a bit confounded in her thinking sometimes. But she's well looked after, she's protected, and she's damn well loved!" And he stalked off, pacing on the lawn for the time it took to smoke several cigarettes.

Upon his return there were apologies on both sides, and acceptances also, and we swiftly fell back into the discussion that had consumed so much of the night before, and which subsequently devoured the remainder of the afternoon and evening.

When the hour came around for the apparition to commence, we were already ensconced in that bleak turret cell and, as Shadwell had predicted, the shrieking began on cue. There, again, was that unnatural ring of glimmering light. There, again, was that white form that convulsed into being before us. There, again, was the horror in her eyes, when those eyes had finally formed. This time, on Shadwell's urging, I noted the dress. It was not, as I'd imagined it, a simple white smock. Perhaps more detail had come through on this night, as I could now make out the embroidered flowers and birds that covered every inch of it. I had seen similar, of course, my more regular career ensuring that I spent much of my time in museums. I believed my tutor to have been correct in dating the garment, and consequently the phantom it clothed, to early in the seventeenth century.

And there, again, was that moment when her eyes seemed to find us, before darting, terror-stricken, away. And since the materialisation lasted yet longer than on my first night in that room, I was now assured that those eyes were watching the progress of someone or something that prowled and circled where she stood. And wasn't that..? Could it have been..? Just before she dissolved away again, wasn't that the wavering edge of a shadow that fell into the circle? I couldn't be definite. If it was there, it was gone again in an instant, fading away with the rest of that ghastly projection. But if it had truly been there, what was it that could cast so monstrously alarming a shadow?

All these questions I would have put to my companion, were it not for what happened in the final second before the girl vanished entirely from our sight and faded from our hearing. It was a whisper, naught more, but in that whisper was a single, pitiful word. "Please…"

This fresh addition to Shadwell's spectre's repertoire led, as you may well imagine, to many more hours of pacing and talking between us. The identity of this poor unfortunate was as yet a mystery, but on one thing we seemed to reach some agreement.

"So many recorded instances of sightings have occurred on sites historically linked with great tragedy, suffering and anguish. I told you before of my uncomfortable night on that blood-soaked battlefield," Shadwell mused ruefully, "though I didn't hear so much as a single clash of sword on shield or a single note from a phantom piper. But others evidently have, and we know the thinking; the trauma of a death in particularly tragic or violent circumstances can leave its imprint. A psychic scar, if you will."

"Like a wound that refuses fully to heal," I furnished, "and continues to ache away over time. I find the conjecture entirely plausible. I think that this girl, whoever she was, died in an agony of terror. I think something she saw in that room terrified her to death. And I also think, no, am convinced, that if we let this thing play out in its natural course, we will catch a glimpse of whatever caused her fatal distress."

My host gave this a moment's thoughtful consideration, before declaring, "Then we have little option but to watch, and to see what there is to be seen."

Over the following days, Shadwell and I slept by day when we could, while by night we would watch and confer. On some days, during our wakeful daylight hours, we would spend some brief time with his ailing wife in her room. During most of these visits she was quite how I remembered her, but on others she was a stranger to me. And on certain days I would not see her at all. On these bleak days the only other company I saw, besides the professor, was that large, and largely silent, nurse.

As I entered my second week at Wraithvale, a feeling of heavy, cloying depression had already taken me in its grip. I could not entirely lay the blame with the distressing nature of the apparition, nor with the worsening mental state of my hostess. No, there was more to it than that. I longed for sunlight, so scarce in that dreary valley. I also longed to be in my own familiar college rooms again, with their own particular sounds; the hiss as the fire died, the steady ticking of my own clock, the accustomed creak as the old timbers settled. I missed these comfortable things, for I was increasingly aware that my hours of attempted sleep were disturbed by vague sounds that seemed more than structural in origin, and that my every movement was followed by echoes that were not of my own making.

Meredith, too, evidently felt some inkling of my anxiety, though I naturally mentioned nothing of it to her. Yet, in her more strained moments, I overheard her tell of sounds, and of smells, 'like the stench of rising decay,' and yet again her concerned plea of, 'What if she comes back?'

What I longed for above these others, however, was

company from outside this troubled household. So strong was my desire to be with another soul, I began to think on that shade of a terrified girl as an ally; one that I would help if I could only find a way. Her face, as stricken with fear as it was, became a familiar, almost welcome sight. And when the realisation that this was the case hit home, I knew that I had to leave that place, before my senses were warped out of all natural proportion. I had to leave and I had, also, to persuade Lucius Shadwell to take himself and his wife from there, for her sanity's sake, if not his own. But how could I simply go and desert that pathetic girl before I could break through what I now thought of as a steadily more flimsy barrier to knowing her and understanding her plight?

My former tutor, too, seemingly sensed my growing mental unease. I had been obsessing about the shadowy form that had first caught my attention on that second night in the chamber. It had passed from my thoughts following the first whispered plea, but as each night saw the girl's torment lengthen in duration, so too did that other, yet more alarming shade make itself more evident. Or was it evident only to my eyes or, perhaps, in my mind? For my friend appeared oblivious to it, despite my repeated efforts to point it out to him as it skirted the edges of that protective circle of salt; apparently kept at bay while it, in turn, held the girl a captive within, her simple cry of, 'Please... please... please...' repeated like a chant. "Some optical effect of the materialisation, perhaps," was the most he would concede. But it was as integral an element of the haunting to me as the girl, and whether it glided or stalked on legs, in my sight it prowled ever onwards with some frightful purpose to its movements.

At the end of that second week, concern for both his wife's well-being and, apparently, my own, saw Lucius Shadwell track me down to his library. Here I was engrossed in some urgent researches, when he announced, "I think it is time for us to cease our experiment. You've become a shadow of yourself, and it would be better that you leave, for a short time at least. I will notify you if there is any significant alteration in the manifestation."

"You intend to stay?" I cried, but my protest was quelled.

"Aye, but alone. Meredith will leave too. You were right, of course, Lawrence. This house is no place for a sensitive creature like her. Paskins has gone to make arrangements with an excellent private nursing home some miles south of here. When she returns tomorrow, she will take my wife and go."

"But you?" I insisted. "What will you do here, alone?"

He smiled a grim smile. "You forget, I am not alone. 'She' is still here. And I will do what I always set out to do. I will watch. I will observe. And I will record."

I could see that he was resolute in his intention, and I no longer possessed the energy to argue the point with him. "Then if Meredith is to go tomorrow, I will do likewise. And, for this one last night, you won't observe alone."

He accepted my offer as an inevitability, stating that he would have expected nothing less, before leaving me once more to my solitary studies. And, when the first cries rang out that night, we were in that tower room together.

Had my loyalty to an old friend not been so strong, I might never have known the grim secret of that dreadful room. I was not quite hardened to the shrieks and the pleas; I think no one with a spark of humanity could be; but they had lost their ability to chill my soul, and I was as detached in my observing as I could possibly make myself. I watched, and I waited. I followed the pale figure's damp-eyed stare around the perimeter of the room, slowly circling back now to where I stood, turning full circle for the first time in my sight. And it was then that the vague shadow that circled in time with her gaze lurched suddenly forward and expanded until some thing appeared to move through the circle and, for a moment, swallow her entirely. Some 'thing' was as specific as I could be at that time, for I could not actually see it. Whatever it was, its image wasn't captured in this impossible light-show. It registered only as a dead spot in the projection, a patch of emptiness that obscured the girl, and through which the present time, the bare boards of the floor and the stone walls, could be seen. From its silhouette only, what I was aware of was a form that loomed up, as thin as a corpse, its stick-like arms clawing and rending at the air. And as it did so, the cry that choked off from that poor girl was enough to break through my attempts at detachment and bring a sob issuing from my own lips.

Then it was gone, moving aside suddenly so that my view was once more unimpeded. And as the unbroken circle resolved itself before my eyes, in its centre lay the still figure in white, her eyes still gazing in horror at that which had rendered her lifeless.

My first thought, irrational since I knew already that this girl was long past any physical help, was to run to her. But the idea of stepping into that circle drove the notion from my mind. Possibly it was the thought of being trapped there, frozen in time, my last moments to be replayed constantly for the amusement or the horror of unseen spectators. Or was it the idea of encountering that lurking dead spot and perhaps seeing its face? Would I scream and beg, just as the girl did?

Lucius Shadwell stared at the prone figure, and it was long moments before she had dimmed and vanished. "I was too late," I heard myself mumbling. "Too late to help her." But he paid me no heed and, even if he had, I would not have been able to explain myself. My own shock had brought a jumble of thoughts crashing and reeling through my mind, and I struggled to snatch hold of any one of them. What kept repeating though was: What was it she saw and why could we not see it? If... oh, but if it was to materialise as a ghost...

Somewhere in the house below us, doors crashed and slammed, and we were shaken roughly from our reverie. There were yells and curses, and as I attempted to follow my host down the spiralling steps, his efforts to hold me back fell on deaf ears.

The creature that leapt on the professor at the foot of those stairs was a frenzied rush of thrashing, clawing arms, and wild hair flying, allowing only glimpses of the scarred dome of bare scalp. It was only when it ceased its banshee howl and shouted its damning, bitter reproaches at my fallen companion, that I realised it was Meredith Shadwell; that devoted, gentle, loving wife, now gone feral. "It's as I heard it before, on that night, that awful, awful night," she cried. "It's the same! It's how she sounded on that night!"

I struggled to wrench her back from her husband, and my hand nearly recoiled when I saw the swirls and knots of scarred flesh that traced their way up her arm, up her neck, and across half of her face and skull. A bundle dropped from her hand, and it too was burnt. I snatched it up, despite Shadwell's breathless protests to ignore her, to watch her, to be afraid of her. "Her mind's gone. It went months ago. She's dangerous! To you. To herself! You see what she did to herself? You see what her madness led her to?"

She seized the bundle from me before I could think to examine it. "In the furnace, it was! You tried to hide it from me!" Then she emptied the charred bag, so that vials of white substance rattled to the floor, before a white mass spilled out. It was blackened at the edges of the collar and sleeves but still instantly recognisable as a long white dress, quite new, but designed to give the illusion of antiquity. And still she raved. "You told me it was an accident. You told me it wasn't meant to happen, but I found this. You tried to burn it, but I saw. I saved it!

"You said she would come back, always. Tell me she hasn't gone, Lucius! Promise me this! Please…"

And as I watched that word form on her lips, I saw! Dear God, I finally saw it all! That familiar quality I'd imagined in the face of that pathetic spectre, I knew now wasn't imagination. It was a memory! The face was Meredith Shadwell's! Not as that scarred and fractured creature now was. The face was that of the indulgent young wife, whose company and friendship I had enjoyed all those years before. The girl was the image of her mother!

And I at last understood Meredith's cries of, "What if she comes back?" They were not the words of protest against an unnatural and harrowing disturbance. They were desperate pleas for the return of her daughter!

"'It has happened!'" I said, coldly quoting the words of that man whom I had once counted as my greatest friend. "It happened because you made it happen. Your own daughter? Sarah?"

"Yes." There was no trace of shame as he gathered himself up to his full height, but it was a trembling hand that raised the cigarette to his lips and tried to light it

I swatted it from his mouth. "Your own daughter! Growing up with you and your stories and your legends. You created another believer, just as you did with me."

"But, unlike you, unlike I, she did not embrace the unknown. She feared it. She believed and that belief frightened her. I realised, were it nurtured correctly, that I could use that fear, use that anguish, to perhaps reopen some of those psychic scars we talked so much about, you and I." Though I could scarcely credit it, his tone as he confessed to this was entirely the same as when he'd excitedly held forth on his theories to my younger self. This wasn't a confession. It was a lecture! "I imagined that I might use her terror to awaken something dormant in this house. And with such an opportunity, such an instrument at my disposal, why should I not use it... use her? Why should I be denied what I've sought so long?"

I scooped up the vial of white greasepaint that had rolled at my feet. The image came to mind of that thin thing, that positively skeletal thing. It had not shown up as part of the haunting because, if it was to materialise as a ghost... it would have to be dead first. And Lucius Shadwell was very much alive. "So you became what she feared most! You trapped her in that room, with its legends already in place and fresh in her mind. And you terrorised her! You scared that girl witless! You scared her to death!" My hands were on his collar now, dragging him closer so that any remorse in his eyes would be clear to me. But there was none to be found.

"It was an accident. Her heart wasn't strong enough to withstand the experiment. An inherited weakness from her mother. I didn't know!"

Possibly he believed it, but I did not think so then and I still do not now. He was not deluded. There was method here. "The circle of salt, from rituals you've studied in depth. It wasn't to keep something out. It was to keep her in! To bind her soul in that chamber, and force her to go through her final agonies again and again, while you watched, observed, recorded!" I thrust him back from me then, unable to bear being in such close proximity to his coldness. Had I the strength, I would have knocked him to the floor and continued to strike him till his cries matched those of his poor, lost daughter in intensity and pain.

However, all I felt then was that familiar heavy numbness that had dogged me throughout my stay. It took my legs from under me, and I dropped, sliding down the panelled wall, falling into a heap opposite Shadwell's wife, who crouched still, hugging that scorched dress to herself.

My head was filled with noise; a pounding that echoed as if from within the walls and floors of Wraithvale itself. A sour smell of cold, clogging earth, and whatever had once lain under it, assailed my nose and caught in my throat. Shadows, or what I at least thought to be shadows, filtered past my already closing eyes, and the vague thought of things long dormant that had gradually been awakened stirred in my mind. The scar had been opened, and who knew what was bleeding through?

The last thing that I was conscious of was the distant sound of urgent footsteps upon stone, becoming even more distant as they spiralled away from me. Then, after a silence that might have lasted a minute or an hour, there came from some chamber above a scream of utter, fatal fear and loathing. Then, mercifully, darkness descended on me.

The great grey figure that loomed into my view, when next

these eyes of mine opened, extended a squat hand and hoisted me to my feet. Paskins would later explain how she had found us both, two crouching figures in that cold corridor, when she had returned that morning. Her first duty had been to her former patient, laying her out in her bed and arranging her so that she looked at peace, before returning to rouse me.

Of Lucius Shadwell, there was never a living trace found. Eventually there was the usual inquest, though the local constables seemed unwilling to pry too closely in that old, once more abandoned priory. What they did turn up were certain remains concealed in the long-cooled furnace. These were later established to be the bones of a young female, disposed of unlawfully. I heard all of this at the inquest where, naturally, I was summoned to testify with regard to my former tutor's, and recent host's, apparent state of mind before the death of his wife and his unaccounted for disappearance. I told them then that I considered him to have been entirely sane in those last hours. Whether this remains the case...

You have asked me to identify for you the most evil entity that ever I was in contact with. I have told you now. Not, as you no doubt were expecting, a ghost or some other revenant, but a living human being. But, as in life, so in death?

To provide a possible answer to my own question, I will inform you only that I spent one last evening at Wraithvale, and I spent it within that turret chamber. There I waited, fervently beseeching The Almighty that Sarah Shadwell, that screaming maiden of Wraithvale Priory, would cry into the night no more. And when the time came and passed, I thanked all that is good, and voiced a hope that mother and daughter were at last reunited.

But that was not quite an end to it. The shrieking may have been stilled, yet that flickering yellow radiance did still cast itself upon that cold floor. For a few long moments, that thin shadow made its habitual circuit around the edges of the light, until, with a lurch, it burst through into the circle, hands outstretched on bony arms to rend the air yet again. The figure was now as visible to my eye as the ring of salt, and as its dark robe brushed through this protective barrier, it obliterated a portion of the powdery trail. Upon realising this, the gaunt face, underneath the greasepaint pallor of its vampiric nobleman's masquerade, grew paler yet. Fearful eyes darted as more shadows began to stalk and slouch and crawl around the edges of the circle; drawing in slowly, but not too slowly, toward the gap in the defensive outline. I had the impression that some of the owners of those encroaching shadows might even have once been human.

It was not very much longer after this that a new voice screamed from that haunted turret chamber.

*

Shortly afterwards, the others of our company left the doctor's study, numbering amongst them that individual who had coerced Lawrence into telling his tale, and whose expression on leaving suggested that he rather regretted it.

I, too, was ready to bid my farewell to my friend, as the sharing of his narrative had evidently worn him down. But he indicated a seat and poured me a generous measure of brandy, before taking his place before the embers in the fireplace.

"There is one last thing to be said, then the story is complete, and I will never tell it again. I didn't wish to share it with the others, but it cannot be left untold. It is not something of which I am proud, yet I cannot claim any great feeling of shame.

"You recall I made mention of some solitary researches in which I'd been employed as my last full day at Wraithvale came around? Well, there was a result to these studies. It took the form of an incantation, a variant form of the rite of exorcism. Whether such an attempt would have had any effect in that house, I could not hope to know, but it had been my intent to at least try to free that wretched spirit from her torment. As you heard, her tragedy played itself out before I

137

had the chance to mount my attempted rescue.

"That next night, as I saw her tormentor find himself consigned to a fate that entirely paralleled that which he'd engineered for her, I became aware that the pages onto which I had inscribed those words of release were still secure in my pocket. Here I had the potential means to deliver my former friend from a possible eternity of terrors.

"Then, I heard only that girl's voice, and still those screams resound in my mind during unguarded moments. But, at that moment, her pleas became a cry for justice. The decision I made in that room that evening may not have been as others would make. You, yourself, may well have chosen differently. We all of us, after all, have our own individual ideas of justice.

"So I left the pages folded up in my pocket, and I closed the door on that chamber, closed the door on Wraithvale, and left Professor Lucius Shadwell to those ghosts he had so long sought."

LOVE IS IN THE AIR

Gary McMahon

As soon as she took off her tiny black knickers, carefully hooking those red-painted fingertips over the tight waistband and flicking them down over her long, tanned legs, I could see that I'd been taken for a mug.

She was what the boys back at the office would call an aeroplane blonde – meaning that she had a black box. Oh, they're really witty those chaps; regular fucking Oscar Wildes.

When I opened the door to find her standing in the hallway with that big Hollywood smile on her face, I'd been fooled completely. Her hair had looked so natural, so *glossy*, and the blue of her eyes was pale and quite stunning in the dim hallway light.

In retrospect, she probably wore contact lenses, but you never think like that in the grip of the moment. Only after the fact, when it's far too late to matter.

So I ushered her into my cheap hotel room, giving a quick glance both ways along the corridor to ensure that she hadn't been seen. I *am* a married man, after all, and as such I have a reputation to keep. Certain standards to maintain.

She wasted no time in getting down to business, stating her terms in clipped, brusque tones, as if reading them from a list. Her prices tallied more or less with those I'd been quoted earlier on the phone, so I readily acquiesced. She stripped off her clothes as she spoke, bored and detached as a cow in a field; I was just another customer, and this was just another job.

That was when I noticed the dark spider-legs hanging down from her gusset – I mean, she wasn't even shaven. These days, that's seen as pretty unhygienic.

I wasn't *too* disappointed to discover that she dyed her hair, even though I'd clearly stipulated a natural blonde over the phone when I called the number from the classified column of the local free newspaper.

She *was* incredibly beautiful, so that part of the verbal contract had been honoured at least. It almost compensated for her having the wrong hair colour. To be honest, if it wasn't for her looks I would've sent her away.

I made a quick mental note to consider using the company again, perhaps next time I was in town on business. Maybe even sooner than that, depending on how this evening went.

She walked slowly towards me, her naked body soft, rubbery and very welcoming in the subdued early evening light. Her smile looked real, and only the emptiness trapped behind her eyes spoiled the illusion.

It always does; that faraway look they all have. As if they're thinking of something entirely unrelated to the job at hand – composing a shopping list, writing a song, or simply deciding what to have for dinner later that night.

I let her take off my creased shirt and tie, watched with rapidly growing pleasure as she knelt down to slip off my shoes, socks and pants. She was good: it only took her a matter of seconds to have me right where she wanted me, naked, eager and twitching. In the palm of her hand.

And when she gently took me in her mouth, smiling round my unruly pubic thatch, I felt more comfortable than I had in quite some time.

We moved over onto the big double bed and went through the usual motions: her on top, me on top, doggy-style, and finally a little bit of light spanking. That always cost extra, so I only ever indulged with my favourite natural blondes or – as in this particular case – the ones who were *especially* attractive.

Flickering porno played in a joyless loop on the hotel pay TV. I'd pre-ordered it earlier, knowing that it always got them in the mood. Just another little trick I'd learned in my time working overseas, in south-east Asia – I'd learned a lot about women over there, and all of it priceless. Well, in a manner of speaking: everything, as I'm sure you already know, has its price.

Afterwards she lay on her back and smoked a smelly French cigarette. I waited for it to come; the moment: it always does, right about this point in the proceedings.

Sure enough, she turned to me with an easy smile, truly seeing me for the first time, and started to tell me about her life. Her poor, tough, misguided life. The reasons why she'd ended up doing what she did: the whole sordid and depressingly familiar little story.

Instantly bored beyond belief, I shut my eyes. Nodded my head, as if I understood.

What I *really* understood was something else entirely. Another one of those priceless little nuggets of knowledge that I'd picked up along the way, during my many travels.

As she babbled at me, the cigarette hanging insouciantly from one corner of her mouth, I leaned across and nuzzled her warm neck to keep her occupied, my right hand sliding slowly across her hard belly and around to her toned back, looking for the nozzle.

I knew it was there. I always knew.

Eventually I found it in the slight crease at the top of her buttocks, hidden away in that moist, dewy cleft. It was tiny, delicate. Like a second belly button.

I popped the cap and felt her instantly begin to deflate.

Once begun, the process gathered speed at a frightening pace. Her large breasts, shoulders, face… all crumpled as the air rushed out of her with an audible snake-like hiss.

The still-burning cigarette fell from her rapidly flattening lips; I picked it up and placed it in a dirty glass that sat on the bedside cabinet next to my keys and wallet. I didn't want any nasty accidents.

I bent her limbs back as she went down, rolling her up tight, like a sleeping bag, for easy storage. I didn't really hear the sharp cracking of bones, only imagined it. Sometimes it's hard to block out, to convince myself that it's just the dry creaking of so much rubber.

Once all the air had left her body I rolled off the bed and

141

folded her up as small as she would go, pressing all my weight down onto her hollow emptiness to rid the floppy husk of any remaining passages of air.

Then I squatted down on my haunches and slid the long, flat cardboard box out from under the bed.

The writing on the label never fails to amuse me:

Love Is In The Air Inc.
Cindy: your blow-up babe!

I carefully placed Cindy in the box, flattening her out as much as I could manage before replacing the lid and tucking in the edges. Then I slid the whole package back under the bed, shoving it right back among the dust and the cobwebs and the countless sticky dropped coins that for some reason always seem to gather in such places.

Feeling dizzy and slightly deflated myself, I then walked to the low dressing table that stood against the far wall, under the small window, and gazed out onto a drab view of a quiet street.

I braced myself against the hard wooden desktop and reached around to the middle of my back, groping for my own worn nozzle. It was in an awkward spot, and it took me a moment to locate it, but eventually my fingers closed around the small fleshy nub.

It was just as I'd suspected. The cap had worked itself loose during our frantic activities.

I retrieved the portable foot pump that I kept in my suitcase, in case of emergencies. Then I carefully affixed the valve to my nozzle and stepped down on the little pedal one, two, three times in rapid succession...

My spirits rose after a few good short bursts – along with various other body parts. It felt good, but I stopped before going too far. The last thing I wanted was to over-inflate. That way led only to serious trouble: another lesson I'd learned a long time ago.

When I was once more suited and booted and full of hot air,

142

I picked up the phone and asked the boy on the switchboard to connect me to an outside line. Then I dialled the number for Love Is In The Air Inc. to place an order for the following evening.

I was feeling... chirpy again, and in need of company.

But this time I had to be firm. The next one, I promised myself, *must* be a real blonde, or I really was taking my business elsewhere.

THE HEAD

Reggie Oliver

It was a clear midwinter evening with the black branches of trees spidering across a dull gold sky: an Atkinson Grimshaw world. I was driving through St John's Wood when the head appeared again. It was on the passenger seat beside me, as before, but for the first time it spoke. It said: "A bit Parkinson this evening, ain't it?" It was Ron's head, of course, but I couldn't be sure if it was his voice. The words were strange. Didn't he mean 'parky'? But 'parky' was not a word Ron would have used. He would have considered it vulgar.

Eighteen months ago I had been sent by my minicab firm to pick up a client in Glebe Place, Chelsea. They knew I liked 'the posh ones'; they also knew 'the posh ones' liked me. I'm young; I dress smart, always the suit; I'm saving money to get a degree and do something with my life. With me it's more like a chauffeur for the night, though I draw the line at a peaked cap.

I rang the bell. It was one of those beautiful little old houses in a row with the fanlights above the door. I waited an age, but I didn't ring twice because I knew clients didn't like that. At last, through the fanlight, I saw a chandelier go on in the hallway and heard heavy dragging footsteps coming towards the door. There was a good deal of fumbling with locks before it opened. Then there was this huge man in an old fashioned dinner suit with watered silk lapels, leaning on an ebony cane.

"I must apologise for keeping you waiting. Thank you for having had the patience to ring but once." He had these little fancy ways of talking.

At a guess I'd say he was in his late sixties, or early seventies, and he was big in every direction. Of course he was overweight, but he was tall – taller than me and I'm over six feet – and broad with it. I guessed he might have been an athlete as a young man, and I was right. He told me later he'd

144

rowed for Cambridge.

His head was big too, with a high shiny cranium, one of those thin beaky noses, and a cluster of reddish grey curls clinging to the back of his head and around his enormous ears. I told him once he looked like a Roman emperor, and he was pleased with that. It was a head to remember.

It took a bit of time to get him into the back seat of the car because his left leg, which was swollen, was causing him terrible pain. Phlebitis, I think he said it was. Anyone else on this job would have said: 'You oughtn't to be going out with that leg of yours,' or some such; but I'm different. I knew at once he was the kind of person who wouldn't take that sort of shit from anybody, so I said nothing.

When he was safely in my car, he said: "I want you to take me to the Royal Academy if you would be so kind."

Of course, I knew this already, but, just by way of conversation, I said: "Are you going to the opening of this new Matisse exhibition, then?" In my rear view mirror I could see his face. He was impressed.

"I am indeed. Are you an admirer of Matisse?" He asked. I said I'd like to study him; I'd like to study art.

From Chelsea until we got to Burlington House he talked almost non-stop. Some of it was about art, but most of it I couldn't understand at all. It was gossip about art dealers and exhibition curators. How this person managed to get to borrow a Velazquez for an exhibition from the Frick Collection but only by betraying this other bloke, that kind of thing. They sounded like a load of bloody sharks, no different from where I was born in the East End. Worse even. I gathered he was a dealer in a small way, but mostly he wrote about art for posh magazines.

When we got to the Academy we were allowed to drive right up to the front steps because of his leg. After I had helped him out he asked me to call back in an hour and a half and take him home. This had not been part of the arrangement but he handed me two twenty pound notes, so I agreed. Then he shook my hand.

"My name is Ronald Pattinson, but you can call me Ron. Everyone calls me Ron." That was funny. He didn't look at all like a Ron to me, but there you go.

After that he would ask for me specially. "I should like Mr Trevin to drive me," he would say to the firm. That's my name, Ed Trevin, though Ron always called me Edward. And the firm would oblige him because he was a good payer which I didn't mind either. And I was learning a lot from him.

If he was on his own and not meeting anyone, he would often take me in to see exhibitions, sometimes at the Tate and the R.A., but most often to private galleries in Cork Street and the Piccadilly area; provided I could find somewhere to park. I hadn't known before that you can just walk into these places. Ron seemed to know everyone, and everyone seemed to know him, though I wondered if this was sometimes just his manner. He'd go into a gallery like you or I would go into our local pub. His voice was loud and he articulated clearly, so everyone heard his opinions good or bad.

Sometimes he would ask my opinion, but in a slightly lower voice. "Now, Edward dear, what do you think of this?" Then he would listen to me – I spoke very low too – with his head on one side. If I said something he thought stupid he made no comment, but if he liked anything about what I said he would take it up and make it seem clearer and cleverer than it was.

I think he got a kick out of my being with him. Once he introduced me to a gallery owner as 'my nephew Mr Edward Trevone.' I don't know why he changed the name, and I didn't ask him. Maybe it was his way of making it all like into a play and me an actor in his play.

It didn't worry me. He was teaching me how to see things and how to get Modern Art. "An abstract canvas looks easy to create;" he used to say, "that is why it is so difficult to create well."

He had decided opinions about everything in art. There were times when I thought he was trying to print his personal taste onto my mind; but I'm not a blank sheet of paper, or *'tabula rasa'*, as he would say. He would come out with things like: "Tracey Emin has only one subject, herself, and that is a lamentably inadequate one... Late Picasso is the work of a highly gifted senile delinquent... Rothko? My dear Edward: Privileged despair; tastefully padded cells for wealthy New York neurotics." I tried to argue with him about that one, but he wouldn't be moved. He had very high standards.

I remember we were going round the Tate Modern once, and somehow I'd wangled a wheelchair for him. We stopped before a Jackson Pollock: "Look at that. Every drip seems meant doesn't it? Now compare it with the Cy Twombly over there. Interesting passages, but hit and miss. Sometimes those scribbles are just scribbles. The man's an amateur by comparison. Every mark must have its meaning."

I saw inside his house once. Most of his things were old, but he had a little Paul Klee water-colour of what might be multicoloured rooftops that I wanted to walk away with, and above the fireplace was a Francis Bacon. It was an early work and Ron said it was a portrait Bacon had done of him when he was young, but I couldn't see how it could be a real portrait. It was this man sitting in a dark bluey-greeny space. He's a big man in a grey suit, you can see that, but where the head ought to be there's just a black space and a few silvery vertical lines. Maybe there's just the suggestion of an open mouth and teeth, but it's hard to tell. I told him it was obvious from the picture that he was a very good looking chap when he was young and he laughed. That was the sort of joke he enjoyed: sharp and ironical, like him.

Of course, when I took him to visit the people he called his friends, I'd stay in the car. In fact, though he was very lame, he did not even want to be escorted to the front door. He sometimes insisted that I park way down the street out of sight of his friend's house and that he should do the painful walk there unaided.

I only once met one of his friends. It was a house in Holland

Park and, as usual, I was parked some way down the road from it. I'd been there about an hour – it was a lunch date, I think – when I heard this tapping on the window. It was a Philippino maid: "Mr Edward, you come," she said. I followed her to the house where Ron was lunching. It turned out that Ron's host, Mrs Argenti, having heard of my interest in Modern Art, had insisted I come in and see her collection of Barbara Hepworth drawings.

You could tell at once it was the house of a very rich person because all the walls and curtains and upholstery were white or cream and looked brand new. Only very rich people can afford the servants needed to keep all that white stuff looking spotless. The furniture was antique French; the pictures were modern.

I was shown into the drawing room where I saw Ron, sitting, hunched over his ebony cane, looking, I thought, rather ratty. Mrs Argenti stood beside him, a small woman in her sixties, thin as a skeleton, in an Armani trouser suit. Her skull of a head was topped by an ash blonde coiffure, like a dollop of whipped cream on a tombstone. She directed me to a wall where the Hepworth drawings hung. Very fine they were too; I hadn't known she drew as well as sculpted.

I suppose I ought to have enjoyed them more, but all the time I was conscious of Mrs Argenti looking at me. She'd heard something about me from Ron and had called me in out of curiosity, I suppose. I was just another thing for her greedy little eyes to take in, like the Hepworth drawings. I hoped that was why Ron was looking so down about it all, but I don't think it was.

He had some funny habits, Ron, as well as a funny way of talking. Once I caught him jacking off in the back of my motor; but he didn't seem much embarrassed. "I found myself having my annual erection," he said, "and sought swift relief. These things are a mere passing nuisance in old age, no longer an obsession. And don't worry, I shall not stain your valuable upholstery: I have tissues to hand." When we stopped at the next traffic lights, he threw the tissue out of the window.

Then he asked me if I had a girlfriend. I said no, they got in the way; so he asked me what I did for sex. I told him I wasn't that bothered, but that I would get a blow job from a tom from time to time if I wanted to get rid of my dirty water. But a high class pro, mind: no dogs, no rubbish. This made him laugh for some reason. I asked him why but he wouldn't tell me.

A couple of months after I'd first got to know him, he asked me to pick him up and take him to an address in Harley Street. When I had delivered him I was to drive around or park up till he phoned me on my mobile and then I could collect him. When I did he was very quiet. He told me to drive up to Regent's Park and go round and round it until he wanted me to stop. I knew better than to start chatting, so we did about two circuits of the park in total silence. I didn't play anything on the stereo either, because he didn't like music of any kind. As we were passing the zoo for the second time he tapped me on the shoulder, so I came to a halt. I heard him give a long sigh, and then he spoke;

"My dear, I want you to do something for me. Don't worry! I'm not going to ask you to put your fair white hand down my trousers. It's nothing like that. The truth is, the very expensive Harley Street gentleman I saw just now has given me the facts. I have at most about nine months to live and the pain is going to get a lot worse. There comes a point, you know, when pain killers don't work. Either that or you're so drugged up to the eyeballs you might as well be dead. Life has ceased to be amusing anyway. Oh, don't look so crestfallen, Edward dear. I was about to say that life has ceased to be amusing but that the only ray of light in the darkness is you, dear boy. Yet even you have not the power to palliate the agony to come. Yes, I know there are hospices and such like for people in my condition, but I somehow don't feel that hospices are my thing. Too placid and pious for me: I've lived life in the world of colour and taste. 'Nature I loved and next to Nature Art.' Do you know those lines of Landor's? Well, with me it has been the other way around. Art was my first love; Nature has always seemed like a pale imitation. Well, the long and the short of it is I am becoming fed up with life. Suffer, suffer, suffer it's just meaningless to me. It's going to be all cross and no crown, from now on, so what's the fucking point? Pardon my vernacular. So what is the favour I am working up to ask you? To put it bluntly I need someone to kill me in as efficient and painless a way as possible, and the only capable person I could think of was you, dear boy."

I had no words to say to this, so there was a long silence. I remember seeing out of the corner of my eye a giraffe in the zoo across the road, peering innocently, aimlessly about.

"You will be handsomely rewarded, of course," Ron continued. "On completing the task, you will receive the key to a safety deposit box. In that box are a couple of early Rembrandt etchings in fine condition, two Cosway miniatures, a Guercino in pen and wash of St Francis receiving the stigmata, and a little drawing in sanguine of a head by Raphael."

"What about provenance?" I asked.

"So! You have picked up a little from me. Well done. Yes. Naturally. Provenance has been provided, bur not traceable back to me so you won't be suspected of theft or anything when you sell. Just talk vaguely of an inheritance. One can't calculate these things exactly, but I shouldn't be surprised if you get about two hundred thousand for the lot. Provided you work through discreet dealers and don't sell them all in a lump, no one is going to ask awkward questions. I have made my plans very thoroughly, you see."

Over the next few days he told me about them. I won't go into every detail but the idea was this. One day in a fortnight's time I would drive him to St Pancras where he would board the Eurostar. He would go down to his house in Provence. On a specified day he would pay off the people who look after him down there, saying that he was leaving and would shut the place up himself. Then I was to arrive and the death would happen. I would dispose of the body – he would give me the details of this when I got there – then shut up the house and leave. It might be some months, perhaps even a year, before his disappearance was noted, because everyone in England would assume he was still in France and those in France that he was in England. Moreover, there would be no body. Suspicion was unlikely to fall on me, and if it did, where would be the proof? Medical records would show that suicide of some kind was the most likely option, as indeed was the case. The fact that it was assisted could only be a supposition.

Did I hesitate? Of course I did. But the way he put it, I was doing him a favour. I asked for some cash up front to pay for my trip into France and he gave it to me. I used it to buy a couple of Paul Nash prints which I later sold at a profit.

*

Ron's house was high in the hills above Collobrièeres. People from the village of Le Charnier about a mile away came in to cook and clean for him; and in France, but only in France, he occasionally drove a car, an old Deux Chevaux which was kept in one of the outbuildings. His house, *Les Buissonets*, had once been a farm.

I arrived there in my own motor at the appointed time one August evening and, as I drove up to *Les Buissonets*, I thought I had never seen a more beautiful spot. For miles around there were nothing but vineyards, fields and forest, punctuated by the ochre-tiled rooftops of a few homesteads. How could anyone want to die in such a place, I thought, at such a time? Then I stopped myself. I had been stopping myself from thinking about it all the way down through France. That was how I got through the journey. I was beginning to get the trick of detachment.

Ron was standing on the terrace of his house to greet me. "Edward, my boy, how delightful to see you!" I might have been an old friend coming for a long stay. On the terrace was a table and two chairs placed so that we could watch the sun set behind the hills. On the table was a bowl of fat green olives, a bottle in an ice bucket and some glasses. We sat down.

"You must sample this," said Ron, filling my glass. "I've been trying to finish off my last bottles of Pouilly Fumé and haven't quite managed it. I suppose you'd have preferred Champagne, my dear, but I'm afraid I never could abide the stuff."

I made some boring comment about the beauty of the view. It was glorious. Ron sighed heavily. He was visibly older, slower, more in pain than when I had seen him off on the Eurostar a month before.

"Yes," he said. "It used to be so lovely and unspoilt until all those ghastly people started writing books about how lovely and unspoilt it was." I could see no evidence of spoiling, but I was not going to argue with him on his last night.

When we had finished the bottle Ron showed me to my room. We had still said nothing about what was going to happen that night, and I suspected it was going to wait till after supper.

Ron said: "Madame Bobelet who 'does for me' as they say has left behind one of her excellent cassoulets to which I am sure you, if not I, will do justice."

The inside of the house was comfortable but quite plain; whitewashed walls, tiled floors covered by rugs, plain modern furniture. One whole wall was a bookshelf and there were a few nice pictures, postimpressionist mostly. Above the fireplace in the main room which contained a large wood-burning stove there was an exquisite little Vuillard. A woman was seated in a garden of chequered shade; the head of a man could just be seen peering at her over the top of a hedge.

We finished the cassoulet and went on to cheese and a *tarte aux pommes*, and still Ron had not got round to the subject. He kept up a steady flow of talk about all sorts of rubbish, mostly gossip and scandal in the art world. I sensed he was doing this with an effort, and I wanted to tell him to relax. It was only when he produced a bottle of Chateau Yquem as we were finishing the *tarte* that he came round to it. He poured two small glasses of the rich golden liquid and held one up to the light.

"I call this the Nectar of the Gods. I wonder if they still drink Nectar in the afterlife; I do hope so. Talking of which..." And he began to give me instructions.

After we had washed up and removed all evidence that two of us had dined that night he would go upstairs to his bedroom. There he would take a large overdose of painkilling drugs which he had stockpiled for the purpose. I asked him why in that case he needed me.

"For two reasons, my dear Edward," he said with a touch of irritation. "In the first place, as I know only too well from the experience of my friends, these things have a habit of going wrong. I do *not* want to wake up and find that my stomach is being pumped by eager French nurses in a Collobrières hospital. In the second place, I have no desire to offend my very dear friends and neighbours, Madame Bobelet and the rest. They are all good Catholics and they would be *most* upset if they thought I had committed suicide. At least if I simply disappear they can entertain some other possibility. May I continue?"

When he was unconscious I was to strangle or suffocate him until I was sure he was dead. Then – "and this, my dear, will be the most arduous and unsavoury part of the process" – I was to convey his body to the bathroom next door and dismember the corpse. ("A hacksaw has been provided.") The extremities, hands and feet, I was to incinerate in the living room wood-burner; the disembowelled entrails were to be boiled in the stock pot, the liquid of which could be poured down the sink. The remaining mess could be minced up and thrown off the terrace to be consumed by carrion creatures. I was to take the amputated limbs and torso in the Deux Chevaux to a nearby wood and there bury them in separate places. "It is a wood not much frequented by huntsmen, but morels and other nutritious fungi are sometimes gathered there at certain times of the year." There remained only Ron's head.

"Ah, yes, the head," said Ron. He went to a sideboard on which stood an old black japanned tin box with sloping sides, like a hatbox. "You must indulge my whim about the head. You are to cut it off and place it in this box. Now, see, I have punctured it with holes. You are to fill it up to the brim with stones – rather heavy but there's no helping that, and when you are half way across the channel you are to cast it into the sea. What with the holes letting in the water and the stones it should sink immediately. I want my head to drop full fathom five to the bottom half way between England and France."

"But why?"

"Because it is my wish. I have always had a fancy to be buried at sea. Obviously the whole body would be too much even for you, dear boy. So I thought just the head, like Orpheus, you know:
'And let the wind and tide haul me along
To Scylla's barking and untaméd gulf
Or to the loathsome pool of Acheron'
I'm afraid you will have to indulge me. After all, I am paying, with my life so to speak."

Once I had disposed of the corpse, with the exception of the head, I was to clean up the house, turn off the mains electricity, and shut it up just as if Ron had gone away. Then I was to return to England, taking with me the head as far as mid-channel.

"And now," said Ron, rising ponderously, "you must excuse me. I have to go upstairs and er... Make my preparations."

I reminded him that there was still the little matter of my reward to settle: the keys to the safety deposit box containing the works of art.

"Of course! My dear Edward, I do apologise, I almost forgot!" He went over to a small bureau, unlocked a drawer, took out an envelope and handed it to me. "The keys and the authorisation codes. And now..." He held out his hand which I shook, as I suppose I was meant to do.

There was a short silence. Through the open window we could hear frogs going 'rivet-rivet-rivet' in the valley below. I wondered what Ron's last words to me were to be. When they came, they surprised me, but with Ron I should have expected the unexpected.

"Now remember, Edward dear," he said "when you are washing away the blood to do it with *cold* water, *not* hot. If you do it with hot then tiny particles of blood become encrusted into the surfaces they come into contact with. A dear friend of mine who had the misfortune to murder his mother made this mistake and went to prison for a *very* long time. The detective told him that had he washed the axe in cold water he might have got away with it. Why they never teach one these things at school I shall never know."

He went upstairs and I finished the Yquem. It was too good to waste. I thought it might make me drunk enough, but it didn't.

None of it was easy. The disembowelling was foul, but the worst of it, oddly enough, was burying the legs and arms and torso in that wood. Helpfully Ron had marked the place on the map for me, but it was nearly dawn by the time I had finished there, and I was in a constant state of terror that some wandering French peasant would come across me and start asking questions. I spent the whole of the next day cleaning up after me and the following night I drove away from *Les Buissonets*, clean, empty and shuttered. I didn't take anything from the house, though I was tempted. There was a little Boucher drawing in his bedroom – a girl's head in red chalk with white highlights on very pale blue tinted paper, a real beauty – but I knew it could find me out, so I didn't. The only thing I took from the house was *his* head.

The head had been difficult too. The neck was a bugger to saw through – he had a thick neck, all bone and gristle – and for some reason the eyes kept opening. It was a horrible thing to hold which was why I let it slip through nervous, reluctant fingers and it bounced on the bathroom floor with a slight crunching sound. You may never have heard a head bounce, and you don't want to. That was when the teeth fell out. I didn't know he had false teeth, you see, so that was another shock I don't know why, but I decided that the best thing to do was to put them back in. Now I wish to God I hadn't.

As instructed, I put it in the tin box with the holes punched in it. You could see the top of the head, all dry and flaky now with a few strands of red grey hair straggling across it, so I filled the box up to the top with gravel. The box now weighed a ton, but I wrapped it in a black plastic bin liner, because it was going to start to smell pretty soon and there would be liquids coming out of the holes.

As I drove up through France that head was on my mind the whole time. I dreaded the moment when I would have to drop it off the ferry into the sea. Ron didn't understand. Lugging that great thing up on deck in a crowded cross-channel ferry, then heaving it over the side: it was bound to attract attention. It made me angry that Ron had been so inconsiderate. I was driving up through France on small roads, stopping for a meal here and there, snatching a few hours sleep in my car, and with every hour that thing in the tin box was getting older and more putrid. The head was doing my head in. (Ron hated that phrase 'doing my head in'; that's why I said it.)

In the end I realised that dropping it off the ferry was out of the question, and one night, as I was crossing the Loire at Chateauneuf, I saw my way out. It was nearly midnight; there was no-one about, so I stopped half way across the bridge. I got the box out of the boot and removed the bin bag covering. I was right. The outside of the box was already slimed and had begun to smell. I hesitated only a moment before I dropped the thing over the bridge and into the Loire. He wanted the sea, I gave him a river: where's the difference? As Ron used to say: 'even the weariest river winds somewhere safe to sea.'

After that my journey got a lot easier. I almost laughed when I reached Cherbourg, and the *Douane* were sniffing through our luggage with dogs. There was something about the boot of my car that interested those dogs, but, of course, they found nothing.

The first thing I did when I got home was to ask after that safety deposit box at Ron's bank, some posh private one in the City. I felt I had earned my reward, but this was the first of my nasty shocks. In the box there were no Rembrandt etchings, no Cosway miniatures, no Guercino pen and wash, only the 'Raphael' head in sanguine, but no provenance.

I took it to a dealer Ron had mentioned and gave him some rubbish about an inheritance, trying to make my voice sound as posh as possible. He sniffed and hemmed and hawed.

"You have no provenance?" He asked.

I shook my head.

"Of course it could be a Raphael. The quality is fine; the paper's right, but it might be a copy. Probably contemporary, though, fifteen twenties or thereabouts. However without provenance I could only offer you..." And he mentioned a contemptible amount of money. I left in a rage.

It was only a few days later that the aggravation really started, and it began with a phone call. Very few people know my number: the minicab firm, of course, a few close mates, and Ron had known. I don't let it out to all and sundry. I answered and it was a woman's voice.

"Where is he?" she said.

"Who is that?"

"What have you done with him?"

"Who the hell are you? What are you talking about?"

"You know perfectly well, Edward *dear*." Then I suddenly recognised that awful upper class quack.

"It's Mrs Argenti, isn't it?"

"Where is Ron?"

"Last time I saw him, it was over a month ago. He was getting onto the Eurostar. I suppose he must be still in France."

"Don't give me that, Edward. I know what's been going on."

"Well, if you know, then why are you asking *me*?" I said and rang off. I thought that was a smart answer, but of course it wasn't because it must have made her think I had something to hide. After that she would often ring, sometimes very late at night when she was drunk. I always slammed down the phone. I considered reporting her to the police as a nuisance caller, but thought better of it. The people at the minicab firm denied giving her my number. I think I believe them; it must have been Ron.

I had to go back to minicabbing because Ron had cheated me out of my reward. There was no way I was going to sell the Raphael head for a few thousand, just so some poncey dealer could sell it on for ten times that amount. It's a nice drawing anyway: probably the head of a young man with this mass of curly hair, but it could be a girl. He – it – is looking round at you with a half smile on his face, enigmatic, almost like the Mona Lisa. (Maybe it's a Leonardo? Ron didn't know everything.) All I can say is that the more you look at that face, the more it looks back at you and the stranger it becomes. The detail is extraordinary. I've looked at it with a magnifying glass and it's as if he's done every strand of red curly hair separately.

As I was driving around I began to see this vague shape of a head on my front seat. If my passenger was in the front seat with me I was all right. The thing that was clearest at first were the teeth, but I was sure it had to be Ron. I admit for a while I used to tell myself it was a trick of the light or some such but it didn't wash. The thing that bothered me was that Ron never used to ride in the front seat; he was always in the back. I'd look in the rear view mirror sometimes, expecting to see him, but he wasn't there.

Then the head became clearer. When I was driving someone I tried never to look at the front seat, but sometimes I couldn't help myself. There it was, half turned towards me with this little smile on his face. Once he winked at me and I nearly went into the back of a white van.

It was lucky that he first started talking when there was

nobody in the car, or I would have given myself away.

"A bit Parkinson this evening, ain't it?"

I said: "What the hell are you on about?"

"A bit Parkinson Grimshaw," it said, and winked.

After that the head was always talking, and it was always rubbish. If I was driving someone I never answered back, but they must have heard him because people began to complain that I was talking to myself when I drove. I lost some regular customers like that.

My God, he talked rubbish. I can't remember much of it; I don't want to. Once I was asked to drive someone to Eton Place.

"Eton Place," says the head. "I've eaten plaice. With chips. Ha! Ha! Eaten Plaice!"

"Will you shut the fuck up?" I said, breaking my rule of silence, and I had to apologise to the old lady in the back of my car. She was very nice about it.

It got so I was hardly driving people at all; I only did long haul deliveries and such. Once I remember, as I was going up to Manchester, the head was yammering at me all the way up the M1.

"If you want to sell a picture it's Provence you need," it said. "You can't do it without Provence."

"*Provenance*, you moron!" I shouted. "It's bloody *provenance*!"

"Hoity toity," said the head, "who's got out of the wrong side of his knickers in a twist this morning? Who made up your bed? Tracey Emin? You ought to be in a fur-lined padded cell, you ought. That might save your bacon. Now then! Now then! No need to go all twombly."

I wanted to smack it round the chops but I couldn't take my hands of the wheel. I was going too fast, and by the time I had stopped in a lay-by it had gone. Sometimes it would just chatter its teeth for hours on end. I tried changing cars but it was no good.

One day I had to go down to Cardiff to deliver some sort of

special birthday present for a rich bloke. It was raining down in torrents and the windscreen wipers could barely cope. They seemed to get slower and slower as if they were tired out, and the rain fell like a waterfall until the road ahead was just a blur punctured by car headlights. Then, as if that wasn't bad enough, the head appeared on the front seat, chattering its teeth and gibbering.

"Pull your trousers down," it kept saying. "Pull your trousers down, pull your trousers down!"

I wanted to punch it, but the idea of actually touching something which shouldn't be there appalled me. I tried to ignore it and concentrated on my driving. I knew I was going too fast in all that rain, but I couldn't help it.

"Edward, Eddy, Ed," it said. "Hey, big 'ed. Pull your trousers down, pull your trousers down or I'll snick your little nipper off with a bloody chopper!"

I balled my left hand into a fist and, without taking my eyes of the road, I struck out in the head's direction. I hit something, mostly wet curly hair, I think, and a surface that cracked on impact like a soft boiled egg. Immediately I took my hand away and back to the wheel. I had skidded slightly so I slowed down. In my rear view mirror I could see through a curtain of rain that the lights of a lorry were bearing down on me, so I speeded up again, but the lights kept coming.

There was something else that I saw in the rear view mirror. At first I couldn't be sure, and then I could. There was a man in the back of my car, a big man in a suit. There was no telling who it was because I couldn't see his head. Where his head should have been there was nothing. Or rather there was something, but it was black darkness.

"Pull your trousers down!"

I swerved across the road and the head rolled off the seat next to me and into my lap. The face side was in my crotch. It began biting me. It bit me in the crotch. The rain was pouring down and I tried to slow but the lights of the lorry were on me. The head bit me again on the prick with its gnashers and I yelled. I was going too fast because in my anger I had jammed my foot down on the gas. I took one hand off the wheel to tear the head out of my legs but I must have lost control because the pain was terrible. I swerved again, this time off the road, down an embankment and into the big black torso of a tree.

When the ambulance came, they had to cut me out. They found most of me, but there was no sign of Ron's head. At least they didn't say they'd found anything like that in the car. I was too sharp to ask anything like: 'have you found a head?' I expect it just rolled away somewhere.

So here I am in hospital, and likely to stay till Kingdom Come. I'm paralysed from the neck down, but they've given me a thing attached to my head, so I can use my laptop and finish the story I started. It's taken me a long time. God! As long as an unhappy holiday, and then some. But I've got time on my heads. Sometimes in the dark the head still speaks. The head in my head I like to call it now. I'm living in the dark, he says, but you, my friend, are with me. Dear boy. Take this grey corridor and walk with me down its eternity. Something gleams somewhere. It is a mirror at the end. Do you see it far off? And what does it reflect? Nothing. Or is there just a hint of a mouth and some teeth glinting and gaping in the greylight? I can still gnash, he says. I can still gnash my gnashers. Ha, ha!

Our food is dust. The dust is thick on the doors which are too heavy for us to lift or shift. No sound but the flutter of dry, dead leaves that blow in from a nowhere that we do not see. But there are some things with us. I see their signs scribbled in the dust. Somethings that bite and gnaw us in the dark where no daylight dims the blackness. But in the greylight we can sometimes see their shadows crawl, or fidget uneasily in the draughty passages. Here we are shut up in dust. Leave me alone! No. Don't! Don't leave me alone. Don't leave me!

I think I've woken up, but it's still dark. Hospital dark, thank Christ. I think. Go away! Don't leave me. Let me feel your scribble on my face, because only my face can feel. I seem to have twombled into a tunnel which is a hole in the ground. A holy tunnel. But Darkness has his trousers on, and will follow me down the hole.

THE DEVIL LOOKS AFTER HIS OWN?

Ian C. Strachan

Nigel and Jennifer walked arm in arm back through the woods to his house as the daylight faded over the Sussex coastline.

"Happy, darling?" she asked, turning her head to smile up at him.

He recoiled inwardly from the sticky sweetness in her voice, while his face smiled back at her with a dazzling sincerity.

What a damn silly question to ask anyone, he thought, and tenderly asked in reply: "What man would not be happy, with you at his side?"

Jennifer squeezed his arm against her. "Nigel, you say the most delicious things! I do love you so."

Experience and intuition told him that this was exactly the right moment to stop, take her in his arms, and kiss her gently on the lips. The trees around them sighed and rustled in the evening breeze.

As they resumed their progress down the path Jennifer exclaimed, "Just look at the colour on those trees! I do love Autumn, don't you?"

Nigel constructed some reply about the season's beauty, linked it cleverly with a compliment about her own, and presented it to her, without having to give much thought to the exercise. Deep in his mind the quick bright thoughts flickered and raced: Autumn – tomorrow is the second of October. Her twenty-first birthday. Her grandfather's money passes to her from trusteeship, and when she is my wife it will come to me – after she dies. And tomorrow her father comes down here to meet his future son-in-law.

There was no shadow of doubt in Nigel Woodford's dark mind that he would be able to win the shrewd old boy over within minutes. Charm was, after all, an essential part of Nigel's profession. Almost every woman adored him, if not at first sight then as soon as he spoke to her.

163

It was not that he was unusually handsome, though the slim athletic-looking six-foot frame, the clear honest blue-grey eyes, the quick smile that seemed to hold something of the schoolboy in it, and the dark hair with the slightest suggestion of a wave all conspired to provide the perfect platform from which Nigel directed that dark spell over those he met.

'Your health and your looks, Maurice,' his doting aunt in the New York suburb where he grew up had told him, 'are precious gifts from God. Be grateful for them, my boy: not everyone is so fortunate.'

His quick silvery thoughts told him, as he smiled fondly at her, that she was a sanctimonious old fool, and then conceived the idea that he could replace her jewellery with imitation stones without her ever knowing. He had been able to think of no other means of raising the price of a plane ticket to England.

The wealthy girls of New York moved in circles he could never enter, would never be allowed to enter. In gentle, sleepy old England, he knew, he could pass himself off as anyone or anything he chose to. He had already decided on a new name, and was making a conscious effort to improve his accent, to lose the gutter slang of his earlier years.

After dinner that evening, he sat with Jennifer in front of the log fire in the big dark-panelled library. "This is a lovely old house," she murmured drowsily. "I love an open fire, don't you?"

The big house was empty and quiet, the cook and maid having gone home after preparing and serving the meal. Jennifer went on: "It's awfully old, isn't it?"

Nigel brought his thoughts back from the question of how long after the wedding he would have to put up with her interminable prattling, and said, "It's Elizabethan. The main part of it, anyway."

The house had belonged to Sarah, his second wife. Like his first victim, she had been rich, rather stupid, and with no near relatives. She had also turned out, after the marriage, to be a remarkably jealous woman. Possessive, Nigel corrected himself, blinking at the flames. She lay now in a concealed chamber upstairs, with a metal skewer driven through her skull.

Ironically, it had been Sarah herself who had shown him the tiny room and thus given him the solution to the problem of what to do with the body. Hiding-places like these, she told him, had been necessary for some families in an age when Roman Catholicism was regarded as a kind of treason in England – but Nigel was not really interested in all that historical stuff. He stepped into the windowless cell and looked all around. "How come the priest didn't suffocate, locked in here?"

Sarah pointed to the two small holes in the ceiling and explained that they led up to the roof. Then she showed him the workings of the handle concealed behind the ornate carving on the wall-panelling of the bedroom. It had seemed to him that a body might lie here, safe from discovery, for many lifetimes.

That night he had selected a sharp skewer from the kitchen and driven it through her ear and into her sleeping brain with one blow from a wooden mallet.

He laid her to rest in the secret room, threw the mallet in after her, and pushed the door closed. He used a cold chisel and hammer to shear off the iron handle, applied an immensely strong contact adhesive inside the little sliding panel that hid it, and stepped back with a pleased smile. The panel, now fastened shut for ever, was invisible to the closest inspection.

He burned the pillow and pillow-case in the kitchen range, and made himself an early breakfast. Two days later he worriedly reported her disappearance to the local police. The neatly folded pile of her clothing found on the shore pointed to suicide, a possibility which was reinforced by the discovery of a fish-nibbled female body in a trawler's nets. This was a stroke of luck that he had not expected, and as he looked at the faceless thing on the mortuary slab he recalled one of his aunt's expressions: 'The Devil looks after his own.'

The detective beside him cleared his throat and prompted: "Can you identify the body as your wife, sir?"

"I – I think so. It is difficult to be sure, with the face like that. But the hands – yes, these are very like my wife's hands. And this little scar on the arm here – she had one in exactly the same place. Yes, I'm afraid it is Sarah."

He would have to be very careful, he told himself, with this polite English policeman. The husband of a missing woman is always under suspicion, especially if she leaves him a large sum of money and a house surrounded by seven acres of valuable land.

The detective said, "You stated that your wife had been depressed recently – was she taking any kind of prescribed medication for this?"

"Tablets, you mean?" Nigel met the other's eyes without hesitation. "No. She had asked me to make an appointment for her with a specialist in London, but that was for the twelfth of next month. She wasn't actually taking anything before she – before she went."

The policeman made a note of the doctor's name and address, and Nigel smiled inwardly. He had in fact arranged just such an appointment for her, but Sarah (who had not known the meaning of the word depression), had been unaware that he had made any such arrangement.

That had been over two years ago, and Sarah's money was now almost gone, melting away as easy money does. He had cast around for a third victim, and found twenty-year-old Jennifer Hudson.

As he slid into bed his mind dwelt on the question of the removal of Jennifer. A tragic accident on their honeymoon – could that be managed? There might be cliffs on the Greek island where they were planning to spend the two weeks, steep cliffs where a silly girl could slip and fall...

He heard her returning from the bathroom and closed his eyes. As she got into bed she said brightly: "I just love this four-poster bed, don't you?" Nigel breathed steadily and made no answer.

"Asleep, darling?" she asked, and added something in a soft murmur about being the luckiest girl in the world.

Will she never be silent? he thought savagely, and consoled himself by letting his mind turn to the fortune that would be his before very long.

The window was bright with sunlight when he awoke. Jennifer's arm lay across his chest, and he moved it aside as he sat up. It was an unnaturally cold and stiff arm, and he looked down sharply at her face on the pillow. Her eyes were closed as if she slept, and a rusty metal skewer protruded from her temple.

Nigel found himself standing beside the bed. Eyes fixed on the dead face. As he snatched up his dressing-gown and pulled it on he saw that a wooden mallet lay on the floor, and that a dusty trail led from the open door to the other side of the bed.

Moving like a sleepwalker he followed it along the gallery, beneath the dark heavy old portraits, to the bedroom at the other end. From somewhere downstairs, the sound of activity could be heard: the servants in the kitchen.

In the empty unused bedroom, the door of the concealed chamber stood wide open. He walked numbly to it and stared inside, trying not to look directly at the unpleasant bundle on the floor. His thoughts no longer flashed lightning-bright in his head. He thought sluggishly: Of course. There is a handle on the inside too.

Wheels crunched on the drive below, a car door slammed, and there came a cheerful hammering on the front door. Nigel's thoughts crawled on: Oh God, what am I going to do? Her father is here. Even if I can hide the body in the secret chamber, he will want to know where she is.

He fumbled to close the door and found that it swung open again as soon as he released it: there was no way of locking it now. He thought: The maid will come upstairs to make the bed and clean sooner or later and find Jennifer, and see that lying there grinning up at her... if only I could think!

He stood shivering, unable to decide what to do, and he thought slowly: Sarah couldn't stand to see me even look at another woman. Possessive, she was. He clutched his hair in both hands and cried aloud, "Oh, God, what am I going to do?"

But God had only given him his looks and his charm, and it may have been Satan, who had perhaps bestowed on him his quick cunning thoughts, who put into his mind the idea of burning the house down.

A fire! The thought seemed to spring from nowhere into his stunned mind and he gazed wildly round the room. He took a chair from a corner and placed it beside the bed. He pulled the lower sash of the window up a few inches to allow oxygen in to feed the flames, and tugging down the curtains, he bundled one up and thrust it under the chair. He spread the other over the chair with one end resting on the mattress.

The flame from his gold lighter scorched the cloth of the curtain on the floor, and fire appeared, grew, spread. In a surprisingly short time the flames were consuming the chair and spreading over the carpet to the dust-sheet he'd pulled from the dressing-table to throw on the floor. The heat became intense and smoke filled the room as the mattress caught fire.

Nigel, coughing, backed slowly out into the passage. He could easily get to the front door before the fire reached the ground floor, he knew: there was no danger and the evidence, the bodies, the mallet, would all vanish into smoke and ashes. He smiled slightly, pleased at how he'd solved the macabre problem he'd woken to find confronting him.

The knocking on the front door was repeated. Jennifer's father, he thought; arriving on his daughter's birthday, to find she has perished in a blazing house. How tragic. Nigel's smile broadened as he loped back along the corridor. In the bedroom, he quickly pulled on his clothes and slipped on his shoes. The dull roar from the other room was now very loud and grey smoke was beginning to drift into this room from the corridor.

Without a glance at the still figure in the bed, Nigel left the room and turned towards the head of the staircase – and froze.

Sarah was standing there, arms hanging at her sides, her blackened lips formed in a dreadful smile. The shrivelled eyes, deep in their sockets, seemed to hold a gleam of mockery.

Nigel tried to move forward, and found his legs were refusing to obey him. He simply could not bring himself to approach the silent being, and if it touched him, he knew, he would almost certainly go insane.

The fire had now erupted out into the corridor, the carpet blazing, woodwork turning to flame, the old portraits falling, flaming, from the wall.

He continued to stand there, the heat already beginning to burn the skin of his face and hands, staring at the figure that stood at the top of the stairs, until the thickening smoke hid it from him. He told himself frantically that he must move, and move fast, or he would be roasted alive. But his horror of the unseen thing facing him was greater even than his fear of burning, and he stood irresolute.

Mr Hudson wrinkled his nose and sniffed. He stepped back and gazed up at the front of the house. He saw that smoke was escaping from below the casement and a dim red glow was becoming visible from somewhere inside the room. He stared, whirled, ran to his car and snatched up his cell phone. When he had made the call and turned, he saw that most of the upper floor of the house was burning; two of the windows now had no glass in their smouldering frames and flames and smoke were billowing out. Two women came round the corner of the house and hurried towards him, glancing up apprehensively at the flame-filled windows.

Nigel had retreated along the corridor, his streaming eyes searching for any sign of Sarah emerging from the smoke. The left sleeve of his shirt flared up and he beat at it furiously, panic seizing hold of his mind. There was a narrow staircase on his right and he ran up it to the third floor. Even up here, the heat was intense, and before many seconds had passed he saw that the stairs were on fire, the flames relentlessly climbing the treads towards him.

There was a skylight further along the passage he stood in, he knew. He had to find a chair, find something to stand on to allow him to reach it and climb out. The middle of the roof was flat: he could wait there until rescuers arrived. As he ran frantically from room to room, the fire ate its way into the passage and raced towards him. He found a wooden crate in one of the attic rooms and positioned it below the skylight, flames touching his trouser legs and scorching his legs. He screamed, fell back, saw that his trousers were ablaze. His hair burst into flames. He staggered to his feet and somehow got on to the crate. Reaching up with scorched hands he tugged at the bar that held the window shut. At last it gave way and he pushed the frame up and, grasping the edge of the opening, pulled himself out, whimpering from the agony of his burning legs and scorched scalp.

Below, Jennifer's father had reversed his car some distance away and he and the two women stood watching helplessly as the fire crept down to the ground floor.

The cook shrieked and pointed. He saw that someone was on the roof, a flaming figure that danced and screamed – desperate cries that could be heard even above the roaring of the fire. It lurched to the edge and appeared to be looking over the parapet, and he saw that it could not be looking, for its face was mostly seared away, and the eyes gone.

In the distance, a fire service vehicle's siren could be heard wailing mournfully.

BAD HAIR DAY

Gary Fry

For once the floor was free of hair. Not that Rebecca Simpson believed for a moment this standard would be maintained. But it was nice to have her impression confirmed that she was regarded by the staff as important enough for them to sweep the salon before her weekly appointment.

Rebecca strutted to the reception desk, her brown hip-length hair swaying in her wake. She knew that she was drawing glances of envy, just as she had during the brief, distasteful walk from her Mercedes. Bradford was a vulgar city, and the car parks could double as dirt-bike circuits, but some of the inhabitants clearly had taste, even if they would never replicate such style in themselves.

"I'm here for my twelve o'clock appointment," Rebecca announced in her mellow public-school voice. "But, of course, I'm expecting you to be aware of this."

The receptionist, a portly woman with the kind of ginger locks one could do little with, replied with a pseudo-professional tone. "Ah yes. Miss Simpson. If you'd care to take a seat. I'm afraid we're running a bit behind this morning."

As if *that* was any concern of Rebecca's. "Young lady, I have a tight schedule myself today. This afternoon, I'm meeting a representative of the Spanish School of Vienna. Am I expected to be delayed on account of a simple trim and blow-dry?"

The receptionist seemed confused; maybe she thought the Spanish School of Vienna was a multinational language-class. Nevertheless, believing that she'd made her feelings known, Rebecca retreated to the window, in front of which three uncomfortable-looking chairs had been placed side-by-side beneath the inverted company insignia: REDZ – HAIR STYLISTS.

Bad Hair Day

Loath to crumple her linen suit, Rebecca sat gingerly, removed her diamond-encrusted compact from the smaller of her Fendi handbags, and then, for perhaps only the tenth time that day, reappraised her unmade-up complexion. It was perfect for a twenty-year-old, let alone someone who was a decade more mature. Buoyed by this reminder of her beauty, Rebecca settled back and, despite the buzzing telephone and an excess of meaningless chatter in the salon, awaited her appointment patiently.

Ten minutes lumbered by... then another... and when the half-hour approached, Rebecca snatched her lean body to its feet and began pacing to and fro on the cheap plastic floor-tiles. There were five chairs occupied, each at varying height settings, and hair was beginning to accumulate around the feet of the stylists. Rebecca intensely disliked the sight of hair detached from its source of life: the roots, the scalp, the *person*. As a child she'd witnessed her mother go bald during a period of manic self-harm, at the culmination of which Rebecca's father had arranged for her care to be transferred from one large house in the country to another: Chatley's Mental Institution in North Yorkshire. Rebecca suspected that this was the reason she'd never had her own hair cut, only trimmed with entrusted precision.

More of the tufts thumped to the floor, and Rebecca found herself turning away in disgust to the window. The view of the city wasn't much better. Ordinary people dragged themselves about, laden with shopping in bags from cut-price backstreet stores. It was a gloomy autumn morning and restless cloud, pregnant with rain, burdened the precinct with too much swirling shadow. Even the architecture, some of which was worthy Victorian, looked grim. It was only the clock on a tower to the left, its third hand clipping away yet *more* seconds, which invested the location with anything like commitment, dignity, duty.

"We're ready for you now, Miss Simpson."

Rebecca spun on the heels of her Manolo Blahniks, her gaze

fixed high, away from the hair. The receptionist was standing before her, fat white hands cupped at the level of her embarrassingly enormous breasts in a gesture of servility. Rebecca knew that there was more commentary to come, and she raised her immaculately plucked eyebrows by way of a forceful prompt.

Indeed, the receptionist went on, "I'm afraid that your regular stylist, Jane, couldn't make it today. She has flu. But please don't worry. We have a new girl – Sozi. She's very good. In fact, she's *magic*."

As the receptionist finished speaking, a tiny woman, so small she might easily pass for a child, edged out from behind a presently vacant chair. *Sozi* – should Rebecca deduce from the name that the stylist was not British? She certainly didn't look like a native of these shores. Her dark, dark eyes and the angularity of her bone-structure perhaps betokened Eastern European ancestry. Only last year Rebecca had spent some time in Yugoslavia on a purchasing trip for raw, young studs. God, some of the *people* she'd had to deal with... their personal habits... Rebecca didn't consider herself to be racist, but the thought of foreign hands running across her scalp...

She would have to say something.

"Is there nobody else? What about the owner – Jacqueline? I can trust her. She's helped out on many a garden-party of mine."

"She's away at a conference, I'm afraid," said the receptionist.

"Typical! *Typical!*"

There was a pause, during which the wobbling posture of the fat woman's body crumpled completely. "Look, please consider Sozi. Honestly, she's... out of this world."

The tiny stylist glanced across at the two women either balefully or dolefully – it was hard to tell; her irises were so black. Thin, ghosted fingers, like nimble boneless insects, were woven into the hoops of a pair of silver scissors. Was she chopping the blades almost imperceptible? Perhaps that was

173

just a sign of nervousness. None of this pointless negotiating could be good for the confidence of the youngster. Indeed, at last Rebecca relented.

"Oh, very *well*." She switched her attention imperiously to Sozi. "Just do *exactly* as I say, okay? Nothing more, and – well, I was about to say nothing less, but as you'll hear, that *won't* be possible. After a wash and blow-dry, I want *only a millimetre* taking off the ends of my hair. *Comprendez?*"

"I'm sure that won't be a problem," the receptionist added. "I'll leave you in Sozi's capable hands."

As the plump ginger woman retreated to her desk, hair on the floor gusted up in a breeze set in motion by the passing trunks of her legs. Rebecca shuddered, looking away immediately. But no, here was *more* hair to her left, mounted inch-high. Then Rebecca stared fixedly at Sozi, but it was no good: in the peripheries of her vision, hair was on the move, scissors glinted in the hands of the other stylists, and hair products – sprays and gels and foams and shampoos – stood all around like weapons awaiting deployment. Snapping her gaze to the ceiling – and spying a beam up there, a bulky stretch of wood whose solidity steadied her to some degree – Rebecca found that she could tolerate no more. Without hesitation, she advanced for the chair beside the stylist for whom this would be a first and final opportunity to minister to the immaculate hair of Rebecca Simpson.

To start with, the chair wasn't right.

"I don't suppose anybody has bothered to tell you, Sozi, that I expect several cushions on my chair."

Without speaking the woman in the black, armless, ankle-length dress rushed into a corner of the salon and returned seconds later bearing three rotund cushions. The eagerness of the act might have impressed Rebecca if it wasn't for the tufts of hair which had been kicked up in the process. She shifted her attention to the cushions that the woman – whose own hair was cropped – was dropping into the leather seat. When Rebecca finally deemed the arrangement satisfactory, she climbed onto the footplate of the chair and then lowered herself gracefully, her expensive handbag clutched possessively in her expensively manicured hands.

The chair's height was adjustable, and as Rebecca scrabbled in her Fendi bag for her eye-mask, she instructed, "Take me up *higher*." In the huge mirror beyond the ceramic scoop of the sink, Rebecca watched the tiny woman: the queerly unreadable expression on her face hadn't altered a bit. "If you have to stand on a box, stand on a box. As is my habit, I intend to use this time to dim my horizon and seek my core. That is to say, I shall be meditating."

Rebecca hoisted the eye-mask and threw the elastic strapping over her angelically shaped head (that was how daddy had always referred to it; bless him! She would telephone him this evening to allay his pitiable solitude). Rebecca pulled and pulled her hair through the elastic band until the whole momentous stream of it spilled across her shoulder and the eye-mask was looped around her swan's neck. As the stylist – *Sozi* – flung a waterproof gown across her client, while extracting the hair, Rebecca decided it was time to render her conditions of employment unambiguously clear.

"The very moment I place this mask over my eyes, I expect *no* disturbance. No talk of holidays this year; nothing thank you for the upcoming weekend; no idle, girly chit-chatter to which I would have little to contribute anyway. My business is with horses, and not with pop-music and fit men and nights out clubbing. *Comprendez?*"

Sozi was pumping up the chair with the foot-pedal to the left of the lever which released its air brakes. The seat reached quite a height, a good yard off the hair-diseased floor. This was *such* a relief. Now that Rebecca's mind was freer, less self-regarding, it suddenly struck her that the stylist had yet to say anything at all. All Sozi had hitherto managed by way of communication were curious stares and an affirmative nod in response to Rebecca's foregoing instruction. Had the cat got her tongue? (That had been one of mummy's favourite phrases before all of the unpleasantness...)

As Sozi tied the gown beneath the eye-mask currently hanging around Rebecca's throat, the stylist passed a hand over one of her own pointed elfin ears and then moved around the chair. With one hand she plucked a showerhead from the claws of its mounting, and with the other she reached for the tap at the head of the sink. As this hand crossed the bowl there was a delicate fall of what appeared to be a fine, black powder... almost not there at all. Indeed, as Sozi beckoned Rebecca forward with one wormlike back-curled forefinger, there was nothing to see on the white of the ceramic but small dabs of dew. Dismissing the matter entirely, Rebecca pushed up the eye-mask until she could see nothing; her hair fell uniformly into the sink as her head went down. Nevertheless, as Sozi's continued silence showed no signs of abating, Rebecca *had* begun to feel unsettled. After all, she was relying on this woman to uphold the greater part of her self-esteem...

Rebecca felt suddenly impelled to say, "I suppose you believe that I'm highly strung by my hair, don't you?"

Then a voice, so minute it could have been mistaken for the squeaking of a mouse, replied rather matter-of-factually, "*Oh, indeed you will be very soon.*"

"I beg your par—"

But before Rebecca could bark any command, the shower was switched on and a roaring, splashing onslaught of water hit the sink and then, presumably once it had attained a bearable temperature, Rebecca's head. Still, maybe those words had been misheard. Amid the merciless deluge thudding against her skull, Rebecca could now detect a torrent of words which sounded even less like English than anything common young people came up with these days. Might Sozi be singing in her mother tongue? Was this a Hungarian folk ballade, perhaps? Or something Bartokian? The phrases certainly possessed a certain idiosyncratic lilt, though the rhythm to which they were set was leaden, march-like, funereal – more a dirge than a delight. Whatever did this mean?

Rebecca decided to drop this speculation in order to indulge in her own mind-game. Once she'd been thrust back into an upright seated position with rather more vigour than she'd cared for, she attempted to lose herself temporarily in her refined psyche. This was a trick she'd picked up at Magdalen from a Buddhist reading philosophy at another of the Oxford colleges (she'd forgotten which). The task was to transcend time and space by the hypnotic repetition of a single word – a Mantra, the friend (whose name she couldn't recall either) had called it. Rebecca's own was MONEY. And then she began: *MONEY, MONEY, MONEY, MONEY, MONEY...* The effort was beginning to work. Rebecca sensed a tingling in her scalp and then experienced becoming distant from her body, as though she was rising up and out of the top of her head. Her whole being soon grew limp with relaxation. She began to breathe in a long, deep cycle.

Rebecca had employed this strategy during the difficult period eleven years ago. Her mother's unruly behaviour had been threatening to shame the family, to such a degree that ostracism from the social sphere with which innumerable generations of Simpsons had maintained contact had seemed a viable and disconcerting possibility. Then the disordered shell of the woman – by now institutionalised and irrevocably insane – had taken her own life by swallowing knotted clumps of her own hair.

How *could* any mother have done that to a nineteen-year-old daughter – indeed, her only child? Without the support of the university, her friends there, and the regular visits by daddy, Rebecca didn't think she could have coped at all. And then every so often, when too much duress had crept up on her, she'd wondered off into metaphysical supra-space (that was the term her friend had invented to describe her destination) and had just, well, chilled, man, out there on the rim of her own private universe...

Rebecca was approaching the zone now. Her body had

assumed a kind of weightlessness which was settled in the chair like a stray balloon. Again she sensed her scalp crawling, as though myriad insects were clambering blindly across its flesh and bone. Here came the sound of a vortex, gusting across time from a rip in the cosmic seas of space: the hair-dryer blowing, of course. Then there were chipping noises, stars colliding, somewhere at the back of her head: no doubt the scissors at work on her split-ends. Rebecca realised how much of this kind of thinking veered uncomfortably short of reality, but as long as it served its purpose – reestablishing the defaults of nature – there was no need to unduly worry.

Suddenly Rebecca felt that enough time had elapsed for the stylist to have effected the minor, barely necessary cosmetic improvements. So Rebecca began to *feel* her way back into her body: her hands clutching the arms of the chair, her legs pinned to the backboard of the foot-plate, her head cocked at a reclining diagonal... and something else... yes, something *wrapped around her neck*.

This was odd. Her mask was still in place; as Rebecca opened her eyes, she saw nothing. Then she felt a tugging at her skull, heard the crisp, clashing blades of scissors. Was the stylist finishing off? Immediately Rebecca was again fully alert. What on earth was Sozi doing at the *top* of Rebecca's head? She should be plying her trade only several feet away, at the extremities of Rebecca's hair. Oh, something *must* be said.

"Stop it! Stop it at once! What are you doing? What have you... you *done*?"

All Rebecca received by way of response was a prompt relinquishment of her scalp. Her head soon dropped freely forward – and yet *still* there was that presence at her throat. Before she could assign this any further speculation, however, she heard a thick padding of retreating footsteps which didn't seem entirely real: they were somehow too soft, too broad-sounding... In a loud authoritative voice, Rebecca said, "Excuse me! *Excuse* me! Where on earth have you gone, you nasty little girl? Just you wait until I get my solicitor onto *this*.

But first let me get up and… and see you…"

Instantly Rebecca made a move to stand from the seat, to snap off the mask: no good.

She'd been *bound* to the chair.

Her wrists were tethered to the padded arms of the seat, and her ankles were attached to the scaffolding underneath it. What with the uplifting cushions beneath her, there was now no possibility of moving any part of her body. The eye-mask suddenly pressed into her face like a relentless branding-iron. And with her enfeebled attempts at resistance, the object around her neck dangled and swayed.

"See here! Let me out of *this*."

Why weren't any of the other stylists responding? Okay, so the foreigner had behaved true to anticipated form, but what about the English girls – Rebecca's own kith and kin? Surely they wouldn't permit any such chicanery. Indeed, if they valued their jobs, they certainly shouldn't…

"I'll have the place closed down on the lot of you!"

But there was no response. Indeed, there wasn't any sound at all: no cars passing the salon, no grumbling pedestrians, and – most disturbingly – none of the buzz and murmur of a commonplace working environment.

Fear got the better of Rebecca, usurping her anger, and she strained again at her confinements anew, hurting herself.

"This is no longer funny!"

There was panic in her voice. Her throat had become chafed, inside *and* out.

If only she could remove the mask. Rebecca flexed her face, precipitating who knew how many wrinkles, while she struggled to hitch the elastic-tight item onto the ridge of her eyebrows. When she frowned, she managed a centimetre of movement, and then more… and more… and a little more. Suddenly the mask rolled up away from her eyes, off her forehead, snapped shut above her scalp, and then perched there until Rebecca, whose eyes remained closed in reaction to the strenuousness of the manoeuvre, canted her head and willed the mask off her. It fell to the ground with a dull, pattering sound.

She emitted a gasp of incongruous joy.

And then she opened her eyes.

Despite her relief, she *had* briefly wondered how the strap round the back of her head had slid so obligingly across the scalp. And now as she stared into the mirror, agonised to her heart and suddenly desperately speechless, she *knew*.

Rebecca Simpson, the most radiant jewel in the crown of the contemporary racing scene, was *completely bald*.

She shrieked. She yelled. She cursed. Then she looked down at her arms – and she *screamed*.

At the points where her flesh emerged from the plastic waterproof gown, her wrists had been lashed to the arms of the chair with thick, plaited rope.

No, not rope at all; Rebecca knew this immediately.

It was hair. Brown hair. Her *own* hair.

She screamed again, and then realised that the tightness of her throat was more than simply anxiety-induced constriction. She threw back her head, confirming her impression of what she'd only half-glimpsed in the mirror.

A rope was hanging from the crossbeam in the ceiling, knotted at regular intervals. It was an elaborate construction of hair: a noose composed entirely of hair which had been looped around her neck and pulled taut against the beam and its fastening... of hair.

Somebody was foolishly implying – the woman, *Sozi* – that her client might be hanged with her *own hair*.

How ridiculous! How decidedly *un*funny a prank!

"*Come...on...out!*" Rebecca yelled with irrepressible rage, amid copious shudders. "*Where...are...you?*"

Indeed, where *was* the stylist? Now that Rebecca decentred to a large degree, she twisted her head around and noticed that there were no other girls about, nor even the fat, ginger receptionist. The salon was in fact deserted, its equipment set aside. Despite her interminable sobbing,

Rebecca imagined that this would be how the place would appear a few hours prior to opening, before the staff blundered in and everyday life went on and on. Even the floor had been swept. Not a whisker of the hair which Rebecca had been evading earlier (and how *silly* this seemed now) could be seen. She snapped her head forwards, staring with disquiet.

There was also no activity out in the city. The streets were empty, closed shop-fronts holding out silence, shadows unmoving as if the cloud above had given up the ghost. Rebecca saw all of this nothingness in the mirror opposite her, behind the sink. However, she couldn't see as much as she thought she might have earlier. This was due to an irregularity in her viewing position, a fact which she'd registered upon first opening her eyes. She could see the hair-rope around her neck, but none of it above her head. The mirror presently ended where her clean-shaven scalp began. She was so much higher now – much, much further from the floor. The chair had been raised to its uppermost setting; it was now very lofty, Rebecca had to concede. What with the cushions under her bottom and the noose around her neck, she thought with some incongruous amusement that if somebody kicked the lever which releases the brakes on the chair then this somebody might actually be able to –

Then she *realised*.

"OHMYGODPLEASELETMEGOI'LLDOANYTHINGAT ALL!" she shrieked in a reckless, entirely unbecoming tide of sheer horror.

After a second's silence, the volume of her cry actually appeared to have awoken something which had been slumbering, or perhaps merely hiding, behind the receptionist's desk. Yes, here it came: a three-foot high figure whose head and body were just a mass of hair. It paced towards Rebecca, the soft sounds of its flattened feet whispering across the tiled floor. It was tinier than Sozi, a remarkable achievement in itself, though this aspect was less noteworthy than what appeared to constitute its physical form. It seemed to be *made of hair.* Its cavernous face was a stunted proboscis; its makeshift torso was bound together with gel. Arms which were twisted lengths of hair terminated in clipped bunches, into which scissors and a can of hairspray had been wedged. Between permed toes, it brandished several razors. As it neared the chair in which Rebecca sat panting, a ragged chunk of its flesh, a cluster of hair, tumbled to one side. The figure slowed, turned gingerly, squatted beside this gel-soaked globule, pressed its damaged hip against the piece, awaited affixation, and again stood complete. A couple of pumps of the hairspray were issued to the repaired flank as an absolute guarantee of solidity. And then the figure – the whole of which was nothing more than an animated collection of discarded hair, held together by products found in a salon, while wielding some of its tools – paced the last few feet towards Rebecca's chair.

Rebecca looked away, numbed by terror, and soon glanced into the mirror in front of her. Her face was a white, gaping parody of itself, shot-through with surging blood. Sweat glistened across her naked scalp, laminating her face with panic. She thought there were as many tears in this sheen. She could still hear the hair-thing, scuttling softly beneath the chair. Was *this* what had removed all her beautiful hair: sitting on her shoulders, its legs and arms working? But Rebecca recalled that she'd also heard a hairdryer. How had it managed to –

It was then that Rebecca suffered this sound again: the angry whirring; the heated exhalation.

Indeed, the hair-thing under the chair had begun to speak.

"*A lever,*" it said, the words just a rising eddy of swirling hair. Perhaps the short proboscis was functioning like the snout of a hairdryer; a fleeting glance into the mirror was enough to show Rebecca that innumerable whiskers had been breathed out onto the floor. And the voice went on, "*This is what my mistress commands. That I* push *it.*"

"NO! *PLEEEAAASSSE!*"

Bad Hair Day

The last thing Rebecca Simpson saw before snapping shut her eyes for a final time was an image which served only to compound her horrified perplexity. Somehow the network of mirrors in the salon had conspired to draw her attention to the evacuated city. And there in the glass was the tower with the clock, bearing its implacable dial. The second-hand had ceased moving as though time itself had, and the soundlessness that infused the world grew utterly unbearable.

Then this silence was broken, just as Rebecca's mind had.

"Here's something for the weekend..." the hair-thing said from somewhere rather close in the dark, its voice an inexorable swishing of heavy hair; and soon it added, *"...courtesy of your mother up there where's she loved. Oh,* you *are not going anywhere half as nice on* your *holiday!* You *are going* down..."

Immediately the lever was triggered and the chair vanished from underneath Rebecca. The final thing she perceived as her neck was shattered, and her Manolo Blahniks flailed an agonising few inches short of the plastic tiles, was a sound like laughter... or perhaps only a breeze-swept random distribution of hair on the floor of just an ordinary, everyday salon.

FLIES

Hazel Quinn

Despite the hot July weather Dulcie Faeroe had the doors and windows firmly shut. She did not want any flies getting in to her kitchen especially whilst she was making a fruit cake.

As she added the raisins and sultanas to the mixture she noticed a fly making its way across the kitchen worktop. Surprisingly quickly for a woman of her advanced years she swatted at the creature with a spatula.

"Got you!" she cried triumphantly.

"How do they get in?" she mused to herself. "It's a mystery."

Busy washing the spatula, Dulcie did not notice another fly land in the gooey concoction. The fly quickly became bogged down in the glutinous quagmire.

Oblivious to the addition to her recipe, Dulcie poured the whole lot into a baking tin and put it into the oven.

Glancing at the clock she noted she had timed things perfectly and the cake would be ready for lunch. She was looking forward to it already.

As she washed-up the rest of her cooking utensils, Dulcie's husband George came in.

"By heck, love, it's hot in here, ain't it? Glorious day like this, you could do with some windows open." And open a window is just what he did.

"George!" Dulcie snapped. "The window was closed for a reason. Now would you be so kind as to close it again."

"Eh?" George was puzzled.

"To keep the flies out," Dulcie explained.

"Oh, right. I get you." George reached to pull the window shut again, but before he could do so a fly buzzed in.

"Oops!"

"George!"

"Too late now, love. Bugger's in. Never mind, I've got the

paper here." He took the rolled up newspaper and swiped the fly with it. "There, got 'im."

But two more had already flown through the open window. And Dulcie could see another watching the proceedings from its vantage point on the wall.

"Hmm." George mused.

Dulcie frowned.

George grinned. "I've got it. Or rather, I will have in a moment. Hang on."

As George went out through the backdoor, more flies came in. Dulcie groaned.

"Here we are," George said on his return, accompanied by more flies. "Knew we had some."

"What have you got there?" Dulcie eyed the small box he was carrying with suspicion.

"Vercoe's Flycatchers. Good old fashioned fly paper, just the thing you need."

"Are they still sticky?"

"Oh aye." George soon got to work hanging the ribbons up, putting one up in the window first.

Soon the whole house was adorned with gummy decorations.

"There we are. Now how about some of that cake? It smells delicious."

"Grand bit of cake this." George Faeroe helped himself to a second slice.

"Mmm." Dulcie seemed distracted.

"You all right, love?"

"No, I'm feeling a little unwell."

"Oh dear. Dickey tummy, is it?"

Dulcie nodded, hurrying to the bathroom.

"Something you ate, perhaps?"

Dulcie closed the bathroom door behind her and groaned. "Oh for heavens sake, George," she muttered, "can't you ever put the lid on the toilet?" As she admonished her husband she

185

noticed there was a large fly sitting in the toilet bowl.

She reached to pull the chain, but before she could flush, the blue-bottle flew up out of the bowl. Straight at her wrinkled face. "Ergh!" Dulcie pulled her head out of the way, getting her hair tangled in a strip of George's fly paper in the process. By the time she had got herself untangled she could not see where the insect had gone, and could not wait any longer.

Sitting on the toilet she spotted the fly sitting on the bristles of her toothbrush. Dulcie gritted her teeth and wondered whether it was doing the same thing as she was.

Dulcie emerged from the bathroom, bowels voided and toothbrush binned. In her absence the number of flies had increased.

"Feeling any better, love?" George did not look up from his newspaper.

Dulcie grabbed the paper out of George's hands, rolled it up and swatted him with it.

"Eh? What were that for?"

"George Faeroe! Just look at all these flies."

"Blimey, there are a lot of the little blighters. You might say this place is buzzing!" George grinned, pleased with his little joke.

His wife was not amused.

"It's like Piccadilly circus," George continued, oblivious to her growing ire. "Never mind, I'm sure they'll soon be getting stuck on the fly paper."

"Look!" Dulcie gestured. "There's not a single fly been caught on any of your marvellous fly paper. In fact the only thing that has got stuck on it was my hair."

"Eh? How'd that happen?"

But Dulcie ignored her husband. An advert in the newspaper had caught her eye. It was for Snelling's Super Spray. *Guaranteed to kill all insect bugs and pests DEAD! Especially lethal to all types of flies*, was the claim.

"That looks just the stuff," she declared. "I'm going to the shop."

"Aye, all right, love. Whatever you say. Oh, and Dulcie?"

"What?"

"Can I have me paper back?"

Dulcie threw the newspaper at her husband, and stormed out.

"Think I'll have some more of that cake."

There were more flies in the house by the time Dulcie returned from the supermarket.

"Did you have a nice time at the supermarket, love?" George asked.

Dulcie glared at her husband, then unpacked her shopping bag putting two cans of Snelling's Super Spray on the kitchen table.

George looked disappointed. "Didn't you get me anything nice to eat?"

Dulcie ignored his question. "Just look at this place, George. There are flies everywhere."

"Steady on Dulcie, love," George said, "they're just flies."

"Just flies? Just flies?"

"Aye, just flies, love." George smiled what he hoped was his most calming smile.

It didn't work.

"It's a plague; that's what it is. Oh God, what did I ever do to deserve this?"

"Calm down, love."

"Nasty! Dirty! Horrible! Disease spreading… things! I hate the horrid creatures!"

Dulcie's attention was suddenly focused on a housefly that had landed on a strip of fly paper. The insect was in no way trapped by the dangling trap, and Dulcie watched in disgust as it rubbed its forelegs together then took off again. It came to rest on the remaining fruit cake.

"George, why didn't you put the cake away?"

"I didn't know where to put it."

"In the cake tin; where it always goes."

"Well, I thought you might want a slice when you got back from doing the shopping."

"And how many flies have been crawling over it whilst I was out?"

"Well, er…"

"And how many of those flies have vomited on it?"

"Um, I don't know, love."

"Because that's what they do, George."

Another fly – a blue-bottle – joined the housefly. Dulcie had her suspicions that it was the one from the bathroom.

"Right; that bloody well does it!" Dulcie grabbed both cans of spray and gave them a good shake. "If I have to use the whole bloody lot, I'll use the whole bloody lot!" Dulcie rarely swore; and for her to do so three times in quick succession showed just how angry she was. George decided to make himself scarce, and hurried off, for once remembering to shut the door on his way out.

As good as her word Dulcie kept spraying until the entire contents of the two cans was floating around her.

"Right… you little bastards," she spluttered. "Die!"

The air was a thick miasma and she began to cough. Violently.

Ten minutes later George returned to see if his wife had calmed down any. But he got no farther than sticking his head through the doorway before he had to stagger away, coughing himself.

Snelling's Super Spray failed to live up to its claims, but it had proved lethal. And as the fog cleared the first flies drifted down to lay their eggs on Dulcie Faeroe's corpse.

NAILS

Rog Pile

Sharon stared at the ceiling, tired, but unable to sleep; it was getting dark now and soon she would have to get up to switch on the light. She had slept badly all day and now her eyes felt so heavy that she could barely keep them open, but she forced herself to sit up in the bed, huddling the blankets around her.

Her gaze shifted across the room, travelled from the cot to the window, the window to the door, back again to the cot – it stood at the other side of the room in front of the dressing table, where she could see it clearly from the bed; but the room was so dark now, only the hood was discernible, a blurred shape against the dressing-table mirror. She heard the toys over the cot rattle as they moved slightly in a draught from the window.

The room was darkening almost perceptibly: picking up her watch she saw that it was ten o'clock. Martin would be home soon, already he was late. Probably there was another meeting at work or, more likely, he was at dinner with a client.

These days he never seemed home on time.

Conscious that her mind was drifting, slipping into semi-awareness, she concentrated on the dim outlines of the furniture in the room and the shapes made by the ridges and furrows in the bedclothes, the expanse of blue carpet that she would have to cross to reach the light switch (but no, she wouldn't think of that yet). Anything to keep her mind active and remain awake.

A dull ache was spreading up her back to her neck, and she sank back against the pillows, wishing she could trust herself to close her eyes, if only for a moment, but knowing that she must not.

That she must switch on the light.

A car passed along the street below the window and when the sound of it had died away she could no longer hear the rattling from the cot. There was only silence and darkness. She opened her eyes and there was still darkness, but she sensed movement in the room.

"Martin?" Sitting up, she propped herself on one elbow, groping for the torch beneath the pillow. "Martin, is that you?"

Unable to find the torch, she swore; then shouted: "Martin, for Christ's sake!"

Full awareness came slowly, like a bud opening in her mind, and with it the knowledge that she could not move, she was totally rigid with fear. An intense deadening stillness had descended on the room, and suddenly she knew with complete certainty that Martin had not come home.

But something had come into this room. She could see nothing and it made no sound, but she felt the sickness it exhaled as it moved through the dark near the wall.

Then in the faint luminescence from the window, something glinted – two things, as the object was reflected in the dressing table mirror. Confused by the reflection, at first she couldn't identify the object; and when at last she recognised it as a bolt of metal, about six inches long – as a huge nail – her sleep-muddled brain was still incapable of grasping the implication.

Only that something was by the cot.

Her mind hung strangely detached, as if no longer a part of her, and she listened intently to the sound of the car idling at the corner, opposite the house; then to it pulling across the street. For an instant the headlights played over the house, the curtains, reflecting off the dressing-table mirror, flooding the room with light; and in that instant, silhouetted in the light, she glimpsed a tall shape leaning over the cot, reaching into it with the nail in its hand. One arm was raised, as if in the act of striking, and there was something large and blunt clutched in the upraised hand.

As if the light had melted unseen ropes from her arms, she felt the paralysis leave her. She leapt up from the bed. And abruptly the shape was gone, vanished into the darkness that suddenly filled the room again.

Something rattled on the floor.

The baby, waking and starting to cry, brought her back to her senses. She was kneeling beside the cot and her face was wet. A voice was saying over and over: "Please, please, don't let it happen again," She wiped her face with the back of her hand and stood up, surprised at how steady her legs were.

"Alright, angel. It's alright. Mummy's here now."

She refused to look away from the cot, but backed across the room and fumbled on the wall behind her for the light-switch.

It snapped down and the light flickered and brightened, harshly illuminating the room. Sharon had never liked the strip lighting, a legacy of the house's previous designer occupant; it made the bedroom look white and cold, like a room in a hospital. She went back to the bed and sat on it, and it was white, too, like a hospital bed.

Now that the light was on, the thing that had happened only minutes before seemed nightmarish, unreal.

"Nightmarish…" Had it really happened?

She stared around, noting that the door was closed, the bolt slid shut. The bolt was a heavy one. Martin had refused to fit it at first, saying that he would only be encouraging her, that she was imagining things. But she'd persisted, and in the end, to pacify her, he'd fitted it.

Now she wondered if he was right after all. Was it possible that the horror was all in her mind; that she had just had a nightmare – too many nightmares? It was true she was on edge. Then was she jumping at sounds, screaming only at tricks of the light?

Feeling suddenly giddy, she sank down beside the bed and cradled her face in her hands, which were cold and wet. Tomorrow she would see a doctor. A doctor would give her something that would make the nightmares go away. Yes, tomorrow; then it would be alright again.

The baby was still crying, and smiling now, she went to comfort her. As she knelt by the cot, she saw something glinting on the floor underneath. With shaking fingers she reached down and picked up the nail. It was at least six inches long. And horribly, it was warm.

She crouched by the cot, holding the nail, her breath rasped in her throat; she wanted to drop the nail, throw it as far as she could, but instead she clutched it tighter, afraid to let it fall because that would make a noise – a hard, metallic noise that would confirm what her fingers and eyes already told her.

But the door was bolted. How had the nail been brought into the room?

Dully, she raised her head, her eyes inexorably drawn by the movement of the curtains swaying gently in the draught from the open window. The curtains had billowed in the windows of the small cottage on the hillside, too, she remembered, when they had first set eyes on it, nearly two years ago. But the curtains in the cottage had been blue, pale blue. They were the first things she had noticed as they neared that place, which was to be their home for a year.

*

For a quarter of an hour the car had climbed the road up the mountain. The village was less than a half-mile below, but the road zigzagged so wildly to compensate for the incline that the journey was at least three times that distance. Sometimes they glimpsed the chalet as the road wound far below and Sharon thought how beautiful it was, with the curtains blowing from its open windows.

"Williams told me he'd arrange for someone from the village to come up and air the place out," Martin said. "I suppose it hasn't been lived in since last summer, at least."

"Thoughtful of him, I'm sure."

Williams was the agent engaged by the firm to arrange housing for their overseas-based representatives; and Sharon's feelings toward him just now were not kindly ones: he had provided them with a road map and a set of handwritten instructions, which they had followed dutifully, and quickly become lost.

Finding themselves on a rutted cart-track, not even indicated on the map, they'd begun to despair of ever finding their way back onto a main road, when the track had curved unexpectedly, almost doubling back on itself – curved again. Then they were driving down the main street of the village.

Clearly visible on a steep slope of the mountain, high above the village, was the chalet.

The last hundred yards of the ascent, a private drive linking the chalet with the main road, was steepest, and at one point Sharon wondered if their old Bentley would make it to the top or slide back down the mountain; but then the road had levelled, dipped abruptly, grassy banks had risen high on either side; then they were driving right under the chalet into a chamber which had once been a stable, but now served as a garage. From here, a flight of wooden stairs led them up to a hatch, which opened onto a spacious, airy room.

"How about a drink or something to eat before we look around?" Martin said. "The kitchen's this way, I guess."

"I can't eat until I've looked around."

The chalet had a comfortable air of habitation. Whoever had built it had intended it to be a home, she thought, not a showpiece for tourists and businessmen to lease a few months at a time.

There were ornaments dotted all over the room, on the windowsills, tables, the mantelpiece; tiny, exquisite things, carved of wood, brightly painted; and someone – probably the same someone who had opened the windows before they arrived – had arranged flowers in a vase on one of the tables. She felt almost as though she had walked into someone's home; and just through that door, perhaps, the family were sitting at lunch.

Inexplicably, she felt suddenly cold at the thought, and walked quickly back across the room to the windows. "It must be really unbelievable here in winter," she said. "Can you imagine that grate, with a big fire burning in it? And out there... Oh, the view!"

"It's certainly beautiful," he agreed.

Perched on a steep slope, as if about to slide into the valley below, the chalet had actually been built into the side of the mountain. Seen from one side, it appeared shaped as a triangle, with the sloping rock itself forming the foundations and back of the building; the front of the chalet and roof, the triangle's other two sides. From the two big windows, each wider than Sharon could span with both arms outstretched, an occupant of the room could look down into the valley, where the red roofs of the village shone in the sun.

"Come on," she said. "Let's explore; and you can tell me all about this place – you've been dropping some very mysterious hints on the way. I'm intrigued."

He smiled. "It has some history," he said; then led the way from the room into a low, windowless passage. They opened doors as they walked along, glancing quickly into the rooms: a study, two bedrooms, a box room.

"And this must be the kitchen," she said, opening the last door.

In fact, it was a scullery rather than a kitchen. Built at the rear of the chalet, some eccentricity in the slope of the mountain meant that the floor was higher than in other rooms, and they had to stoop slightly to avoid touching their heads against the ceiling.

"What's through there?" Sharon pointed to a low door set in the far wall of the room, "A pantry?"

"No. This is part of that history."

The door was stiff. He had to use all his weight to open it. When he did, there was only darkness beyond. He flicked his lighter and held it into the gloom. "They never bothered running electricity into this part of the chalet," he said.

Behind the door was a natural tunnel running straight back into the mountain.

Sharon was delighted. "Is this the chalet's dark secret?" she said, laughing.

"Something like that."

"I suppose it comes out further down the mountain, and they used it to bring dead bodies up for some well-meaning sociopath to dissect?"

"Not quite. Come on, I'll show you." He stepped into the tunnel, holding the lighter in front of him. "Mind your head; it's pretty low here."

The tunnel stretched almost a quarter of a mile into the mountain; at the end of it, they came to another door. The door was heavy, built of whole unsmoothed logs. Two of the logs had been cut away near the top of the door, and iron bars were set in the opening; at the bottom of the door, a small gap, less than four inches high and not quite two feet across, had been cut between it and the floor.

There was a massive bolt set in the door which slotted into a niche in the rock wall itself, Martin shot the bolt and stepped inside, holding the lighter high so the small chamber beyond, was lit dimly by its glow.

"This is where Joseph Elliot kept his wife," he said.

Sharon stepped reluctantly into the chamber. She would have much rather not, but Martin was there, and there was a little light. Her feet pressed into some soft pulpy stuff, and she shuddered as something brushed her ankles, then she realised that it was only rotten straw – bedding of some sort?

The chamber was strangely angular, not quite square, the curious planes of the walls only giving that impression: it was cut by nature, not human hands.

"It's horrible."

Martin nodded. "Her name was Kate; she was mad. If she wasn't to begin with, I guess she would have been after five years."

"Five years. In this place?" After less than a minute, the abysmal cold of this stone prison deep in the mountain had begun to penetrate the thin summer clothing she wore.

Martin didn't answer, and they stood silently in the chamber; though the place was not quite silent; there was a persistent sound, so faint that it might almost have been the rushing of their own ears, possibly a subterranean stream. Sharon imagined the icy water melting from the snows higher up the mountain and plunging down rivers and streams, until finally it roared into a gaping black hole in the rock. She thought of Kate Elliot, lying here in the darkness, listening to that sound, imagining the water rushing through the rock close by, thinking how it would emerge further down the mountain, erupting in a spuming torrent which would flash and sparkle in the sun before continuing its journey to the sea.

"Did she ever get out?"

"There's a story; it'll take some time to tell."

"Not now, Martin, please. I don't like this place. Let's go back."

He pulled her closer, kissed her lightly on the forehead; she pushed him away. "Not here," she said.

The day passed quickly; night came. They were lying in a huge bed in a huge room at the end of the chalet. The room was dark.

"Tell me about Joseph Elliot's wife," she said.

He turned, thumped the pillows into shape. "Why'd you want to know about her now for God's sake?" But he sat up and reached for the cigarettes on the bedside table anyway.

"I only know the story as I've heard it from Williams," he said. The lighter flickered in the darkness and Sharon lay closer to him.

"Begin," she said.

"Originally, the chalet was built by Joseph's father. He was a woodcarver, and a good one too, by all accounts – the carvings here are probably his – but unfortunately Kurt didn't inherit much of his father's talent. Only the chalet. When his father died, and his mother soon after, he set himself up as a carpenter. It was the only thing he knew. That was how he met

Kate; she was employed in a house he visited in the course of his work. Not to make a long tale of it, it wasn't long before they were married.

"He probably loved her at first. She was quite beautiful and he was proud of her. But he wanted a son, and Kate had a strange fear of children. The truth was, she hated them, or at least the thought of giving birth.

"When she was at a particularly impressionable age she had watched her mother dying in a consumption during pregnancy; and since that time she had been unable to think of children except as parasites, feeding off their mothers."

"But Joseph was persistent?"

He nodded. "Much against her wishes, Kate became the mother of a fine healthy boy named Daniel. Joseph was pleased; he had a beautiful wife and a son to carry on the family name. But Kate became convinced she was ageing before her time. In the end, she refused even to breast-feed, the child, claiming it was sucking the life out of her." He paused, to draw slowly at the cigarette.

"When the baby was three weeks old, Joseph had to return to the village to work – at least, that was what he told Kate. In fact he was becoming tired of her and her idiosyncrasies and had begun seeing a girl in the village. One night he got back to the chalet in time to find Kate trying to smother the child with a pillow.

"After that he didn't waste much time. He'd used the chamber behind the chalet to store materials and tools for his work. Now he emptied the chamber, built a strong door, and imprisoned her there. He never opened the door again, even to feed her; just slid a tray under the slot in the bottom of the door. He had everything worked out.

"He could talk to her through the grid in the top of the door, but after she'd been there a few months it's not likely they had much to say. People who visited the chalet and heard Kate thought he kept a dog in there. Williams told me about some of the things they found in the chamber when they were restoring the chalet, dishes and the like; only they weren't dishes, just troughs."

"Who was looking after the baby all this time?"

"Joseph. But he wasn't making a good job of it. After Kate was locked, up, the baby got sick and began wasting away. Possibly it was pining, though that seems unlikely. Kate had never wasted any love on it.

"Understandably, Joseph was reluctant to let a doctor into the chalet to examine the child; awkward questions might have been asked. He cared for it the best he could, but he realised the child needed a mother.

"Most of the people in the village secretly believed Kate had died long ago. It was a small, rather incestuous community; there weren't many complications when he wanted to marry Elaine, the other girl.

"Elaine knew about Kate, but she was smart enough to know that her own security depended on her keeping the secret."

He exhaled smoke slowly. "On the day the child was a year old, Kate escaped. How she did it exactly, no one's sure. But she was in an emaciated condition by that time; it's just possible that she managed to reach the bolt through the grid in the door. Apparently the only one to see her when she escaped was Elaine, and they didn't get much out of her; whatever she saw shocked her badly, and she never fully recovered. He found the child himself, murdered in its cot, with a nail hammered through its head."

Martin felt Sharon's body shudder against him. "Perhaps it was here," she said. "In this room."

"It's possible, of course. But there's a footnote to the story; probably just local gossip, you know how these things get about – but when the police arrived and searched the chalet, they found Kate dead in the chamber. She wasn't long dead, and the door was open alright; but from her condition, it looked as if she hadn't done much crawling, let alone walking, for quite some time. How she found the strength to reach the cot and..."

He turned over, stubbing out the cigarette. "Now get some sleep."

Sharon settled back in the bed. "You tell lousy bedtime stories," she said.

The next morning she awoke feeling the first tiny kicking in her womb. And for a while she forgot the prison in the mountain.

*

She walked across the blue carpet, parted the curtains and stared down into the street. A mist had begun to fall and the street was shiny; the mist was visible as a halo, flickering in and out of existence around the orange streetlamp across the road. She studied her wristwatch, shook it, then looked up and jumped at the sight of her own reflection in the windowpane. The flickering streetlamp was beginning to get on her nerves. She went back to the chair by the bed. It was three in the morning, and Martin had not come home.

She was considering going downstairs and making herself a hot drink, when she heard a car draw up outside the house. Hurrying to the window, she opened the curtains in time to see Martin get out. In the uncertain light he seemed to be smiling. She supposed the meeting had been successful. Before he could look up and see her at the window, she let the curtains fall back into place and got back into bed, not wanting him to find her still up. At the last moment she remembered the bolt, and there was just time to unfasten it and get back to the bed before she heard his footsteps on the landing outside the door.

She sat up, rubbing her eyes as he walked in. "What time is it?" she said. "Did I fall asleep with the light on again?"

"The baby keep you up?" He peered into the cot.

She nodded and wondered if it was only her imagination how his expression changed as he turned to look at her. "How did the meeting go?" she said.

"Meeting...? It was alright." He went over to the window.

"Hell, it's stuffy in here; I don't know how you stand it." He slipped the catch, began raising the window, "Let's have some air in the room."

"No!" It came out as a hoarse shout. Quickly she tried to cover up by saying, "It's misty outside. Damp air's bad for a baby's chest."

He looked at her strangely; then she remembered that the mist had only begun falling in the past half-hour.

He shrugged and turned from the window; went back to the door. "I'm making myself a drink before I turn in. Like me to bring you something?"

"No. I won't sleep. Martin?"

He paused in the doorway.

"All these meetings lately; this is the third time you've been late this week. And then there was last week…"

"What about it?"

"Couldn't you bring them back here? Your clients, I mean. I could make dinner; and if you wanted to talk there's always the lounge…"

"Sorry, no. It's out of the question."

"What's that supposed to mean?"

"Have you taken a look at yourself lately?"

She stared at him.

Abruptly, before she had time to protest or even think about what was happening, he had pulled her from the bed and was half-carrying, half-dragging her across the room to the dressing-table. He locked his hand around her neck, pushing her head forward until her face was inches from the mirror. "Now why don't you tell me?" He stepped back and let her go, "You look awful. When was the last time you slept? This has been going on for weeks, not sleeping, locks on the doors. Why won't you see a doctor?"

Her head swam; she no longer recognised his voice. A stranger had walked into the room. He looked like Martin, but Martin was not like this.

She stood swaying in front of the mirror long after he had

gone; then, methodically, she reached, for a brush and began to pull it through her hair, slowly at first, then faster and faster. When at last she was calm, she lowered the brush onto the dresser with exaggerated care, wanting to hurl it into the mirror. She went back to the bed and lay down, waiting for the sound of his feet coming back up the stairs. The stranger who looked like Martin. The click of the light switch. Then he was in the room. She felt the mattress give slightly as he got into bed, and she stayed still until she sensed that he had turned over, away from her. Despite her weariness she didn't sleep but lay staring into the dark room a long time. Finally there was only blackness, like an abyss.

*

"Will you be late again tonight?" She stared deliberately into her cup as she spoke.

"Probably." He folded the paper he was reading, putting it to one side. "I don't know for certain. You'll just have to expect me when you see me."

She nodded, trying to ignore the tightness in her stomach.

As soon as he was gone, she heaped the dishes in the sink and hurriedly but methodically tidied the kitchen and bedroom. Then, looking out of the window and seeing her neighbour hanging washing out, she went into the garden.

"Janice, would you be a love and look after Angela for me today? I've got to go into town. I'm not sure when I'll be back."

"No trouble at all. Going to have your hair done?"

Sharon shook her head.

"Sorry. I don't mean to pry. I just thought an afternoon being fussed over in a salon wouldn't do you any harm. You've been a bit pale lately."

"This is just something I have to attend to," Sharon said.

After taking the baby next door, she drove into town, parking her car in a side street near a small cafe. The cafe overlooked the parking lot at the back of the office building where Martin worked. She spent most of the morning wandering around the shops, having lunch in a restaurant by the river; the rest of the day she walked in the park. At a quarter-to-five, she returned to the café.

From a seat by the window, she watched the flood of office-staff emerging from the building. Then a quarter of an hour later, the arrival of the cleaners in their ones and twos. The waitresses in the cafe began wiping down tables and stacking chairs, and for a while Sharon thought she might have to leave; but just then she saw Martin appear on the steps of the building. He was alone. For a moment, hope surged through her; then he stopped and turned, and she saw a tall, dark haired girl descending the steps behind him.

Though she had suspected precisely this, the reality came as no less of a shock. She had planned to follow him – follow them, if her suspicions had been founded, but now she only sat and watched as they got into the car and drove away.

She was still sitting there when a hand touched her lightly on the shoulder and a voice, polite but insistent, said: "Excuse me, miss. We're closing now. You'll have to leave."

As she left the café, Sharon collided with an old woman, almost knocking her to the pavement. Before she could reach out a hand to help, the woman had recovered her balance, and Sharon's stuttered apologies were addressed to her quickly retreating back.

Forgetting the car parked nearby, she walked back along streets which were empty now except for a few late shoppers weighed down with heavy bags. She walked uncertainly, like a somnambulist. In a space of less than twenty-four hours, the foundations of the secure world she had once believed surrounded her, had crumbled. Now she felt no bitterness, or even self-pity; inside her was only a terrible emptiness.

But no, not quite emptiness; there was still the baby.

Her mind was suddenly icily clear, and she stopped and

looked around, realising she had taken several wrong turnings and was now in a part of the town totally unfamiliar to her. The houses at either side crowded close to the pavement behind their iron railings, and the walls were cracked and stained. Newspapers and broken glass littered the pavement and gutters.

Remembering the car, she thought of retracing her steps to it, but then decided she was in no fit state to drive; for the baby's sake, if not her own, it was even more important now that she take no unnecessary risks.

After passing along three more streets, each more squalid than the last, she had to accept that she was utterly lost and began looking around for someone to ask directions of. The only person on the street apart from herself was a woman walking along the pavement some distance in front of her. The woman turned the corner, and Sharon hurried after her, but reached the corner only in time to see the woman disappearing into an alley further down the next street.

She called, but the woman either did not hear, or simply took no notice, and Sharon ran down the street and into the alley in time to see her briefly silhouetted at its far end.

The walls of the alley were high, topped with barbed wire; occasionally there were peeling gates, all closed. At the end of the alley she emerged onto a towpath above a stinking canal.

The path curved, away in either direction, until finally it disappeared behind the high wall bordering it. The woman was nowhere in sight.

She toyed with the idea of going up to one of the houses and asking for help, but uncertain of the reception she would get in this forbidding part of the town, decided against it and went back up the alley to the street.

By now, she was beginning to have difficulty reading the names of the streets; she realised with a vague sense of apprehension that it was almost night. Despite her tiredness, she forced herself to hurry, breaking into a run. It began to rain, and her feet slipped on the wet uneven paving stones.

Twice, she found herself running in the middle of the road.

Travelling much too quickly for the wet conditions, a car swerved around the corner in front of her, and she tried to wave it down. It shot past, horn blaring. Exhausted, she leaned against a wall, luxuriating in the reassuring firmness of the stone against her back; her fingers traced the smooth edge of a sign set in the wall. Hardly daring to look, she turned and read the sign. A wave of relief swept through her. Then she began to run, and didn't stop running until she stood in the pool of orange streetlight opposite her house.

*

Janice opened her door almost as soon as she pressed the bell. "You're late," she said, "God, you look all in."

"I got lost." Sharon walked into the warm hallway and tugged the scarf from around her neck. "Has the baby behaved herself?"

"No problems. She's entertaining a guest right now."

"Oh?"

"Here, let me help you with that." Janice took Sharon's wet coat and draped it over a banister. "This woman just called; said she was collecting for prisons or something – I just can't seem to get rid of her."

From along the hall, Sharon heard Angela crying.

"You've saved my life, arriving like that. It'll give me an excuse to get rid of her. You'll stay for coffee of course? Go right on in, I'll just go and put the kettle on."

Sharon opened the living-room door and smiled as she saw the woman leaning over the cot. Then the woman straightened, and an impossibly dead white face was staring into her own. It swayed under its unkempt hair, white and smooth, obscenely grimacing.

Sharon opened her mouth, but only a dull moaning sound came out. The room whirled sickeningly. From a great distance, she heard Janice saying: "That's odd. She was here

204

just a minute ago. I suppose I'll have to go around and check nothing's missing. Hey, are you alright?"

She helped Sharon to a chair. "You really have been overdoing things, haven't you? Just sit there a moment, and I'll bring you something." She shivered slightly and pulled her cardigan closer around her shoulders. "It's cold in here. I could do with a drink myself."

*

Half an hour later, Janice's husband came home, and Sharon reluctantly went back to her own house. As she was closing the door, something made her pause and look back across the street. At first, she thought it was deserted, but then, as the streetlamp flickered and brightened momentarily, she saw a tall shape standing in the orange light. It might have been a trick of the light. The figure was absolutely motionless, and it was impossible to distinguish its face, but she knew that it watched her. She shuddered and closed her eyes.

When she opened them again, the figure was inside the gate. She grabbed at the door and slammed it shut; leaned against it. She waited until she had regained her breath before trying to think what she should do next. It had already been inside the house, so locking the door against it would accomplish nothing, she knew. It was playing games with her, trying to frighten her; and it was succeeding. She wondered how long it would be before she fell apart completely under the strain.

She thought of the way its hands had once reached through the bars of a dismal prison deep in a mountain. Had it already been dead, then? Had it been Kate Elliot who had escaped from that cell, long ago, murderous and deranged, or her spirit?

She made her way upstairs to the bedroom and sat on the bed. She lay back and exhaustion, mental and physical, crept over her.

She remembered.

She was sitting in the warm, sunlit bedroom at the end of the chalet, cradling the baby to her breast. It hadn't snowed in three days, and now the sun flashed off the peaks around, flooding the room with its reflected light and heat.

"It's awfully quiet for a baby." Martin was leaning against one of the windows, the mountains a soft white backdrop in the distance.

"She, not 'it'", Sharon said. "And she's an angel." She looked thoughtful for a moment; then glanced up at him, "What do you think of Angela for a name? Not too prissy, you think?"

"Oh, lord. Yesterday it was Sarah. The day before – what was it the day before?"

"So I changed my mind, dammit. Woman's privilege. And you're not to upset me, I'm to have lots of rest; the doctor said so."

"That settles that then. Doesn't it – Angela – ever cry? I thought that was what babies did."

"Sometimes, when she isn't feeding. Now go away and leave us in peace. I'll have to change her soon, and I don't want you standing there screwing your face up."

Martin got up. "Mrs Jansson will be up from the village later on," he said as he walked over to the door.

"Then hadn't you better make sure you've cleared away the dishes? Mrs Jansson is not, remember, employed to perform menial tasks."

Martin grinned as he recognised the stern tones Sharon had mimicked. Mrs Jansson was the woman who had opened the chalet before they arrived here, more than half a year before. She had been a frequent visitor since and had stepped in quickly (if with no great show of enthusiasm) to offer assistance when minor complications had made it impractical for Sharon to be moved from the chalet for the birth. She was an austere woman, as hard on the surface as one of the wooden carvings which decorated the lounge, but, Sharon had found, kindly enough, and a more than capable nurse.

Martin hesitated at the door, undecided whether to speak. At last he said; "We'll have to leave here soon. You know that, don't you? My business here's almost finished, and I can't go on claiming executive's privileges much longer."

"Don't remind me. I don't want to leave here ever."

She waited until the door had closed behind him, then looked down at the feeding baby. "Angela," she whispered quietly.

That night she was awakened by someone entering the room.

She sat up, glancing into the cot at the side of the bed where the baby was sleeping soundly. The room was cold and her breath condensed in white clouds in the bright moonlight. She realised that Martin's side of the bed was empty; then she saw the shadowy figure of a woman standing near the window.

"Mrs Jansson? You're very late."

"Your husband has had an accident, Miss Sharon." (Mrs Jansson always called her that: Miss Sharon, never Mrs Brown.) If you come with me, I will take you to him."

"Martin? Something's happened to Martin?"

"You must come with me quickly."

Confused and frightened, Sharon got out of the bed; some instinct made her take Angela from the cot. "Where is he? How did it happen? What's happened?"

"Please, there is no time for questions. We must hurry; he asks for you."

Stumbling in the dark, clutching the baby closely to her, Sharon followed the other woman out of the bedroom and along the passage to the kitchen. "Through there?" She could smell the stale coldness from the low open door. "What was he doing in that place?"

She groped for the switch and winced as the light struck her eyes. She glimpsed Mrs Jansson's back disappearing down the narrow passage and hurried after her.

The door at the end of the passage was open and she stepped into the chamber. "Mrs Jansson, for God's sake, haven't you got a match or something?"

There was a gentle, almost inaudible thud as the door closed.

"Martin? Mrs Jansson? What's going on? Is this some stupid sort of joke?"

She knew it wasn't a joke.

With her free hand she groped around in the darkness until her fingers came in contact with the wall; she felt her way along it to the door. Her fingers closed over a metal bar, and pulling herself up to the grid she could just see a dim light filtering along the passage from the kitchen. She pulled desperately at the bars, but they were solid as if set in granite, and the door had been bolted. Turning back into the chamber she found that her eyes had begun to adjust to the dark, and now she could vaguely distinguish the angular planes of the walls. They showed, with an odd phosphorescence in the dim light from the grid. She began to call out, and after a while to scream, but the sound reverberated from the stone, hammering against her ears, and she became quiet again. There was nothing to worry about, she thought. This was just a room. She did not like it here, but it was just a room, and before very long Martin would start wondering where she was and would come looking for her. She leaned back against the wall, aware in the silence of the subdued roaring – the *unsound* of water rushing through the rock, perhaps only a yard, a foot away.

And in any case, there was no need to worry about the baby. She had Angela with her. Tenderly, she parted the shawl from around the baby's head and looked down at her.

Then her eyes widened in utter disbelief as she saw the thing she had been carrying.

She dropped the bundle, the horrible small dead thing, and flung herself against the door, banging, tearing her nails against the wood. The roaring in her ears increased until it seemed that it would burst her head, and the door and the very walls of the chamber began to shake and pound madly around her, throbbing like the inside of a giant's heart.

Something struck her a stinging blow across the face.

"Sharon! Wake up! What in God's name are you doing in this place in the middle of the night?"

Martin had hold of her shoulders; he was shaking her as a dog shakes a rabbit. She tried to speak, but only an unintelligible choking sound, came out. "What are you doing here?"

"She said you'd had an accident, and I came down here, but she locked the door, and... Martin, the baby! Something terrible's happened to the baby!"

"The baby is in her cot in the bedroom, sleeping. And that's what you should be doing. Who told you I'd had an accident?"

"Mrs Jansson. She came into the room and you weren't there. She said you'd had an accident. She said you were asking for me, and I had to come at once."

"Sharon." Martin spoke slowly, deliberately, as though he were speaking to a child. "Mrs Jansson couldn't come today. She phoned earlier, while you were sleeping. She said she had a migraine and wouldn't be able to make it."

Sharon wound her fingers into Martin's shirt, bewildered.

"Who locked the door?" she said.

*

Someone was coming up the stairs. She had been woken by the sound of the front door slamming, and now someone was coming up the stairs. It was a light confident step that she recognised immediately, but she lay still on the bed, not daring to call out or even move, in case she should be wrong. The footsteps were halfway up the stairs. Now they were almost at the top. Her eyes moved anxiously, shifting their attention to the door, the handle.

It turned.

"Sharon?"

She began untangling herself from the curtains and tried to stand. Almost crying with relief she began to cross the room.

"Hurry it up, will you? I've had a rough day."

Now she was almost at the door, her hand reaching out for the handle; in just another moment she would slide back the bolt, she would turn the handle. Then everything would be all right again. She wouldn't be alone and everything would be all right. Her left hand closed on the handle; her right was already at the bolt.

"Still taking no chances with the door? Very wise of you."

And immediately, she knew that something was wrong. Her stomach muscles tightened; she stepped back a little way from the door.

"What's keeping you? Are you going to keep me standing out here all night?"

"The bolt's stiff. Just give me a moment."

But if only she could be *sure*. Memories flickered by like grainy slides through a magic lantern. And voices.

'She came into the room and you weren't there.'

"Sharon?" There was an impatient edge to Martin's voice now. "Are you listening to me?"

'An accident. She said you'd had an accident and you were asking for me and I had to come at once.'

"I hear you," she said. Her hand was moving slowly, as though of its own volition. Another quarter of an inch and now the bolt was almost free.

"Sharon, will you please open this door?"

But if only she could be sure.

'Mrs Jansson couldn't come today.'

"Why are you torturing me?" she said.

There was silence.

She knew that it could enter the room whenever it wished. It could have no reason for these mind games except breaking her down mentally. It had been in the room before. She had seen it standing above the cot, the hideous nail in its hand. Yet somehow it still wanted to break her down, and now she realised that it needed to do that. Why? What else did it want or need? She remembered the thing that she had held in her arms in the dank chalet prison; the thing that she'd not been able to find later. Martin had said that she'd imagined it.

So it was able to manipulate her perceptions, change what she saw and heard.

Was it able to manipulate her in other ways? Could it make her do things she had no wish to do? Could it possess her? Perhaps it felt pleasure in twisting her to its will?

But then the footsteps were going down the stairs; and they were quite different now, not like Martin's at all.

For a long time she lay on the floor, staring at the door, waiting, her hands tracing aimless patterns in the nap of the carpet. Then she turned back to the chair, to the vase, which still lay on the floor where she had dropped it that night.

There had been no sound from the other side of the door since the footsteps had descended the stairs, but she knew it wasn't over.

It hadn't left. It was still in the house.

She went back to the cot and looked down at Angela. Stroking aside the dark hair fringing the baby's forehead, she leaned over and kissed her, barely brushing the skin with her mouth in case she should wake and cry out. Then she took the bronze vase, which she saw was dented now, and opened the door.

From the top of the stairs she could look down into the hall at the closed front door. Then the hall led away behind the stairs, out of her angle of vision. She descended the stairs, clutching the vase ready before her. At the foot of the stairs, she turned along the hall, past the lounge and kitchen to the study at the end, where light glowed dimly around the door. She hesitated for only an instant before turning the handle, then stepped into the room. She blinked in the strong light. Martin's books lined the shelves or were stacked untidily on a low table beside one of the two armchairs; a typewriter glinted coldly under the harsh light, surrounded by different coloured folders and sheets of paper. The windows of the room were closed and the curtains open.

It wasn't here.

She felt an icy prickling touch her back as a faint rattling came to her from above. The rattle of a baby's toys. The room above was the bedroom. The journey back along the hall and up the stairs was no more than a blur of closed doors, endless stairs and thick carpeting on which her footfalls were silent. And then there was the door of the bedroom, open, which she entered. With all her strength she drew back her arm to hurl the vase at the woman's shape standing behind the cot. And immediately it dissolved in a noisy flashing rain of glass.

Slowly she went to the dressing-table and lifted the vase from among the bottles and hairbrushes, ignoring the broken shards of the mirror stabbing deep into the soles of her feet. She looked down at the baby: pieces of the mirror lay scattered over the hood of the cot or caught in the folds of the woollen blanket; yet amazingly the child was unharmed. She had awoken, but was not crying. She made pleased gurgling noises in her throat and looked up at Sharon with something like a smile – as close to a smile as she knew how to make – enjoying, Sharon supposed, what she must think was a new kind of game. Carefully Sharon reached down and picked a jagged splinter of glass from between the baby's fingers before she could put it to her mouth.

"Go back to sleep," she said. "Nothing will hurt you while Mummy's here." She went back to the chair and sat down; the vase lay in her lap beside the winking length of glass. What would Martin say, she wondered, when he came home and found the shattered mirror, the broken door? What would he think?

But what did it matter *what* Martin said or thought. Where was he now, after all, when she needed him? But that was a stupid question. She knew exactly where Martin was now, or at least, whom he was with. He was with another woman. She wondered who the girl was. A secretary, she supposed, just some girl from the office, after a quick promotion, not particular how she got it – a slut. Yes, Martin was with a slut, while she... she...

But he hadn't always been like this. When she had first met him he had been considerate, kind, nothing had ever been too much trouble for him, just so long as it made her happy. What had made him change then? When had this begun? She remembered how he had always come straight home from the office when they had first been married (so that they'd have more time together, he'd told her). He'd always been generous with his time; with everything. They were always going out; there was no doubt about it, he'd spoilt her. But of course, that was before the baby was born. With so young a baby, she had been reluctant to leave her in the charge of a babysitter; she'd heard how careless they were. A babysitter might have been neglectful, and perhaps Angela would have smothered, or swallowed something. No, she could never have trusted her baby to one of them.

And what was the alternative? To stay home and look after Angela herself.

Now the child was lying sleeping in her cot, oblivious to anything that might threaten her; and Martin was...

She imagined them rolling in bed together, doing things, talking. Did they ever talk about her? The thought made her feel sick, and she leaned her head forward on her hands. But it was clear in her mind now. Things had been perfect before the baby had been born. A few minutes pleasure and it had taken root inside her, it had grown like a worm, feeding off the stuff of her body; she had given it existence and it had taken away her reason for living, left her drained, a husk. If it had not been born then Martin would be here now, and she would be lying with him, not sitting in this chair, keeping watch, waiting.

Waiting for what? A memory? A ghost?

She wondered why she was thinking this way, it wasn't like her but she couldn't seem to stop. Her hands twisted, wringing together.

Perhaps she slept then. The only thing she was certain of was that when she opened, her eyes, there was a shadow on the

213

wall where no shadow should be. It was tall and hunched, and it carried something blunt in one hand. She was vaguely conscious then of standing above the cot, of looking down into it. As if in a dream she watched her hand sliding over the edge of the cot, over the blankets; she watched as her hand stroked aside the dark curls of hair from the baby's forehead and lowered the heavy glass splinter. She tried to move the hand away, but it only moved a little. The glass spike stopped above the baby's eye. She was conscious of a weight in her other hand; it was difficult to move her head, but from the corner of her eye, she saw that she still carried the vase. Then she was raising it, lifting it high above her head. In the broken mirror she saw the figure over the cot do the same. Outside she heard a car door slam, footsteps coming up the path. With a dreadful gentleness her hand was lowering the glass sliver.

*

Martin climbed the stairs slowly. The representative sent by the contracting firm had been an attractive woman, and he had realised too late that she had been using her femininity against him; he had been cleverly manipulated and had made a poor deal for the company. Now he felt tired and only wanted a stiff drink and some sleep. Walking up the path he had noticed that the bedroom light was on; now he supposed he'd have to go through another scene with Sharon. Climbing the stairs he was surprised to see light falling through the open doorway. The door was usually shut and locked.

Then he reached the door and stopped, seeing for the first time the figure by the cot.

"Sharon?" It was a question. The figure did not move at the sound of his voice but remained hunched over the cot, a heavy bronze vase gripped in one hand like a hammer. Though it was motionless he was conscious of tremendous stress concentrated in the slim frame; idiotically, his mind conjured up a picture of a girder trapped in a press, which would crush and twist until the steel turned white and snapped like a twig. Then he saw the head of the figure turning; saw the deathly white mask framed in the tangled mess of hair. Her eyes seemed strange.

He felt cold, and a sound seemed to fill the room as he watched, a sound like a mountain stream, or the rushing of water through rock. The lips of the mask were unmoving, frozen, but a voice seemed to be screaming inside his head as if from the bottom of a black pit. Then the lips of the mask began to part.

"Martin, it's you at last." Sharon's voice seemed unnaturally calm, flat; a sharp contrast to her face and rigid stance. She had turned completely toward him now. "Things are going to be different now," she said. "I know this has been difficult for you, but now things are going to be alright."

He moved forward uncertainly and began to reach out for her, his hands still uncertain.

Then he looked into the cot.

THE LORD OF THE LAW

David Conyers

I'm forced to sit upon the ceiling, because gravity has reversed for me. I'm trapped in a hotel room. I dare not look out the window, afraid of what I'll see. At least I had the courage to confirm the window is locked, so I can sleep at night.

This morning the Lord of the Law has returned. He deems to reverse gravity and sit with me. His clothes don't hang downwards like mine, bunching at my neck and armpits. His clothes are clean.

"Are you ready to apologise?" he asks me.

I look at him. He wears the shape of a man, but his density is all wrong. When he's still it's like he's painted on the wall, a two-dimensional picture of him on a canvas. The occasions when he does move I feel it is the room that shifts and warps around him, propelling him forward in its flux.

"I still don't know what you want me to apologise for?"

He won't look at me.

"Haven't you tormented me enough?"

He doesn't say anything. Instead the cracks in the ceiling and walls extend. They open silently, run before my very eyes. I feel an unseen density press upon me, like swimming in water.

"Please?"

"Mr Skolling, self-denial serves no one. Not me and especially not you."

"But I don't know what I have done."

He doesn't say anything. He doesn't move.

So I sob. I've been sitting on the ceiling for two weeks, trapped in dirty clothes, trapped with nether-light that casts shadows on every surface. All the time I'm wondering if I'm ever going to escape.

"What do you want me to do?"

"We'll talk again tomorrow."

"Please, just tell me?"

He rises, walks onto the wall, turns, walks to the floor, turns and goes to the bar fridge, every step silent as if he is not there. He takes a beer, opens it, and pours it into a dirty glass. I can smell it. I want it. He knows this. He places it on the side table, its liquid suspended above me.

"What did I do?"

He leaves me, not through the door, but by melding into the wall, vanishing like a shadow surprised by a bright light.

*

I'm haggard, I know that. I look like a drug addict when I have a cigarette dangling in my mouth. I stand on the bathroom ceiling, stare into the dirty mirror and see a man who has lost ten kilograms, whose skin has greyed and whose eyes are bloodshot.

I light the cigarette and watch the smoke coalesce around my toes. I feel the nicotine eat my lungs, both loving and hating my insides. At least when air, smoke, water, beer or food enters me they then match my gravity, but not before.

I reach up, turn on the bathroom tap and pour a glass of water – I've worked out how to do this now. When I hold it to the lamp it's tainted brown, even beer looks dirty in this hotel. Then I have to press my head into the ceiling if I'm going to drink it, unless I can find one of my straws.

I sob again. I've been sobbing for fourteen days. This isn't fair.

I've lost my mobile phone. In the bedroom I have to jump to snatch the hotel's handset, five attempts before I reach it. I can only ever remember two numbers. I only need to dial one.

"I won't be coming in today."

It's my secretary who answers. I can hear it in her voice that she doesn't want to ask if I'm okay. The previous thirteen times we've had this conversation the question has been raised, and I either scream at her or wail in torment.

217

"Is anyone paying the bills here?" I ask. "I'm still in the same room, same hotel."

"Mr Skolling, you were supposed to be back in the office thirteen days ago. The company isn't paying your bills."

"Then who is!" I scream at her.

"I think you are depressed, sir. I think you need help. Professional help."

I scream louder, inaudible words even to my ears. I throw the phone to the floor where I won't be able to reach it until room service tidies my mess. I sit in a corner and fight my sniffles, wondering why I pretend that calling in is important. A tear runs up my forehead, falls, splashes up there somewhere on the beige carpet.

I light another cigarette from my near depleted pack, but it's lost all its taste.

Eventually I pull down the desk chair, flip it and stand on it. My weight stops it falling, and I feel lighter by exactly the same amount the chair displaces. I snatch the beer and snort it through the straw I managed to save from last night's in-room dining. The beer is flat, but the Lord of the Law knows I'll want it anyway.

He's just letting me know who's in control here.

*

"Are you ready to apologise?"

He lies on my bed, the bed I haven't slept in for fourteen days. He looks like he's become the crumpled sheets. Two lamps, our only light, seem dimmer when he visits, like he's sucking the photons out of the very air itself.

I lie on the ceiling, looking down, looking up at him. It's feels hard, concrete just beneath the plaster where I rest my back. I only notice my discomfort because he's comfortable.

"This is unfair."

Like one of his cracks, a smile runs across his lips, changes his mouth. "You need to take responsibility for your predicament, Mr Skolling." An eyebrow shifts upwards. "You do know what responsibility is?"

"Of course."

He looks at me like I'm a liar.

I snort. I know I'm a successful business development manager for a medium-sized kitchen fittings company. I've always commanded respect because of my accomplishments.

But I'm lying to myself. Once I was a successful business development manager for a medium-sized kitchen fittings company, and then something went wrong. So I question what responsibility really is, what it really means to me, but only in my head. I'm not yet ready to share.

"What gives you the right to question who I am?"

He shrugs, and it's like someone has just tugged on the sheet and the imprint of his shoulders moved. He doesn't say anything.

"What is it, with this Lord of the Law thing? I mean, really?"

"It's just a title, no more. It helps mortals understand."

I roll my eyes. I want to get drunk, but there is never enough beer. I wonder again who is paying for all this, my time here, while I'm tortured.

"Lord of which laws exactly?"

"Entropy, density, the weight of all things... I'm not the only Lord of the Law. We are many, many thousands. We each control our own dominions, and we are each very precious about them. You..."

He stops, looking worried, like he was about to tell me something I should already know, but changed his mind. This is the first human characteristic he's let slip, and I feel relieved to have seen it. Perhaps there is still hope I might relate to his human nature, and he will release me.

"Don't tell me, your dominion includes gravity?"

"In a sense, yes."

He pours me two beers, into two dirty glasses, and doesn't explain why. Everything in the hotel is dirty and dark, even the

219

amber liquid. I notice the walls are stained with rust, and that the curtains look to have fed moths for centuries. The sheets are the same texture as the tap water, the faintest brown. The beer is all that I enjoy, and it's not even good beer. Or the occasional cigarette when I'm desperate enough to ignore their dwindling numbers. It's like nothing can ever get clean in this place; me included.

He points to my drinks. He knows me and yet is cruel to me. I'm depressed, and alcohol is like a revolver or a noose for a suicide. I quickly drain both glasses and then light up.

"Tomorrow, I think you will apologise," he says just before he leaves, by melding into the wall.

I snort again. He's said that before.

*

Room service is tricky. I don't want to be seen, not in clothes that are soiled, not in skin that hasn't been washed in eight days, and especially not while I'm a freak pressed into the ceiling.

I tried to shower a couple of times, water pounding into my nose and crotch. I filled the bath once, sat under two hundred litres of tepid liquid, tempting it to fall on me. It didn't. So I tried standing up, to drown myself. The bath was too high.

Room service is once a day, at eleven.

Before she arrives I hide in the cupboard, pressed in with the spare pillows and blankets. This is also where I sleep, the only place I can stay warm. The only place blankets don't fall to the floor when I roll over.

The maid who cleans my room is young, pretty and thin – too thin actually, like a holocaust victim. She doesn't really clean the room either, but she is young.

When she opens the door to enter she runs inside. It's like she fears something in this hotel too. I'm convinced she takes solace in my space.

I haven't complained about the conditions, about her

questionable cleaning skills. I leave her alone, so she can rest in my space and feel safe, if only for a few minutes. I tolerate her for her company, to stare at her, even if she doesn't know I'm watching.

She likes to lie on my bed. She daydreams, stares into the ceiling, traces the cracks with her eyes, and probably wonders where all the stains on the roof came from. Sometimes I will her to see me, but I'm too afraid to move or call out, in case she does.

Once she touched herself, as she lay upon my bed, moaned, and I was aroused.

I realised then what I had become, a pervert hiding in a cupboard.

Nothing to do, my world forever out of reach, the Lord of the Law had cursed me with too much time to think, to much solace to darken my soul. My thoughts are not my own. My mind is unravelling. The locked doors of my subconscious are opening again and it's his fault. I wanted to fuck her, and then I want to hurt her, and then I want to fuck her again while I hurt her.

She has fifteen minutes every day to clean my room. She only cleans for five, and then rests for ten.

Today she does something she hasn't done before. At fourteen minutes she opens the desk drawer, as if she's not even thinking about what she's doing. She sees what I see but misses its importance, looking for something else but I can't guess as to what it might be. What I see is a leather bound book. It isn't a bible. Its title says something about 'The Law'. I feel my stomach become butterflies.

Her time with me is over. Standing she adjusts her stockings, smoothes down her uniform. I watch her without blinking. Stare down her cleavage hoping to see more.

Screwing up her nose, I can tell she smells something she doesn't like. She goes to the window to open it.

I tighten my eyes. I tighten every muscle in my body.

I can't see outside. I won't see outside.

She rattles the latch, until she realises that the window is locked, so leaves it alone. I'm relieved, but I keep my eyes clenched until she closes the curtains again, and shuts the door behind her as she leaves.

*

Today the Lord of the Law joins me on the ceiling. He has brought a beer, a glass and a fresh packet of cigarettes. My lips are dry in anticipation. I lick them. He opens the bottle and the liquid inside does not run to the floor, dirtying the carpet.

He takes his time to pour the beer. It remains upside down like me. He leaves the glass next to the packet and the light bulb. It becomes the centrepiece of the room because of how light shines through the glass.

Unable to control myself, I crawl towards it.

The glass shatters, but doesn't explode outwards like I expect it to. It compresses as the cigarettes disappear with it. The grinding noises are indescribable. Within moments they've become a tiny compressed ball barely a millimetre across. I see that it's still shrinking.

"What did you do that for?"

"That was one hundred thousand times the pull of your planet's gravity at sea level. Force enough to crush rocks under their own weight."

The sphere is so small now I can barely see it.

"So that you have some kind of comparison, Mr Skolling, one thousand Earth gravities will crush a tree. A mere twenty gravities would kill you. Five will immobilise you better than any maximum security prison ever could."

"I wanted that beer, those smokes."

More cracks thread through the room, forming a web-like pattern around my keeper. I remember that this is how he expresses disappointment.

"This is not a game, Mr Skolling. I'm not some client you can swindle, not some cheap girl you can take out on the night with the promise of love and then dump her."

My mouth feels dry, my clothes crusty. I scratch the coarse hairs grown wild on my chin. I don't know what to say. I certainly don't understand what he is trying to tell me.

"That was a demonstration. If you think you are uncomfortable now, your circumstances can be made much worse. What if I double the gravity you are experiencing? Triple it?"

I shake my head. I have no idea of the things he is talking about. I am just a salesman. "Please, just tell me what you want me to do?"

"Apologise!"

"For what?" I scream at him. "I've done nothing."

He looks at me, holds my stare. His eyes are like black holes, without definition. He wants me to provide all the answers.

Eventually I feel compelled to say, "You've turned me into a pervert."

He laughs at me, but he is not happy. "You've always been a pervert, Mr Skolling. But what did I say the other day, about taking responsibility?"

"But it's your fault!"

"Is it?"

"Well who else?"

He's on the edge of losing his temper. I can see it in his flesh, trembling like a plate of jelly astride an idling motor. I question if he is really the godlike manifestation of a cosmic force, or just a man who knows too much.

"You blame me for being a pervert? By all means blame me for trapping you in this room, that I can accept, but not for what you already are, what you have always been."

Wetness fills my eyes, runs down my forehead. I'm sniffling, because once my snot enters my nostrils it cannot run out my nose.

"This isn't about my…" I look for a kind word, a nice word, but I can't find one. "About my perverted sexual lusts at all. Is it?"

He shakes his head, or more precisely the room appears to warp so it looks like his head is shaking.

"Please, give me something to work with?"

He leaves, without rewarding me with beer or smokes.

What remains of the crushed glass and cigarette packet is now so small I can no longer see it.

It is so easy to hate him.

*

I didn't tell him about the book. I've been afraid to even glance at its hiding place, until I know he's come and gone again. I don't want him to surprise me while I'm reading it. The book must play some part in why I'm here. I think the Lord of the Law doesn't know it's in the room. I'm thinking it might give me leverage.

Getting the book is going to be tricky.

I grab the chair, turn it upside down. I feel odd standing upon it, when it wants to fall to the floor and I in the opposite direction. It's like it can sense I'm not right.

But the chair and I cooperate. Astride it, I reach the drawer, take out the book.

The title is the first thing I read, *The Law Vol. MCDXLIII: The Realm of Gravity.*

I know immediately I'm on the right track.

I flip through the pages. The book is old, although there are no publisher notes to date it. It reads like a mathematical theorem melded with studies of demonology. I don't understand a word or symbol inside, except to guess that these are formulas to control gravity, much as a sorcerer might try to bargain with a summoned creature raised from the underworld.

I read for hours.

I fail to comprehend a single word.

Eventually I place the book back into its drawer. It's hard work reading when I have to keep holding it tight; trying to stop it from flying out of my hands. When it's back where it belongs I don't miss it. The book is not my answer, not for someone like me.

I sit and just stare at the wall. If I had the courage to kill myself, I would. But I don't even have courage to go near the curtained window. At least the window is locked, so I can feel safe in my cage.

I didn't call work today. I don't care anymore.

I light a cigarette, my last one.

Eventually I decide I must dial the second number I've always kept in my head.

I get a ring tone.

"Hello?"

It's her. I savour the moment, the briefest seconds when she doesn't know who I am, when she'll still be pleasant with me.

"Who is this?"

"It's Doug, your husband."

"Doug? I told you, I'm with someone else now. Don't call again."

"Wait!" I yell. "Please, I have something to say."

I don't know why, since our split she's never waited, but this time she does. Maybe it was the way I asked.

"What do you want, Doug?"

"I just…" The words stick in my throat.

"I don't have time for this."

"I just wanted to say I'm sorry."

There is a pause – a long pause.

"Sorry for what, Doug?"

"For whatever it was that I did to hurt you."

Silence again, but I can hear her on the end of the distant line. She cries. She's crying like I've been crying for sixteen days now. If only she knew the hell I'd been through to make me want to contact her.

"You don't know how long I've been hoping to hear you say that, Doug."

I don't know how to respond, so I hang up.

I let the telephone slip from my fingers. It falls upwards, smashes on the carpet.

I know what I'm capable of now. I can do it. I can apologise to the Lord of the Law, even if I don't know why.

*

He comes back to me the next day. When he arrives, he appears by shimmering through the wall. Today he and the scene behind him resemble a crumpled piece of paper, as if someone just screwed them into a ball, then unravelled and pinned it to the wall. He soon unbalances me again, by not immediately demanding that I apologise.

I think he already knows that I found his book.

He sits in the lounge chair, lies back so he can see me on the opposite side of the hotel room, from where I can only lean against a wall. We both stare at upside down faces.

"I'm sorry!" I blurt before I can change my mind.

"What was that, Mr Skolling?"

"I said I'm sorry, for whatever it was that I did to you. I feel really bad about it."

He nods, but he does so very slowly. It's as if he's become the uncertain participant in our dialogues.

I feel my stomach churn. I'm waiting for him to say something, hoping they will be words I want to hear.

"That's very interesting, Mr Skolling."

"What do you mean?"

"That you feel the need to apologise to me."

The muscles in my chest tighten. "But that's what you wanted, an apology."

"Do you know what you're apologising for?"

I shrug. This isn't proceeding at all how I expected.

"I ask, Mr Skolling, because I made a mistake."

"What – what do you mean?" I crush my knees against my chest. I fidget, interlace my fingers and press my palms together until they hurt.

"You see this is very interesting, because I made you suffer only because someone in this very room manipulated the laws of my dominion. They did so to achieve their own selfish purposes, without first seeking my permission to do so."

I sit bolt upright. "You mean from the book, that volume?" I point to the desk drawer.

He raises an eyebrow, and it's like the eyebrow has just been drawn. "So you knew about the book?"

"Actually... not for very long... only yesterday, I..."

He is silent again. He's waiting for me to finish what I have started. But all I can feel is the sensation of flies crawling over every centimetre of my skin.

"The book doesn't concern me, Mr Skolling. People and their lies concern me. Let me explain, someone in this room used my laws disrespectfully. I thought it was you, because the hotel records show you checking in here on the very day of the violation. However, I forgot to investigate who checked out that morning. It seems that the man who did – a man called Kendal – is vastly more capable of tapping into my dominion than yourself."

"You mean...?"

"Yes, I made a mistake. I got the wrong man."

"So you're going to let me go?" I'm trembling now. I can't believe this nightmare is finally over, that I'm going home.

"That would seem to be the logical conclusion..."

"But?" I say the word. I know I don't want to. 'But' is such a horrible word, because it always begins sentences that never lead anywhere pleasant.

"But you still felt the need to apologise to me, Mr Skolling, and this worries me."

"That was a mistake. I didn't know what I was saying, why I was saying it."

"Do you know how many people tell me what they think I want to hear, just to get something from me? That's what Kendal did, what they all do. I respected you more when you were telling me the truth, defying me."

227

"But—"

"But you still felt compelled to apologise, so that means, logically—"

"No!"

"Please, let me finish, that logically you feel that you have done me wrong, the 'wrong' being lying to me to get what you want. If you feel this way, I should honour your conviction."

"No! Please, no, I…"

He stands, washing through the edges of the room as he does. I know he only stands when our daily conversations are at an end, but this conclusion feels more definite.

"Goodbye, Mr Skolling."

"But…" I stand with him. "What about the gravity? Are you going to restore me to normal? Can I leave now?"

"Yes, you can leave now. I'll allow that. If you choose to stay however, I will no longer be covering your expenses."

"But the gravity…"

"What about the gravity?"

"I… I didn't mean to apologise…"

"Really, Mr Skolling, I don't believe you. You lied to me deliberately, like they all do, for your own selfish ends."

He goes to the window, reaches behind the curtain and unlocks the latch.

"Leave any time you want, Mr Skolling. We won't meet again."

Today he doesn't disappear through the wall. Instead he steps into the corridor, and locks the door behind him.

He leaves me standing on the ceiling.

I hear the sounds of his footsteps vanish in the long hall, and then when I hear nothing, I scream to fill the void he's left behind.

The Black Book of Horror

18 Tales of Terror

Nominated for Best Anthology 2008 British Fantasy Society Awards.

A provincial museum that's not dull but certainly deadly, satanic skinheads, demonology and alien invasions are just some of the nightmares that await you in The Black Book of Horror

'Black Book stands squarely in the great literary tradition of horror and supernatural fiction...'
Peter Tennant, Case Notes, Black Static #2

'A superior example of its type.'
Guy Haley, Death Ray, issue 10

'...this anthology is well worth your time. Solid writing and great ideas.'
Tony Owens, Oz Horrorscope

The Second Black Book of Horror

An undertaker's dozen of frightening fictions

Spectres and killers, monsters and the mad stalk
horrifying hospitals and vile villages in The Second
Black Book of Horror

'...*this is an excellent anthology of solid, enjoyable,
pleasantly scary fiction.*'
Mario Guslandi, The Harrow

'...*an ideal read if you like your horror gutsy,
suspenseful, and with unfortunate endings for your
protagonists.*'
Albedo One

'...plenty of violence, blood and mutilation.'
Adam J. Shardlow, Prism

The Third Black Book of Horror

17 macabré chillers

The Third Black Book of Horror, where you'll
encounter a hound from hell, practitioners of dark
arts, vengeful women, and the restless dead. Tales
of ghoulish delight and blinding terror.

'...*another enthralling horror anthology. I hope
many more will follow.*'
Mario Guslandi, The Zone

'...*an almost uniformly great collection of short
stories...*'
Lee Medcalf, Pantechnicon

MORTBURY PRESS

The horror anthology publisher

Tales of terror and the macabré, the supernatural
and the occult, the gruesome and the ghastly.

Selected by Charles Black

http://www.freewebs.com/mortburypress/
mortburypress@yahoo.com

Lightning Source UK Ltd.
Milton Keynes UK
26 November 2010

163500UK00001B/49/P